BRAT

The application of his hand to my bottom had been firm, almost a smack, as if to chivvy me along, a bad girl who needed to be guided by having her bottom patted. I had been bad – he'd said so – and it seemed more than likely that he'd want to punish me with the spanking I so desperately wanted. Maybe he would even make me pee in front of him and then spank me as well, which would be lovely. In any case I was lost, willing to do just about anything for the chance of getting my bottom smacked.

A NEXUS CLASSIC

BRAT

Penny Birch

This book is a work of fiction.
In real life, make sure you practise safe sex.

First published in 1999 by
Nexus
Thames Wharf Studios
Rainville Road
London W6 9HA

Copyright © Penny Birch 1999

This Nexus Classic edition 2002

The right of Penny Birch to be identified as the Author of
this Work has been asserted by her in accordance with the
Copyright, Designs and Patents Act 1988

www.nexus-books.co.uk

ISBN 0 352 33674 9

*All characters in this publication are fictitious and any
resemblance to real persons, living or dead, is purely
coincidental.*

This book is sold subject to the condition that it shall not,
by way of trade or otherwise, be lent, resold, hired out or
otherwise circulated without the publisher's prior written
consent in any form of binding or cover other than that in
which it is published and without a similar condition
including this condition being imposed on the subsequent
purchaser.

Typeset by TW Typesetting, Plymouth, Devon

Printed and bound by
Clays Ltd, St Ives PLC

One

Had anybody ever had the courage to tell me that I needed more discipline, I would simply have laughed. Then I would have told them that I have a successful career teaching and writing about wine, that my flat is my own property and that I am more than capable of looking after myself. I would then have pointed out that few twenty-four-year-old women can say as much and walked away with my nose in the air. If it had been a man I might even have taken the opportunity to use a few carefully selected and amusing put-downs that would have made him feel like a bully and a wimp at the same time.

Just recently my real feelings would have been different to say the least. Instead of being filled with righteous indignation I would have been deeply embarrassed, and not by what they had said, but by my own reaction to it. While they would probably have been thinking of discipline in the sense of organisation and efficiency, my thoughts would have been of something rather different as I walked away with my cheeks red with blushes. In my imagination their suggestion would have been that I needed to be taken across their lap with my arm twisted into the small of my back, my neat woollen skirt lifted up to my waist and my silk panties pulled down into a tangle around my thighs. Then I would have thought of how it would have felt to be spanked by them. Yes, spanked, with my bottom bare to humiliate me and make my pain worse; spanked while I kicked and blubbered and begged; spanked like the snotty, spoilt, impudent little brat that I am.

1

I am rather spoilt, being realistic about it. As the only child of comfortably wealthy parents I never really had to struggle. My school reports used to say things like 'Natasha is a bright child but could try a great deal harder'. Then I'd come top in class and Dad would laugh and call me 'smarty pants', a reaction which always made me thoroughly pleased with myself. As I became more senior and more sure of myself, words like 'disrespectful', 'indolent' and even 'conceited' began to creep into the reports, but I still came top and Dad still laughed, so everything was all right. After a year off swanning around Europe on a decent allowance I went up to Bristol University to read English, then came home to tell my parents that I wanted to be a wine writer.

Dad was delighted. He bought me a flat in Primrose Hill and a nice car, and spoke to enough old friends to ensure that I got a foot in the door of my chosen career. After that it was a breeze. I've always had a thing about wine, and had spent most of my European tour visiting vineyards and flirting with the owners to get free samples.

I pitched my writing style to be fashionable and light-hearted yet backed by enough knowledge to give me authority. This worked, and after just over a year I added another string to my bow by taking on an evening job teaching wine appreciation in an adult-education establishment. This came through Charlotte Petersham, who had the attic flat in my house and taught all sorts of energetic, physical things at the same college.

It was this new aspect of my life which led to my fascination with being spanked. Not that anybody at the college wanted to spank me or anything, they were all thoroughly respectful and politically correct, but it was while buying samples for a class that I overheard a bit of conversation that pushed everything else out of my head. I was walking up Haverstock Hill and a couple were coming the other way. They were typical young professionals, smartly dressed, self-confident and relaxed. She was a little taller than me, say five foot seven, and had her dark hair cut short. I don't remember him at all. As they approached

2

I caught the words 'You're joking!' and noticed a surprised, perhaps even worried look on her face. Being inquisitive I perked up my ears and heard him reply, and I remember the exact words: 'I'm telling you, he spanked her. He sat on her back and told her she needed discipline. He took her jeans and knickers down and he spanked her bottom . . .'

That was it, nothing more, but it was enough. I had heard the delight in his voice as he described the incident. I had sensed the relish with which he said the word 'bottom', making it seem somehow incredibly rude. The thought absolutely overwhelmed me that some female friend of theirs, presumably as smart and modern as they themselves, had been sat on, had her bottom stripped and been smacked on it. From the way he had expressed himself it had even sounded as if he had seen it happen!

I had also seen the look on the girl's face. She had been torn between disbelief and worry. Disbelief that such a dreadfully undignified thing could be done nowadays. Worry that the same thing might happen to her.

Worst of all, though, had been the way he had said 'discipline', as if smacking a woman's bare bottom was a perfectly reasonable thing to do if she was naughty, made a mistake or got above herself. He had said 'needed' as well, as if to imply that it had actually been necessary to spank her; as if he was doing it for her own good; as if spanking her had been an irksome but unavoidable task.

I was trembling as I continued up the hill. The whole episode terrified me, and it was as if I could feel everything the poor victim had. First surprise as she was pushed down and sat on. Then there would have been fury as strong male hands fumbled at the button of her jeans. Then frustration as she fought to stop her jeans and panties coming down but was unable to do anything about it. Next there would be humiliation as her bottom was exposed, bare and pink in front of at least two men, maybe more and maybe other women. Then pain and worse humiliation as he set to work spanking her, stinging her flesh, making her bottom bounce and wobble, perhaps even making her

3

cheeks open so that her anus and pussy showed. Finally he'd have left her lying sobbing on the carpet, feeling thoroughly sorry for herself with her bare, red bottom naked for everybody to see how she had been punished.

It had to have been a punishment – you don't do that to someone just for fun. Maybe it had been his girlfriend and she had cheated on him or something. I didn't know, but I did know that my pussy was hot and wet and that if I didn't get home quickly there was going to be a highly embarrassing wet patch at the crotch of my tight white cotton trousers.

I hastily bought my bottles and started back, trying desperately to come to terms with my own feelings. I had been genuinely shocked by the thought of the girl getting a spanking, but it had turned me on more than anything else, ever. There had also been something else in the expression of the girl who had been listening to the story. Possibly it was just my overactive imagination, but I was sure that there had been something hopeful, almost hungry, about it. She had been worried that it might happen to her, but she had also wanted it to, and I was the same.

My fingers were trembling and there was a lump in my throat all the way home. On the one hand I could barely believe that I could enjoy the thought of being punished, let alone so badly humiliated. I mean me, Natasha Linnet, who always went on top and never, ever, let a man call the shots for her! On the other hand there was no denying my wet crotch and stiff nipples, nor the other feelings of a sexual arousal stronger than on some of the occasions when I've been to bed with a man.

It was no good; I was going to have to do it. Even though I hated myself for it, I was going to have to masturbate over the idea of the girl being spanked and I knew full well that when I came it would be myself who I was imagining with my panties down and bum red and sore. Well, not really hated myself, because I never do hate myself. I was certainly ashamed of myself though, but that just made it even more exciting.

4

So it was back to my flat, on to my bed, out with my mini-vibrator and down with my trousers. I got into a kneeling position because I wanted the feeling of having my bottom raised, and that was when my shame really hit me. I have a big mirror on the wall to one side of my bed, and as I looked back I found that I had a full view of myself from the rear.

There I was, kneeling with my bottom stuck up in the air and my tiny white silk panties stretched taut across my seat. My trousers were well down, exposing my thighs, while my blouse had ridden up enough to leave the undersides of my lacy bra-cups on show between my legs. I held the vibrator in one hand, leaving no doubt as to the dirty little game I was intent on. It was my bottom that really drew my attention. I am proud of my figure, but at that moment my bum looked really plump. Most of my cheeks were spilling out because the white trousers tended to make my panties pull up between them as I walked. My crotch was wet too, and with my thighs a little apart I could see the outline of my pussy lips through the damp silk, like a little peach, rounded and divided down the middle. My face was a picture too, with my brown curls in disarray, my mouth half-open and my round glasses adding a strange touch of innocence to the whole scene.

It really did look as if I was offering myself for spanking, crawling on the bed with my panty-clad bum pushed up in the hope that some bastard of a man would beat me on it. It felt so shameful to be doing it, but it was too delicious to stop. I pulled my bra up and watched my breasts fall out, then began to swing them so that my nipples brushed on the surface of my coverlet. They felt extra-sensitive, and just the sensation of rubbing them made me desperate for my orgasm. Looking in the mirror once more, I reached back and took hold of my panties by the elastic. With my eyes fixed on my bum I began to pull them down, imagining that it was a man exposing me for a spanking. I could really feel the humiliation of it as my bottom slowly came on show. I looked rude anyway, but my panties covered the naughtiest, and prettiest, details. Then the full, raised upper parts of my cheeks were showing, two humps of flesh parted in the middle. Then my full, pink moon and the tight, puckered spot of my bumhole with its little corona of pale-brown skin and a rose-pink centre. Finally the tuck of my nates and the pouted, furry bulge of my pussy, the lips swollen and parted and all the little, secret folds of pink flesh blatantly on display. I was so aroused that my vagina was a little open, as if she had just been full of cock, which I could imagine happening before my spanking. Best of all was the tiny, shiny bud of my clitoris, half-hidden by her hood of flesh – the target for my vibrator.

I settled my panties around my thighs so that I could feel the silk straining against my legs, then took my vibrator and applied it to my clit. I do like a nice cock, but I've yet to find one that can vibrate, although several men have let me bring myself off by rubbing their erections against my clit. What I wanted a man for now was to punish me. As the exquisite thrill of the vibrator ran through me I started to think of what it would be like. A modern man would really have to lose his temper to spank a girl, especially one like me. I would have to flirt and tease, refuse his advances, only to start flirting again and once more refuse him. Finally he would snap and haul me across his lap. I would kick and struggle desperately, but it would be no good. He would twist my arm hard into the small of my back to keep me in place and simply ignore my attempts to bite or scratch him. Down would come my trousers or up would come my skirt, exposing my fancy panties to him and any onlookers there might be. Not that I would even be allowed to retain that tiny scrap of modesty. He'd pull them down, agonisingly slowly, then off completely, and cock a leg between my thighs to hold me in place and incidentally expose my pussy and anus. I'd be able to feel the hard lump of his cock pushing against my tummy, and would know it was destined for my pussy when he'd finished chastising me. Then he'd start to spank me, his big, hard hand smacking down on my poor little bottom to make my cheeks bounce and redden. Soon I'd be crying,

6

blubbering over his lap in a welter of pain and humiliation, a humiliation made worse by the sure knowledge that as he spanked me my pussy would be getting wetter and wetter, more and more ready for his cock.

I came, screaming out my pleasure with my eyes locked on my naked bottom and wishing it was red and throbbing with the pain of my imagined spanking. I saw my vagina tighten as my muscles spasmed, pulsing as if to squeeze on the cock that might have been inside me. My anus clenched to, bringing me the utterly filthy thought of having a cock up my bottom as I hit a second peak. The combined thought of being spanked and then sodomised took me to a third, and then I was slumping down on to my bed, happy but exhausted, only for a flush of pure shame to hit me even as I took the vibrator off my clitoris.

Prior to that episode I had never really thought about spanking at all. It was one of those things that simply didn't happen to me, like being in debt or having to pay rent. Nor do I have any idea why it had such a powerful effect on me, because my parents never smacked me at all and my schools had all dropped corporal punishment years before I was a pupil. So much for Freudian psychology, because all it took was that one single hint and the desire became indelibly fixed in my mind.

I did feel thoroughly ashamed of myself after that first wonderful orgasm, but it had been possibly the best of my life and I know myself well enough to have no illusions about needing to do it again. Just about every time I felt the need of an orgasm I would pose my bottom for myself and use the vibrator to bring myself to a climax as exquisite as it would be shameful. For all that, fantasy is one thing, reality another, and the thought of actually surrendering myself to a spanking was completely horrifying. Yet with my eyes open to the possibility it was impossible not to think about it, and I started to wonder if any of the men I knew would like to do it to me. I quickly realised that the answer was probably yes, which in itself filled me with outrage.

7

Two possibilities seemed to exist, one of them actually quite titillating and one that absolutely scandalised me. The titillating one was the tutor on the advanced French course that I was taking, it being a tutor's privilege to attend one other course for free. He was called Antoine Barras and was a dark, swarthy, rather serious man from the Catalan part of southern France. He was intensely masculine and I think every woman in the class fancied him, at least a little. I certainly did, and used to flirt and tease but without any real intention of taking things further. The thing was that I generally prefer men who'll do as I like in bed – especially letting me go on top without making a fuss, and licking my pussy without automatically expecting their cocks sucked in return. I couldn't see Antoine being anything like as pliable, as he was more than a little chauvinistic and rather old-fashioned. There was also something stern about him, which made me wonder if maybe, just maybe, he was the sort to lose his temper and spank my bottom for me if my behaviour became really unbearable.

Secondly there were my fellow wine-writers, and this was where the fantasy reached its true peak and also its most degrading depths. Several of them, mostly the older men, clearly fancied me and would often perform little courtesies, indulge in minor intimacies or make half-joking sexual suggestions. I tolerated this and even used to flirt a little, but that was all, and I kept them firmly at arm's length. Among them were some pretty lecherous old goats, and I found it easy to imagine them thoroughly enjoying the idea of having me wriggling over their laps with my panties down and my bum bare for punishment. They were dirty old men, not like tramps or anything really disgusting, but at least in the sense that any older man who likes the idea of sex with a younger woman is a dirty old man, and I was sure that they were far more likely to enjoy the thought of spanking girls than were younger men.

It didn't quite accord with my original fantasy of being spanked purely in order to chasten me, but it was as good and was what I mainly fantasised over when I masturbated. My feelings of shame were even stronger after coming over the thought of being put across some dirty old man's knee, and I was sure I'd never submit to it in reality.

Possibly the worst of them was a big ginger-haired man with a bristly moustache called John Thurston. He always called me 'my dear' in the most condescending way, and twice he had patted my bottom when holding doors for me. More and more he would creep into my spanking fantasies, and the more he did the more ashamed of myself I would feel after I'd come. Despite the fact that my best orgasms always came over the dirtiest fantasies, I was determined that if I tried it for real the person who spanked me would be someone that I was not ashamed to be seen with, preferably Antoine.

Two

I didn't find the courage to do anything about Antoine, and I really couldn't face the idea of trying to goad any of my colleagues. So for a month things stayed much the same, but halfway through May my spanking fantasies were given a new impetus. I was walking across Regent's Park on my way home when I found myself headed for a group of rough-looking, leather-clad types. People like that fascinate me in a way, but they always make me feel nervous. They were on the bridge over the lake, which I always walked across. I am stubborn enough to feel silly if I change my route just because of some louts and so walked determinedly on.

They were mainly men and were laughing and drinking beer out of cans as I approached. They seemed to find the spectacle of people minding their own business in the park intensely funny, which annoyed me and made me feel even more nervous. I pressed on though, despite being sure that they would make some remark at my expense. Sure enough, the biggest of the men made a comment on the tightness of my vagina that sent the blood straight to my cheeks. Another agreed, stating that anyone dressed as I was had to be a virgin. I had just come from a tasting and was wearing a trim two-piece in fine, dull-red wool, a frilly blouse and sensible heels. I suppose I did look a bit prissy, especially with my glasses and my curls pinned back, but I still felt that their remark was really unfair and also uncalled for. Of course my resulting blushes made it worse and they started to catcall and jeer as I walked down the far side of the bridge.

At that point I saw a pair of policemen walking across the park in the distance and knew that I had a perfect opportunity to give the louts a piece of my mind and get away with it. Normally I wouldn't dare cheek anyone so tough looking, never mind a whole bunch of them, but I was pretty cross and the police in the middle distance gave me the perfect chance to air my sarcasm. I turned back, several suitable comments already ripe in my head, only to see something that stopped me dead.

One of the girls was leaning on the railings with her back half turned to me. She was small and pretty, despite having several facial piercings and some really striking black and green make-up. She also had green and red hair and a red-leather dress that left most of her legs showing. I'd been thinking of making a remark about parrots, but as my eyes came to rest on her bare legs the words died in my throat. Her position and our relative elevations left me looking pretty well straight up her dress, and I could see that she had no panties on. That was shocking enough, but worse by far were the three broad red stripes that decorated her upper thighs and the tuck of her bottom. Somebody had taken a belt to her.

She was small but seriously tough looking, and I simply couldn't imagine her accepting that sort of treatment unless she wanted it. Nor did she seem unhappy. Just the opposite – she was laughing and joking with the best of them. I decided against my tirade and hurried away to the sound of their laughter, although they didn't realise why I was so flustered. The girl had been given what I so badly wanted, and presumably by the great hulking brute of a lad who she had been kissing when I first saw them. The idea of what it must have felt like to be belted by him had me in an absolute lather, and I knew that there was only one thing for it: back to the flat for another session with the vibrator.

I did it kneeling again, only this time nude. I imagined that they had stripped me, whipped me with their belts and made me kneel for sex with all of them. For the first time I imagined the girls joining in, punishing me with all the

11

malicious delight that girls can take in being horrid to one another. The orgasm was exquisite, a mind-blowing experience that left me weak and shivering with reaction.

The fantasy became even stronger after that – a desperate need to be physically punished. My ideas of what I actually needed became clearer as well. A willing spanking across a boyfriend's lap would have been no good at all. Fun perhaps, but not nearly shameful enough to really hit the spot. It was essential that the person who did it was unaware that I was enjoying it and thought that he was either genuinely punishing me or that he had tricked me into accepting something that gave him sexual pleasure but which I thought was a punishment.

If that all seems a little complicated and demanding, then that's just the way I am. What's more I tend to get my way and so seldom feel the need to tone down my desires. That was the other thing that I began to realise. I do nearly always get my own way. What I wanted was for someone to put me across their knee and give me a really good spanking, instead of allowing me to push them around.

That was something I could really see the big lad who had been with his friends in the park doing. He wouldn't be impressed by my missish behaviour, nor spend his time crawling after me because I'm pretty. On the contrary, he seemed the type to put me firmly in my place, and if he could take his belt to his girlfriend's bottom, then why not mine?

Of course, the last thing I wanted was to be under the thumb of someone like that all of the time, and if he didn't give me my much-needed spanking then I could see myself getting fed up with him pretty fast. On the other hand he might just do it, and I needed that spanking so, so badly.

The idea of getting to know him and his girlfriend also appealed to another part of my nature. I know that it is quite common for girls from wealthy families to like rough men, and there had always been a streak of that in me. For all that they make me nervous, there's a certain glamour to people like that. Twice before I'd had brief flings with similar men, but in neither case had it worked, and the reality of rough sex had proved to be a big letdown on the fantasy. Admittedly this had mainly been because I had still wanted to call the shots in bed, and perhaps things might have been better if they hadn't let me.

I decided to try in any case, and was pretty confident that however much they despised me in twin-set and frills they would be interested if I presented an image they thought was sexy. Doing it would also mean leading a double life of sorts, which seemed a fun idea. I was also sure I could find them again, because I remembered seeing them before and was fairly certain that they were from the estates between the park and Hampstead Road.

So it was in a thoroughly happy mood that I visited Camden Market the following weekend. From what I had seen of them, leather was definitely the thing, along with lots of cheap jewellery, bizarre make-up, weird hair and plenty of leg and cleavage on show. There was no shortage of what I needed in the market, but I was keen for my look not to seem contrived or merely a fashion statement and so spent plenty of time choosing.

For a start their clothes were not entirely typical of current fashion and, for all I knew, might be associated with some particular type of pop music. Then there was the fact that the small girl had had no panties on under her skirt, which argued a sexual bravado that made me tingle just to think about. In my line of work I find I need to look both smart and conventional – a mini-skirt with no panties would have been totally out of the question.

The first thing I found was a really sweet leather skirt. It was bright purple, flared, and while it fitted me nicely around the waist it looked likely to leave a truly indecent amount of leg showing. I was so pleased with it I began to feel really bold and I decided that, whatever I did, my outfit would include only four items. My next purchase was a pair of wonderful boots. These were in black leather, had four-inch heels and came right up my knees, attaching with a series of large shiny buckles. That was two items and

13

I was beginning to feel deliciously naughty, even to the extent that I considered getting a piercing. There were plenty of booths for this, which offered to pierce not just noses, tummy buttons and other slightly cheeky things, but nipples, tongues and even labia. I wasn't at all sure if I could handle the idea of having a ring through my pussy lips, but it sat quite well with my spanking fantasy because it would have been so humiliating when it was discovered. A really stern person might even give me extra for it, or make me take it out in front of them; the thought had me blushing and hastily turning away from the stall.

I decided that I didn't have the courage for a piercing, at least not that day. Feeling slightly cowardly, I continued my search for clothes. A black leather jacket with a nipped-in waist attracted me, and after a bit of thought over whether it was too fancy I bought it anyway. That left me with one item to buy, either top or bottom. Knowing that I was going to be either leaving my bottom bare under my skirt or my breasts bare under my jacket increased my feeling of naughtiness. I was thinking of buying a really fancy bra and going without panties when I found a stall that instantly changed my mind. They were selling knickers, quite big, rather like the ones I'd worn at school, only made of rubber. I was entranced, especially as with a skirt so short it was likely that someone might see – see that I was in a pair of rubber knickers.

There was a bright-red pair with a small frill around the leg holes which I simply couldn't resist. I was blushing furiously as I bought them from the couple behind the stall, and the woman gave me a knowing look that sent my pulse fluttering. I had a knot in my stomach as I walked away, aimlessly at first because I was in such a state, then in search of a jewellery booth. There was an excellent one in a cluster of stalls by the road, run by a tall girl with long white hair. She was more than keen to help me choose and wanted to know about my birth sign and all sorts of other, apparently irrelevant details first. There were rings, bangles, chains, studs and all sorts of strange body jewellery, most of which I could imagine the girls I had

14

seen wearing. I came away with a big bag full of the stuff and an uncertain feeling as to whether she regarded me as a great customer or a sucker.

I went back to the flat absolutely dying to try everything on and intent on taking a trial run to see what reaction I got from people. Unfortunately I had no sooner put the bags down and turned the kettle on than the bell rang. It was Charlotte, my upstairs neighbour and fellow adult-education teacher.

Charlotte and I had got on well from the first day I moved in. Her background was similar to mine, and within ten minutes of meeting we had been swapping school stories and giggling together as if we had known each other for years. She also looked up to me and valued my advice, which I liked. I freely admit to being vain, and I've always liked friends who see me as something special. Charlotte was like that, always wanting my opinion and never one hundred per cent sure of herself. She was taller than me, had a lithe, muscular body, short cropped blonde hair and big innocent eyes, all in all making her someone I was more than happy to be seen with.

About a month before, she had started going to a non-denominational church in a rather seedy part of town. Religion has never interested me at all, having had it firmly drummed out of me by two chapel attendances a day for my ten years at school. Charlotte seemed to find it comforting, which was fair enough, yet she was becoming almost obsessive about it and I was starting to feel concerned for her. The priest was apparently an angel in human form, and I was sure it was him rather than any deep belief that drew her. I had repeatedly declined her invitations to join her, hoping that my disapproval would change her mind, but, rather to my irritation, she only continued to grow more enthusiastic.

That was what she was after on this occasion, and it was the last thing I wanted to do. I couldn't bear to be cross with her though, which would have been rather like smacking a kitten for wanting to come up on my lap and tearing my tights. In the end I promised to come the following week, not to a service, but to meet the priest who she assured me was so wonderful.

I waited until she had actually left the house before starting to change, unsure if I wanted her to know about my intended new image. Certainly I was much too shy about my desire to be spanked to confide in her, or anyone else for that matter. I love to appear confident and in control; in fact I am confident and in control – it's just that wanting to be spanked for being a little brat doesn't suit the way I like people to see me.

Dressing in front of the mirror was fun. I like the sight of my own body; I always have, otherwise I wouldn't have put the mirror there in the first place. I'm not like some women either, always desperate to be taller, or slimmer, or have bigger breasts, or smaller breasts. I like being me, and if I occasionally wonder how it might feel to be really tall or perhaps have a slightly less cheeky bottom, then it's not often. A mirror is also nice to masturbate in front of; I can watch the way my vulva swells and moistens and opens as I become more and more excited.

I was certainly getting that way as I began to dress in my new outfit. The rubber panties alone had me pushing my bottom out and looking over my shoulder to see how I looked from behind; I very nearly reached for the vibrator. The panties came right up to my waist and covered most of my bottom in a snug fit, leaving just two arcs of soft girly flesh peeping out from beneath the frills at either side. My pussy looked sweet too, with a little crease of rubber caught up between my lips.

It looked even better once my skirt was on, the high hem providing teasing glimpses of rubber panties if I bent forward even a little bit. The contrast between the red rubber and the deep-purple leather was shocking too, making me look a fine little tramp, which was exactly how I wanted it. The leather jacket added a slightly rough but definitely feminine look, especially with the waist belt pulled tight and the zip adjusted to leave a good slice of my cleavage showing. The shoes really added the final touch, the heels making the muscles of my calves, thighs and buttocks tense. Plenty of make-up in tones of black, red and yellow, the removal of my glasses and spraying my hair into tighter ringlets were the final touches, leaving me looking such a little slut in the mirror that I wanted to spank myself, never mind have anybody else do it.

The next step was having the courage to go out. I was sure I would get propositioned, but that happens to me all the time anyway and I'm quite capable of handling myself. On the other hand when men proposition me it tends to be 'Would you care for dinner tonight, my dear?' and not 'How much for a blow-job, luv?' In the end I decided to put my coat on over it all and drive round to the south of the park on the off chance that my quarry might be there.

I made it out of the house without being seen, drove around the outer circle once and then parked in a side street. I was more than a little nervous as I got out of the car, but quickly found that nobody paid any more attention to me than they normally do. Perhaps one or two of the stares I got from men were a bit more lecherous than usual, but not really all that much. Feeling bolder and more than a little mischievous, I walked over to the park. It was a glorious day and there were plenty of sunbathers on the grass, many wearing less than I was, if not in such dramatic style. It felt deliciously naughty just being so different, and it was quite hard to resist the urge to bend over and show everyone that I had rubber panties on. Even if it got me nowhere with my spanking fantasy it was a great experience. I had just decided to make a full tour of the park and maybe even find someone to flirt with when I found out that my luck was really in.

The big guy who I had seen on the bridge was there, just lying on the grass minding his own business with a collection of beer cans at his elbow. Well, sometimes things are hard and sometimes they're easy. He was drunk and I was turned on; the idea of rejection never even entered my head as I strolled over in his direction. He noticed me and called me over, full of boldness and arrogance. I went, and five minutes later was sitting by his side drinking a fairly disgusting beer which nevertheless gave me a pleasant buzz of alcohol.

He was a big lad, well over six foot and broad

17

shouldered, and would have appealed to me even if I hadn't been angling for a spanking. He also couldn't keep his eyes off my legs and breasts, and as I'd walked up to him while he was propped up on one arm I knew that he would already have had a good look at my rubber panties. So it wasn't so much a question of whether we would have sex as of when and where.

Inevitably he was completely different from the way he had been with all his mates; men generally are. Nor did he recognise me from our brief encounter on the bridge. I think he'd have been amazed to learn that the eager little tart beside him was the same person as the trim professional woman he had seen just days before. As it was, within half an hour of meeting we were kissing and he was soon on top of me. It was all a bit public, but I let him put a hand up my skirt and have a good feel of my panties. The next thing I knew he had pulled the zip of my jacket down and my tits were out. It felt lovely with them bare in the middle of Regent's Park, but it was really taking exhibitionism too far; I squeaked and hastily put them back.

He wasn't particularly inclined to take no for an answer, and I really think he would have fucked me right there on the grass, even if he had had to pull my pants off to do it. I was in no mood to resist but insisted on at least some privacy. He just laughed, stood up and pulled me up after him. I followed, a dishevelled mess with my jacket half-undone and my red rubber panties on show to anyone lying on the grass. It was also quite obvious why he was pulling me towards a clump of rhododendrons, and I caught more than one knowing smile as we crossed the hundred yards or so to the shelter in which we were going to fuck.

Once there it was quick and rough. He pushed me down over a convenient branch and pulled my skirt up. Then he slowly rolled my pants down to my thighs, the sticky rubber peeling away from my skin, exposing first my lower back and then my bum cheeks and finally my pussy. I could smell my own excitement as I lifted my bottom, ready to have my pussy entered, or, just possibly, to be given the spanking I so desperately wanted.

18

I was there, bent over with my bare bum showing to a big, rough lad with hands like hams. I wouldn't normally dream of showing myself off to a man in such a rude position, but it was exactly what I wanted. I looked back to find him pulling at the buckle of his belt, a wide one made of thick, embossed leather. For one blissful moment I really thought he was going to take it to my bottom, but he simply undid it and slipped his jeans and pants down in one smooth movement. His cock was already stiff, if not exactly erect, and the next moment he was offering it to my mouth. I sucked willingly, acutely aware of the rudeness of my position and that it was unlikely that we were completely hidden. He fumbled my jacket open as his cock came to full erection in my mouth and took one dangling breast roughly in hand as they came free. I was just beginning to get the taste for cock sucking when he pulled it out, went behind me and put it to my vagina. I was soaking wet and it went in easily, sliding up to give me that blissful full feeling as he took me by the hips. He rode me hard, grunting and shoving me against the branch while I panted and gasped at the sensation. I opened my legs, intending to reach back and masturbate while he was in me, but he was too fast for me, pulling out and spraying my bare bottom with come.

That was it. He was finished and had no intention of obliging me with a licked pussy. I had to come though – I couldn't help it and was quickly rubbing at my clitty. He called me a slut and once more I had the wonderful feeling that he was about to punish me. He didn't, but I still came, clenching my teeth to stop myself crying out as I thought about how I'd been taken roughly from behind in the bushes.

I was blushing as I cleaned my bottom up with a tissue, but I don't think he noticed. He said nothing anyway, except to suggest another beer.

That incident really set the seal on things. It was all just too much fun, too much of an adventure, to back out of. Also, the two moments when I really thought I was going to be spanked had been so good, so heady with expectation and apprehension, that I knew that I just had to have it. The guy in the park, who turned out to be called Steve Monk, had actually quite scared me when I thought he was going to take his belt to my bottom, but that had just made it even better. My only regret was that he hadn't done it.

Being realistic, the idea of spanking me before sex had probably never even entered his head. On the other hand I knew that he had smacked his girlfriend's thighs at least once, and unless it was something she had specifically asked for he must have had a reason. So he had to be a possibility.

So did she, because she was more than a little suspicious when he introduced me as a new friend. I could see the light of jealousy in her eyes immediately. I didn't mind the idea of the spanking coming from a woman, in fact in many ways it would be even more humiliating to be put across a woman's knee than a man's. I did want to be fucked afterwards though and so preferred the idea of it being done by a man.

I saw them twice over the next week and applied most of my charm to the girl, Lydia, so that she wouldn't cut me out. On each occasion I made an effort to dress to their expectations, if not with quite the flamboyance of my first time. Despite this I couldn't help but feel that they didn't accept me one hundred per cent. There was always a subtle feeling that I was someone who was just amusing to have around, even to make fun of, and that I wasn't really one of them. I suppose I wasn't really, being something of an impostor, but then I wasn't the only one. Despite her best efforts to cover it up, Lydia's accent betrayed a somewhat different social background from the one she made so much effort to lay claim to. There was also something familiar about her, something in her face or perhaps her figure, but nothing that I could actually put a finger on.

Three

I had hoped that among Steve Monk's group the idea of punishing girls to keep them in their place might have been standard, but either it wasn't or they weren't telling me. Realising that my bottom wasn't going to get her treatment quickly, I decided to play it easy with them and turned my attention to Antoine Barras.

The situation with him was already quite tense, as I had flirted outrageously before, only to pull back. As he was so good-looking and so masculine it was more than I could resist. He also had a hot, emotional nature, and I knew that my behaviour really got to him, which made flirting all the more fun. I have always enjoyed teasing men, and the better looking and more self-confident they are the better. It's no fun at all to tease the sort of guy who has difficulty with girls anyway, because they are used to rejection. Arrogant, cock-sure ones are much more fun, because I can drive them mad with lust and then just coolly turn them down. Sometimes I accept, of course, but what matters is that by that time I'm the one in control and I've turned a big, blustering macho man into a faithful, whining little puppy dog.

I had never intended to go all the way with Antoine, because he was so full of lust and pride that I couldn't see him bowing down to me. True, social conventions prevented him simply ripping my panties off and ravishing me on the classroom floor, but I'm sure that that was what he would have liked to have done. He was certainly getting fed up with my behaviour, and that was what prompted me to hope that he might just be the sort of person to spank my bottom if I finally surrendered.

His classes were on Friday nights, and after spending most of an afternoon with Steve, Lydia and the others I decided to give Antoine the full force of my femininity. Just being near Steve turned me on, but with Lydia around I was unable to suggest a replay of our first meeting. There was something about her which aroused me too, perhaps a reflection of my own natural energy. By the time I had to go to class I was feeling extremely naughty and just in the mood to be seduced by an ardent Frenchman.

I changed, not only because ripped jeans and a leather jacket would have looked out of place in his class, but because I wanted to drive him to distraction. The room he taught in was set up with rows of tables that I knew gave him a pretty good view of the girls in the front row. At the least he would get smart shoes and elegantly turned calves, and possibly even flashes of thighs or panties. I chose high-heels, a tight skirt as short as I dared in front of the other girls, black stockings and lacy panties in dove-grey silk. For two hours I sat in the front row, attentive and respectful while I showed off my legs. I stopped short of making my actions obvious, only allowing him one glimpse of my panty crotch and making sure it looked accidental. It was enough, though, more than enough. My previous behaviour had been judged to give him the impression not that I was a wicked little tease, but that I was an angelic little innocent who had no idea that she was making such a display of herself nor of the effect it was having on him. It is always best like that, because then the man can't harden himself and gets even more completely sucked into my web.

Before, when he had suggested an after-class drink I had always declined, judging my excuse to ensure the maximum frustration. This time I didn't, although I had to hang around until the others had gone and look out of the window with my bottom rather pointedly stuck out before he asked me. From the instant I accepted I could read him like a book. He started off full of hopeful lust and caution.

He wanted to lure the innocent little English girl into the sack and was determined not to do anything that might scare her off until she was back at his flat. Then he would turn on the full force of his charm, produce some spiel about respecting her but believing that a man and a woman should express their feelings. He would then flatter the poor little moth into bed. Once there he would be able to indulge his beastly passions to his heart's content. After his thrusting cock had given her a dozen orgasms she would be putty in his hands and become a grateful, servile little playmate who he could use as he pleased.

Perhaps that is a little unfair, but it is certainly the impression I got. He took the lead from the start, charming and flattering me in a condescending, macho way that would normally have had me running for the nearest taxi. He gave me the bit about respect and the bit about love. He gave me the bit about my beauty and the bit about my innocence. He even had the nerve to choose the wine in the restaurant.

I let it all flow over me, concentrating on his smouldering eyes and sensuous lips rather than his banal seduction technique. I giggled a lot too, and played the coy, uncertain maiden perfectly until he was absolutely certain that he had me properly hooked. He may even have thought I was a virgin, poor lamb, but he certainly didn't expect to be turned down when we'd got back to his flat and he made the final, crucial move towards the top button of my blouse.

What should have happened is this:

I should have slapped his hand and asked him who he thought I was, thus completely destroying his carefully constructed castle of seduction. With a hard cock in his trousers and his fingers itching to get my breasts bare, he would have pressed the point. I would have smacked his face and insulted him in a way judged to make him look inadequate, then leant forward across his lap to get my bag. Furious, and presented with my bottom in tight, lightweight wool, he would have grabbed me around the waist, pulled up my skirt, dropped my panties and started

23

to give me a sound spanking. I would have kicked and thrashed and sworn, calling him every name under the sun and further arousing his temper. I would have lost control as the fire built in my bottom, reaching the ecstasy of pain and humiliation that I imagined in my fantasies, maybe even coming as my bare pussy rubbed against his knee. My bum would have been a bare, red peach, framed in lace and silk, a sight guaranteed to keep his cock stiff. When his anger was spent I would be left sobbing across his lap, making no effort to pull my panties up. Inflamed past reason, he would have rolled me over, ripped my blouse open, pulled out my boobs and then his cock. Finally he would have entered me, first with my legs held up and my pussy stuck out over the edge of the settee, then with me face down so that he could admire my hot red bottom and come all over it in a vain effort not to do it in my vagina.

What really happened was that instead of losing his temper he went off in a sulk. This left me sitting on the settee with a soaking pussy, nipples fit to burst and an all-over body flush. He went into the kitchen muttering about cold English girls and wishing he was back in Perpignan. Not willing to give up, I followed him and suggested that he didn't know how to handle English girls, hoping to imply that the knack was to spank them first. It didn't work, but succeeded only in hurting his pride. He got in a fine state, calling me a prick-tease and a flirt. I pretended to get angry back and suggested that if I'd been so bad then I should be punished; my words dripped with sarcasm.

That didn't work either, and if I'd dropped any heavier hints it would have ruined my fantasy, because the one crucial point was for the man to be genuinely beating me as a punishment. He carried on ranting and I burst into tears, not as he supposed because he was being nasty, but out of sheer frustration. That changed him completely; the next thing I knew his arms were around me. He kissed me on the neck and then the lips. I responded, and a moment later he was pulling my skirt up and had taken a good handful of panty-clad bum-cheek.

24

I just melted. He was pulling my panties down even as he pushed me to the floor. I sat down quite hard, my bare bottom smacking on the cold quarry tiles. He pulled my legs up and slid my knickers down them and off. I spread my thighs, offering my soaking pussy as I fumbled frantically with the buttons of my blouse. He was pulling his fly down as they popped open. I pulled my breasts free of my bra even as his cock appeared in his hand, half-stiff. A few quick tugs and it was hard, a rigid pole of flesh aimed straight at my vagina. He mounted me with his weight on his arms and entered me without preamble, making me gasp as my pussy filled. Then he was humping away, sending me into dizzy bliss as I lay back and stroked my boobs.

He was really urgent, desperate even, fucking me as if determined to come before I changed my mind. I wasn't going to, and begged him to slow down. I wanted a long hard session and then a lick to make me come. He took no notice, going faster if anything, so that I was too breathless to speak. I wasn't completely lost to reality though, and was aware that he was inside me with no condom and about to come. He slowed and I was about to protest when he pulled out. He grabbed his cock in one hand, still supporting himself on the other. I realised what was going to happen and squeaked in protest. It was too late. His cock jerked and sent a jet of sperm all over me, spattering my skirt, my bra and my blouse. Having opened my mouth to protest only resulted in a couple of large gobbets of come going right in it. I don't mind spunk, but it was a bit of a shock and I was instantly cross about my nice clothes. I did need my own climax though, and the taste of his come in my mouth made the need even more urgent.

For a moment I was torn between annoyance and lust. Then the lust won and I was lying back with one hand on my pussy and one rubbing sperm into a nipple. He had sat back, his still-hard cock in his hand and an expression of surprise on his face as I began to masturbate. I pulled my head up and focused on his cock, admiring the thick shaft, all slick and moist with my own pussy juice. That was enough. My middle finger was on my clitty, circling and dabbing as the muscles around my pussy began to tense. Then I was coming, a long, hot orgasm that made me sigh and arch my back, abandoning myself completely to the sensation.

Once my climax had subsided I just lay on the floor, feeling limp and exhausted and wondering what was going to happen next. He got up and turned away to put his cock back in his trousers without even bothering to wipe it. Then he turned and looked down at me with a strange mixture of curiosity and disgust. I know I was lying on the floor with my thighs open and my boobs out, but if my pussy was wet and dribbling then he was the one who had made me like that. He was also the one who had come all over my expensive clothes.

I was cross, at the way he taken me without any consideration for my needs, at the mess he'd made of me, and because after he had come he seemed to find my sexual response indecent. On the other hand I am nothing if not practical, and if you let sperm dry into silk the garment is ruined. So I ignored him and went into the bathroom to put my blouse, skirt and panties in cold water. Once I'd saved my clothes I turned the bath on, stripped completely and wondered how to get home.

His flat was somewhere in Kilburn, and all I had in the way of spare clothes was an extra pair of panties. Given that my blouse and skirt were both soaking it looked like I was stuck. I resigned myself to a night with Antoine, which was fine as long as he stopped being moody. Physically he really pushed my buttons, but his domineering arrogance really didn't appeal unless he was actually going to spank me. That didn't seem very likely, but I was still in the mood for sex and hopeful that he might be a bit slower and more considerate on the second go.

Of course all of this depended on his not still being in a mood, but his temper proved to fade as rapidly as it built. I was in the bath and making a leisurely job of soaping myself when he knocked politely on the door. I told him to come in, as it seemed ridiculous to worry about him watching me bathe after he'd seen me in the throws of orgasm.

He had made me a coffee, which I drank while he sat on the edge of the bath and sipped his own. We started to talk, more openly now, but with no mention of the tempestuous circumstances of our first bout of sex. I suppose I'm just a natural show-off, because I soon began to enjoy being nude in front of him. At first he kept glancing at my breasts, the tops of which were sticking up out of the water. When I made no objection he became bolder, frankly admiring my body. I responded by starting to soap my boobs, thoroughly but casually, while we chatted about southern France.

It didn't take long before my nipples were erect, their pinky-red tips poking up through a froth of soap bubbles. He was getting visibly agitated, his fingers drumming against the side of the bath. I was still in a tormenting mood and determined to prove to myself that he didn't really find the idea of me playing with myself off-putting. I moaned and slid one hand down to my pussy, cupping my mound and easing my middle finger down between my sex lips. He made no move to touch me, but his eyes were riveted on me.

After the way I had surrendered, my pride demanded that I get a bit of control back. Showing off to someone is actually a good way of taking control, because I decide what to show and how to show it. Men generally like to watch as well, and so don't interfere; certainly Antoine didn't. I really started to let myself go, moaning and moving my hips in time to the motions of my finger against my pussy.

I suggested he got his cock out and he complied, then he stripped completely and began to stroke his erection in front of me. It was lovely masturbating together, and it soothed my earlier misgivings about him. In ways it is an act even more intimate than intercourse, because it means being completely open to each other's gaze. I've always liked it and often had men do it with me, especially if there's no contraception available. Now was no exception,

27

but as my pleasure rose my need for a spanking returned, stronger than ever.

As I always concentrate on what I want rather than what a man wants of me, I can't really claim to know a lot about men's sexual desires. Sure they all like to feel girls' breasts and bottoms, they all like to watch us undress and they all like their cocks sucked, but I wasn't at all sure about the more subtle points. Most importantly, I wasn't sure whether the sight of a girl's bottom normally fills men with the urge to smack it. I knew they normally didn't, but that might just have been uncertainty about the acceptability of spanking a girl. The modern girl isn't really supposed to like that sort of thing – certainly not without asking for it – so it was entirely possible that men had wanted to do it to me without ever plucking up the courage to try.

I determined to test Antoine in any case, and when his cock was nicely erect I turned on to my front and knelt up, presenting him with my bottom and sliding a hand back between my thighs to carry on masturbating. He must have been able to see everything: my up-raised bottom, all wet and slippery, my open pussy with my fingers working in the wet mush of my vulva; my anus, pinky-brown, wrinkled and pulsing as my pleasure rose.

The position was a blatant invitation to spank me, or so I thought, and I was hoping that he might still feel that I would benefit from punishment. The alternative would normally have been to mount me from the rear, but there was no room. I looked round, finding him stroking his erection and eyeing my bottom. The look on his face was hard to read, but contained lust and a curious uncertainty that I hoped was doubt as to whether I would accept smacks on my bum. I wiggled, hoping he would do it, but it only increased his look of discomfort.

'Enough games,' he said suddenly. 'Come to my bed.'

'Don't you want to . . . watch me?' I asked, nearly saying 'spank me' but stopping at the realisation that if I said it the fantasy would be ruined.

'It's . . . it's childish,' he said, gesticulating in a way that showed just how uncomfortable he felt.

'It's nice,' I protested. 'I like it.'

'I want to make love to you,' he said hotly. 'To watch your response as a woman, to hear you moan as you come from the pleasure of my penis inside you.'

Well I could have told him that I only came when my clitty was stimulated, but it would probably just have started an argument. If he insisted on us taking what he saw as the conventional (natural was the word he had used earlier) female and male roles, then I was prepared to put up with it. Besides, my clothes were still wet and if the choice was between him taking me to bed and sulking in a corner then I preferred to go to bed.

So I let him have his way. He really took control after that and was thoroughly pleased with himself. I dried and went into the bedroom, where he had a fine double bed with a rather hard mattress. He laid me down on this and began to kiss and caress me. I suppose he was good, in his way. He made a lot of effort to stroke my thighs, neck and other erogenous zones instead of just grabbing my tits and bum. He also kissed well and spent a lot of time on my neck and breasts before going slowly down to my tummy and finally my pussy. He didn't lick though, just kissed, as if reluctant to get his face messy with my juice. When the time came to want his cock sucked, as it always does, he pushed my head down gently but firmly, as if overcoming an imaginary resistance on my part.

I made no objection and took him in my mouth. Sometimes I can't be bothered to suck cock, and it's not something I'm ever really desperate for. I don't mind though and gave Antoine a nice long session, first taking him deep into my throat and then giving his shaft long licks as if it was a lollipop. As I sucked I moved my body round, hoping to straddle his face and get into a sixty-nine. I love to sit on men's faces and make them lick my pussy, or even my anus, but Antoine was having none of it. Instead of letting me mount his face he pulled his cock out of my mouth and took hold of my hips. Once more I let him have his way, because with him the choice seemed to be either his way or nothing, which was selfish but I was too turned on to object.

29

Keeping a firm hold on me, he knelt up, got behind me and entered me from the rear. Doggy position is nice but always makes me feel rather subservient, so I don't often let men have me like that. On the other hand it makes for good, deep penetration and I was soon moaning away wantonly as he rode me. I thought he might come before too long, and put a hand back to play with my clit. He immediately stopped, turned me over and mounted me between my open thighs. He seemed to have something against me using my fingers on myself, and of course I couldn't with him between my legs.

He took off at a hell of a pace, as if determined to make me come just with the feeling of his cock moving in my vagina. Maybe I'm not as sensitive as some girls, but I never come that way and would have told him if I hadn't already resigned myself to accepting sex on his terms. So I laid back and enjoyed what was available, only getting obstinate when I decided it was time he put a condom on.

What followed was the classic condom argument, with him complaining that it was an insult to his masculinity and me pointing out that that was all very well but that I had no desire to get pregnant. I didn't mention that I was also on the pill, but gave him a straight choice of either putting one on or not coming in my pussy. He sulked a bit and then asked if he could bugger me. I turned him down but offered him a choice of coming in my mouth, between my boobs or along the crease of my bottom. He went on a bit more about how he had been going to ensure that we climaxed together and how beautiful it would have been, but eventually accepted the offer of my boobs.

I then sat on the bed while he straddled me and took his erection between my breasts. It looked nice sticking up between the fleshy pillows and he quickly forgot his sulkiness in the pleasure of fucking them. He came pretty fast, and I licked his sperm up to make up for not letting him have his way, but he was still a little grumpy afterwards.

We slept together and had sex once more in the morning, again with him on top. He seemed to have accepted my limits and came on my belly with no more than a minor grumble about how I was denying nature. He still wasn't keen on me frigging off either, and I had to sneak my climax in the loo, which was all a bit sordid.

Despite everything we got on quite well afterwards, as we had a lot in common notwithstanding our sexual differences. I helped him make breakfast and chatted merrily, still stark naked and oddly enough not in the least self-conscious. It was only after a chocolate croissant and a cup of black coffee that I remembered I had promised Charlotte that I would to go to her church with her.

I dressed hastily and left, unspanked but at least fairly satisfied, and in two minds as to the benefits of another encounter with Antoine Barras.

Four

Inevitably Charlotte was long gone by the time I got back to my flat, but I knew the address and so had a quick wash and set off. The church was in among that rather fiddly area of housing opposite St Pancras Station, getting on for two miles from my flat. It was a nice day and I didn't want to leave the car in what really isn't a very nice area, so I walked, finding the place after a couple of false starts.

The church was classical in style, with one of those spires rather like a wedding cake. To the best of my rather sketchy memory of architectural history, that made it a Regency building, and it must have started life belonging to the Church of England. A sign now proclaimed it as the headquarters of the Church of Universal Salvation, which sounded pretty pretentious for an organisation built entirely around one man's ego.

The high doors were painted a sort of duck-egg blue and firmly shut. I knocked on them but only managed to hurt my knuckles. I was late, it was true, but under an hour and I still felt that Charlotte might have left the door unlocked for me. Feeling cross, I stood back and wondered how to attract her attention.

The church had also obviously been built long before the buildings around it. This meant that it was now packed in between a pub on one side and the end of a Victorian terrace on the other. It also had a thin fringe of land around it, once presumably sacred ground but now a tangle of unhealthy-looking undergrowth. On the terrace side this was a chasm no more than two yards wide and wired off from the pavement. I could see a light coming from a round window at the end of this.

I couldn't really see, but the wall of the building with the window in it looked to be of the same greyish-yellow stone from which the church was built and so presumably belonged to it. Someone had loosened a corner of the wire, leaving a hole big enough for me to get through. I hesitated, feeling a bit silly, and then ducked through, determined that I hadn't walked well over a mile for nothing. The alley was fairly disgusting, dank, muddy and littered with old beer cans and cigarette packets. It ended in an algae-encrusted wall, in which the round window was set, about a foot higher than I could reach.

One of the scrub sycamores had grown up right in the angle of the walls, and I managed to get a foothold on this. It was pretty awkward and I had to hitch my skirt up, but I managed to get level with the window. I craned forward, almost lost my balance and managed to steady myself in a position that gave me a clear view through the window. It was quite a view as well.

Charlotte was standing with her back to me in the middle of what looked like a vestry. It actually took a double take to be sure it was Charlotte, because she certainly didn't look her normal self. For a start she wasn't wearing her normal combination of track-suit bottoms and sports top. Instead she was in a smart pinstripe suit and a pair of what looked like Y-fronts. It was hard to tell, because they were pulled down to her thighs along with the suit trousers, leaving her rounded, muscular little bottom quite bare. She was holding up the tails of her suit and a white shirt beneath it, standing quite still while a man in a black suit knelt behind her. He was fondling her bottom – in fact, worshipping would be a better word. As I watched with my mouth open, his fingers traced a slow pattern over her nates, exploring every curve and crevice with a fascination that I can only describe as reverential.

I know this sounds pretty slow, but it was only when I realised that she was wearing men's shoes that it dawned on me that she wasn't just dressed in a suit: she was

33

actually dressed as a man. She made a pretty man as well, or rather a youth, because with her slim figure and short blonde hair she looked eighteen at most. The way she was holding up her tails was particularly sweet, displaying her bare bottom to be touched by the man who could only be the priest, Evan Dunstal. Combined with the thrill of being a peeping Thomasina, the sight was really turning me on.

The sound of a car on the road behind me brought me sharply back to earth. I climbed down quickly, but was feeling more than a little hot under the collar and decided that I didn't want to miss out on watching Charlotte. The vestry had a flat roof, and I had been able to see the inside of a skylight through the window. It didn't take a moment to scramble back up the sycamore and on to the roof. My nice cream two-piece got covered in algae, but I didn't care.

The roof was perfect, a flat expanse of lead ringed on three sides by high, windowless walls. The fourth side was the sloping roof at the rear of the church and the small opening by which I had climbed up. Confident in my solitude, I moved carefully over to the skylight and peered in. Things were much as before, but I had a better view. Charlotte had her eyes shut and her face was set in an expression of utter bliss. She had a tie on, confirming my suspicions about her being dressed as a boy, while the front of her pants were up high enough to cover her pussy. As I watched she stuck her bottom out a little and her lips came apart as his fingers reached the more sensitive areas of her bottom.

I was in a squatting position, with my skirt hitched up from climbing on to the roof. This left the front of my panties open to the air, and I could feel that they were moist. I moved back a little to get a better view of Charlotte's bottom and locked my eyes on the neat pink hemispheres which he was caressing with so much devotion. I was relishing the naughty feeling of spying on them and wishing someone would treat my own bottom with the adoration that he was giving her. Of course in my case I'd want it spanked after they'd had a good feel, and

34

then fondled some more afterwards. I'd let them open my cheeks and touch my bumhole, maybe even put a finger in me. Then they'd start to explore my pussy, tickling me, teasing me, exploring every little fold and crease until I was soaking wet and begging for their cock.

My hand was at the crotch of my panties as Charlotte moved into a crouch. The silk was soaking, but I forced myself to stroke the soft skin of my inner thighs instead of going straight for my pussy. Below me her bottom was stuck right out, a really rude position that left her crease open to his lewd, intrusive gaze. He was doing it too, holding her bum-cheeks open and inspecting her anus in minute detail from a distance of inches. I wanted to touch my own, but held back, wary of committing such a dirty act outside.

I began to stroke the front of my panties as Charlotte sank to her knees, lifting her pretty bottom in open invitation to entry. He paused and rocked back on his heels, his hand going straight to his fly. I watched as his cock came out, big and very pale, already fully erect. I expected him to simply edge forward and slide his cock into her pussy, but instead he reached to the side and took hold of a tube of some sort of jelly.

I suppose I should have guessed from the men's clothes and the position she was in, but it was only when he squeezed out a long worm of the jelly between Charlotte's bottom cheeks that I realised what he was going to do. I know men like the thought of putting their cocks up girls' bottoms, and I've fantasised over the idea a few times, but I had never let anyone do it to me. I was actually a little shocked, and not just because it's so dirty and undignified for a woman to accept sodomy, but because Charlotte was not just accepting it but obviously welcoming it.

She had a look of absolute rapture on her face as he put his cock between her cheeks and began to rub the lubricant into her bottom hole. My fingers were still on my pussy, and I couldn't help but rub myself. It was just so dirty. Charlotte was such a sweet, clean girl, and here she was, on all fours while her priest prepared to put his cock up her bottom. I mean . . . a man's cock, inserted into her anus!

I could see everything: the red, swollen head of his penis, her greasy bottom hole distending as he tried to force entry; the blissful, breathless expression on her face as it popped inside. Then the head was inside her and he was pushing, each time sliding another inch or so of penis into Charlotte's rectum. It was a sight at once so obscene and so exciting that I was cross with myself for enjoying it even as I pulled my panties aside to find my clitty.

With one hand on the roof to steady myself I began to masturbate as I watched the priest bugger my friend. His cock was right up her bottom, so deep inside that I could only see the fuzz of his pubic hair between her sweet little cheeks. He had adjusted his clothing so that it didn't get greasy, exposing muscular buttocks and a firm stomach. Charlotte's bottom was very obviously female, as was her waist. Otherwise she could have been a skinny young man, and even as I masturbated myself into dizziness I was wondering exactly what he was getting off on. True, it must have felt pretty nice with Charlotte's bumhole clamped tight around his cock, but from all appearances she was a boy in his mind.

He had her by the hips and was speeding up, making her grunt and pant in a wonderfully unladylike manner. My own fantasies had started to run, and I was wishing I had a cock so that I could do the same to her and make her groan and wriggle with her anus stretched around my own thick, solid penis. Even with a fake one it would have made me feel completely in control, just as when she returned the favour I would be completely out of control with my poor little bumhole straining around eight inches of thick, cock-shaped rubber.

I started to come, thinking of how I'd feel in her position – only after a good spanking had left me grovelling on the floor with my bottom in the air, begging for his cock inside it. I moaned as I came and lost my balance, sitting down hard on my bottom. Too far gone to care, I just carried on rubbing at my clitty. I fell back on the lead as my climax tore through me, heedless to where I was or the display I was making to anybody who saw me.

Before I had really finished coming I was struggling back up and pulling my skirt down to cover my panties. I was sure they would have heard, but I could still hear their groans of pleasure; it seemed that I had got away with it. Chiding myself for letting go so completely and feeling a little ashamed of myself for coming over the thought of being buggered, I bent forward and peered cautiously through the skylight.

He was still in her bottom but was obviously near coming. His face was screwed up in a mask of ecstasy, while she was clawing frantically at the floor and kicking her feet in a beautifully anguished response to the penis in her rectum. He gave a final hard push into her and she cried out as he came up her bottom, a sight that had me trembling despite my recent orgasm.

I didn't wait to watch them clean up, but climbed down quietly from the roof. As I pushed my way back through the trees I struggled to come to terms with what I'd seen. Evan Dunstal was obviously fascinated with Charlotte's bottom, which I could appreciate. On the other hand it had looked to me pretty one-sided, with Charlotte doing as she was told in order to satisfy his perverse fantasy. A lot a men are like that, expecting all sorts of curious things but not prepared to give and take. I'd had a boyfriend once who had been obsessed with my shoes, which was fine until I took him home for sex, went to shower and came back into the room to find that he had come all over my beautiful new black suede high-heels. I was furious, not only because he had ruined a pair of expensive shoes, but because I had to do without the sex I had been anticipating.

Evan Dunstal struck me as similar, basically selfish. It was true that I had been turned on by the sight, but then I am a lot tougher and more in control than Charlotte; it seemed to me that he was abusing her. Even before, I had been suspicious of his motives and it had always seemed to me that his church was simply an excuse to get the gullible to part with their money. In Charlotte's case she was also surrendering her body; and while she might have been enjoying it I felt it was my duty as her friend to put a stop to it.

I waited in the street until I was sure they would have had a chance to tidy up, then knocked on the door again as loudly as I could. I had no intention of admitting to having watched them, not even to Charlotte. After all, in some ways the taboo against being a peeping Thomasina is even stronger than that against buggery. Instead I intended to play my cards carefully and eventually make Charlotte see that she was being used.

So when they finally answered the door I greeted Charlotte with a friendly kiss and shook hands with Evan Dunstal. She was no longer wearing the suit, hardly surprisingly, but had on a long floral dress. His appearance also gave no hint of what they had just been up to, but I could tell that they were both slightly flushed.

We spent the next hour or so talking, or rather Evan and I talking and Charlotte occasionally putting in a comment to support him. I had to admit that there was something attractive about him, and also alluring, even magnetic. Not only did he have smouldering good looks, but he was so convinced, so intense in his beliefs that had it not been for the fact that they were so obviously utter twaddle I could easily have found myself being drawn to him. I could certainly see why Charlotte was attracted to him and why she was prepared to do just as he said sexually.

His beliefs centred on what he saw as the increasing depravity and low moral tone of society, and the need for belief in God to save the population from disaster. I thought this was a bit rich coming from a man who had just had a girl dress up as man so that he could indulge a bizarre homoerotic anal fantasy. It was also obvious drivel, as society is really no worse than it ever has been and in many ways better. Still, a lot of people like to believe in imminent disaster, especially if they can convince themselves that they will be among the few saved. Basically he enabled rather stupid people to feel self-righteous and superior to the rest of humanity.

I could easily have told him that he was talking rubbish,

but I could see from the way Charlotte reacted that she was completely besotted with him. So I pretended to be impressed and agreed to come along to a service and even sing in his choir, all the while trying not to think of how he had looked with his erection up Charlotte's bottom.

Charlotte was delighted that I seemed impressed with Evan and chattered incessantly as we walked home. She even admitted that she was in a relationship with him, although she made no mention of the juicy and perverse details. Instead she painted him as a gentle, saintly character, more than worthy of adulation.

The more I heard of it the less I liked it and by the time we got back to Primrose Hill I was absolutely determined that her relationship with him was not going to last. I was also fed up with the way she kept talking about him as if he were some sort of ideal man. In the past she had always looked up to me, and while she still wanted my support, she expected me to see Evan as an icon on a plane far higher than either of us.

The discovery of a large bunch of flowers outside the door of my flat cheered me up considerably. I like my admirers to send me flowers, and this was an obviously expensive bouquet, if a little vulgar. It consisted mainly of big, crimson roses but had all sorts of little things like forget-me-nots and stock as well as lots of greenery. Charlotte cooed over it and asked who it was from, so I told her about Antoine, leaving out only the muckiest bits and painting a much more glowing picture of our love-making than the reality deserved.

What with telling Charlotte about my encounter of the night before and my memories of watching her and Evan at their dirty little games, I was feeling pretty steamed up by the time she left. I confess to being a bit of an addict for my baby-sized vibrator and for playing with myself in general, but left to my own devices I like at least two orgasms a day. It was impossible not to in any case, because it was the first time I'd really had a chance to concentrate since getting together with Antoine.

Also, the implication of the roses and the attached note was that he wanted to make our encounter more than a one-night stand. I wasn't sure if I was going to accept his offer or not, but it was flattering in any case and not many things make me more turned on than men chasing after me.

So it was off with my clothes and on to the bed for a nice, leisurely play in the nude. So many erotic things had happened over the previous day that it took me a bit of time to sort out what I wanted to come over. For a start there was the rough, manly way Antoine had controlled me during sex, which seemed a lot more exciting now that he wasn't actually doing it. Then there was the thought of having been a peeping Thomasina and of having watched Evan bugger Charlotte while he fantasised over her being a boy. Finally there was the spanking fantasy that had led me to go to bed with Antoine in the first place.

I let my mind run for a while, lying on my back and playing the vibrator over my belly and thighs. My first thoughts were of how it would have felt if Antoine had buggered me in the bath, using soap as a lubricant to make my anus sting and doing it really brutally while he slapped my wet buttocks and called me dirty names. From there it went to Evan and Charlotte catching me on the roof and making me strip to be beaten with a thick leather belt. I imagined how it would feel to be naked in front of them with my bottom covered in welts and my face stained with tears. My open, wet pussy would show that I'd been excited by the beating, adding to my shame and giving Evan a hard cock. He would then bugger me in front of Charlotte and come all over my well-whipped bottom.

My head was beginning to spin with pleasure and the anal part of the fantasies was starting to come out on top. I rolled over and stuck my bottom up, using the vibrator on my cheeks. It felt really dirty as I moved the humming plastic tip in slow circles towards its inevitable target. I sighed as it found the crease of my bottom, turning to watch myself in the mirror. I looked so good, stark naked with the vibrator inching towards my bumhole. I pulled my

40

knees up and there it was, pinkish brown and tight above the sweetly pouted lips of my pussy. I put the vibrator to it and pushed but couldn't get it in dry. A quick dip in my pussy solved that problem and an instant later I was sighing as the hard little plastic rod eased my anus open and slid inside.

It felt glorious and looked glorious, me kneeling in the nude with a vibrator protruding from my anus. I wanted it to be Antoine's cock, and I shut my eyes to imagine it was, easing it in and out of my tight little hole as I thought about him buggering me after a good whipping. Best of all would have been if he'd caught me peeping and beaten me for it, stripping me and taking his belt to my nude bottom until his passion became too much for him and he forced his cock up my hot virgin back passage. He'd be filled with disgust for my behaviour, and when he had finished with me he would leave me there, tied in a kneeling position with one of the roses he had been meaning to give me inserted in my anus.

I had to do it – it was more than I could resist. Getting quickly off the bed I scampered into the main room and chose the biggest rose. I picked off the thorns to stop myself from hurting my tender bumhole and stuck my bottom out in front of the mirror. Using one hand to spread my cheeks I poked the rose stem at my anus and watched it slide up my bottom. I put it in a good long way and then knelt back on the bed, bum to the mirror so that I could admire how I looked stripped naked with a big red rose sticking up out of my bumhole. It looked every bit as rude and humiliating as I had expected and I turned back to the thought of Antoine doing it to me while I put the vibrator back to my clitty and started on what I knew would be the final climb to my orgasm.

It didn't take long. In fact, I had nearly been there when I decided to stick the rose up my bottom. I thought of Antoine's fury at catching me peeping and of his strong hands ripping my clothing away until I was grovelling nude at his feet. Then of my terror as I watched him pull his belt free of his trousers and lift it over my naked haunches.

Then of the pain as it came down hard across my unprotected bottom. Finally of him completely losing control of his lust and fury and mounting me with his cock wedged to the hilt up my bottom.

I came, my third of the day and much the best, with no distractions and my whole mind fixed on my fantasy and my reflection in the mirror.

Five

The week passed quietly although not without a little apprehension. This was because I had seen Steve, Lydia and the gang on the Sunday. I had finally got fed up with being treated as an outsider and had said as much. Steve had laughed and gone off to whisper with a couple of his male cronies and then come back to tell me that if I wanted to be accepted by them then I would have to go through an initiation ritual. Steve wouldn't give details but said that it needed to be done somewhere lonely, implying something erotic and probably either painful or humiliating. I was pretty sure they were making it up on the spot and expected me to run a mile at the idea. They weren't the only ones who could play games though, and I actually found the idea rather titillating. I agreed as long as the other girls were there, because although I was a bit scared of them I couldn't see them taking me off and gang raping me with Lydia and the others around. Besides, there had to be a fair chance that whatever it was involved a smacked bottom for me, and being held down with my bottom bare and spanked with a piece of wood or something appealed to my fantasy. It also scared me a little, but not enough to put me off. At the end of the day I can look after myself – I was confident in my ability to keep things under my control.

So the prospect of the coming Sunday kept me on edge all week, adding a delicious erotic frisson to everything. I masturbated every evening, long, lazy sessions with fantasies that invariably involved me being made to do unspeakably rude things. My keyed-up state must have been detectable as well, because at both the tastings I attended my male colleagues were even more attentive than usual. One, a fat Yorkshireman called Percy Ottershaw, even gave my bottom a sneaky squeeze, and I was so lost in an erotic reverie at the time that I didn't even manage a cutting look, never mind a verbal put-down.

Sunday came and I dressed in my full gear, frilly red rubber panties and all. I looked pretty cocky and did my best to act it, but there was a knot of tension in my stomach as I walked down to Steve's flat. It had been a very long time indeed since I'd enjoyed such a thrill of nervous anticipation, simply because I handle life too well to get into that sort of position unintentionally. I was already a little moist and had had to make a conscious effort not to have a quick session with the vibrator in front of my mirror. As it was I arrived at Steve's looking good enough to eat and was immediately the centre of male attention.

We took the tube from Euston up to Highgate, where we got out and started down the hill with Steve and another man, Paul, holding my arms. They seemed to be heading for a completely built-up area, and I imagined that I was being led to some sordid squat where I could be abused at leisure. Instead they turned down a steep bank and I found myself on a disused railway, the existence of which I had never suspected. It had obviously been turned into a formal walk, as the path was clear and had signs along it. The end, though, was very different: a twin tunnel bored into the hillside and closed off by tall iron grilles. This produced what was in effect an enormous cage, some two hundred yards long and completely hidden. The atmosphere got to me immediately: the dim light, the cool dank air, the feeling of being trapped, all combining to bring my sense of anticipation to a sharp peak. We walked the full length, nobody speaking, the only sounds being the crunch of boots on clinker and the drip of water from the roof. At the far end was a grille identical to the first except in that the gate was chained shut.

'Well, boys, what's it to be?' I asked, trying to sound brave.

I was leaning against the bars at the far end of the tunnel while they stood around me in a semi-circle. Steve grinned and produced two candles from his jacket pocket. They were black and looked cheap. A shiver went through me and I coloured up, thinking that I was going to have to masturbate in front of them. He made no move to give me them, instead producing a vicious looking knife and carefully cutting two rings in the wax about halfway down each. My heart had given a little jump at the appearance of the knife, and so I was relieved when he put it away but puzzled at why he had marked the candles.

'Strip,' Steve ordered, staring at me with an expression of cruel pleasure.

Everyone was looking at me, the men dirty and furtive, the girls tense. I could see that they really didn't expect me to do it, although they were certainly hopeful. I fought down the knot of tension in my stomach, looked Steve squarely in the eyes and put my hand to the zip of my jacket. You could hear the water dripping in the tunnel as I drew it down, slowly, purposefully. My jacket was a little tight across my breasts, and as the zip catch undid with a click it fell open, exposing them. Paul licked his lips as I shrugged the jacket off, making no effort to hide my breasts from them.

My skirt followed, eased down over my hips to leave me standing in rubber panties, hold-up stockings and my stack-heeled boots. I knew that when he said strip he meant me to show my bare pussy and that anything less would make me look timid. It still took a lot of courage to take my pants down though, with nine of them staring at me. If I'd been born poor I would have made a good stripper, and I like to think I did it well. I turned, threw Steve a coy glance over my shoulder, stuck my bottom out, put my thumbs into the waistband of my panties and started to push them down.

One of the girls called me a slut as the taut rubber rode slowly down over the cheeks of my bum. I had never done anything like it before, for all my bravado, and was trembling as I exposed myself to them. With the panties off my bum, I let them drop to the ground, turned and kicked them to Steve. He caught them and Lydia shot me a warning glance while the others focused on my bare pussy and boobs. I put my hands on my head to lift my breasts and stuck one hip out, posing for them insolently as if being nude in front of an audience was something I was used to.

I knew that at least one of the girls, Sally, stripped in pubs, and I was determined not to look naive. I knew I looked great too, standing there in my boots and stockings, otherwise nude, but inside my stomach was fluttering and I could feel my skin prickling with arousal.

'Nude,' Steve said wickedly, his eyes burning into my body while he stroked the candles as if they were his cock.

I complied, kicking off my boots and peeling my stockings down to stand bare in front of them. It felt a lot more vulnerable stark naked than it had done with just boots and stockings, even though I wasn't showing any more. I suppose it's because a girl in boots and stockings, or just boots for that matter, looks poised and artistic, while a naked girl is just that – naked.

'Now do a handstand, up against the bars,' Steve ordered.

'A handstand?' I demanded, wondering what they were doing.

'Just do it,' Steve growled.

I obeyed, feeling a bit silly doing something I last did when I was about thirteen. Of course I hadn't been nude then, and there hadn't been nine people about to put me through a sexual initiation. As my ankles touched the warm metal of the bars, Steve and Paul took hold of them and pulled them apart. I gave a little gasp because it spread my sex wide open. Lydia sniggered and I saw that she was now holding the candles. Two of the other men, Darren and Phil, started to undo their belts. Steve and Paul took a firmer grip of my ankles, as if expecting me to struggle. It was the last thing I was going to do. My eyes were locked on the thick, heavy lengths of leather being slowly pulled free of the other men's trousers.

In my fantasies it had always been my bottom that was beaten, but if they wanted to do my breasts, belly and legs I certainly wasn't going to back out. Maybe they would even whip my pussy. I was trembling, and scared, a rush of emotion and sexual excitement that combined with the pressure of the blood in my head to make me weak and dizzy. Darren got his belt free first and stepped forward. I braced myself, only to find that the belts were to be used to strap my ankles to the bars.

I actually felt a twinge of disappointment, so strong had been my response to what I thought had been going to happen. Not that I needed to worry about being let off, because Steve and Paul had lifted me up so that the belts could be attached to a horizontal bar. This left me dangling and I had to grab the bars to stop my whole weight going on to my ankles. It hurt and I squeaked in protest but they just laughed and pulled my legs a bit wider to make an even more indecent display of my pussy.

'Stick them in, Lydia,' Steve said as he stepped back. 'One in the cunt, one up her arse.'

I was completely helpless, upside down with my pussy spread and my legs lashed in place as she stepped forward. My trembling became stronger. Lydia, another girl and one who I had fantasised about more than once, was going to put candles in my pussy and bumhole and there was absolutely nothing I could do about it. Maybe I wasn't going to be beaten, but for the first time I experienced for real the feelings of helpless shame and consternation that had so appealed to me when I had heard about the girl getting spanked.

My groan echoed in the tunnel as Lydia's fingers touched my pussy, opening my lips with the casual intimacy of someone who has another completely at their mercy. It wasn't the first time another girl had touched my sex, but it had never before brought on such a strong reaction.

'I think she's going to come!' Sally laughed, a light,

amused sound that sent a sharp pang of humiliation through me.

I probably would have done as well, had Lydia turned her attention to my clit. She didn't, but held my labia open and slid the butt of the candle inside me. I groaned again as my pussy stretched around it and the hard, waxy shaft was pushed deeper. Sally giggled again at the obscene sight of me with a candle sticking up from my pussy; Lydia wiggled it, making me moan again.

I knew what was coming next, a piece of degradation perhaps even more intimate than having the candle in my pussy – and certainly dirtier. Lydia put an arm up behind my bottom and spread my cheeks between finger and thumb, exposing my anus. She giggled at the sight and put the butt of the second candle to it. I moaned loudly, feeling the firm stub pressing on my anus. Then it began to force the tight hole open. I relaxed, accepting the candle in my bottom. My anal ring tightened on it as it slid right up, a sensation so dirty, so debauched that I was whimpering out my pleasure without the slightest thought for what they would think of me.

Then Steve lit the candles, grinning down wickedly at me as he put his lighter to the wicks. I had expected it as soon as I realised what the candles were for, but the reality was still a shock. With the candles burning, my breath started to come in little sharp pants. At any instant I was going to get hot wax on my vaginal and anal skin; the thought filled me with panic yet at the same time a need for the pain I knew was coming.

Then it happened, a burning sensation on my bumhole that made me scream and jerk, flicking more wax on to my open vulva. I screamed again and writhed my hips, mewling and squirming in my pain as more wax fell on my anus and then in-between my pussy lips and right on to my clitty. I screamed again, almost fainting, yet close to orgasm.

'For fuck's sake shut the little bitch up,' someone said – Lydia, I think.

'I think she's had enough,' Sally suggested.

Steve stepped forward and blew the candles out, leaving

48

me hanging limp and breathless with my pussy burning and itching. I had been out of control and quite unable to handle the pain, yet when it stopped I wanted more even though the thought terrified me.

'Do it again,' I said, hearing the weakness in my own voice.

'Slut,' Lydia said and turned to Steve, who shrugged and passed her the lighter.

I started to shake violently as she stepped forward, not at all sure what I wanted but desperate for that ecstatic feeling of a totally uncontrolled orgasm to which I had been so close. She lit the candles again and I closed my eyes, trying to calm my breathing as I waited for the first drops of hot wax.

I screamed again when it happened and started to thrash. The drop had gone right between my pussy and anus and really stung. Another touched me, on the rear of my stretched anal ring, then another, full on my pussy. I was writhing and whimpering as the drops started to come faster, hanging in my bonds with the pain in my ankles and the dizzy sensation in my head building along with the pain between my legs. A drop hit my clit and I knew I was going to come if it happened again. Then someone's knuckle touched my pussy and I started to rub, opening my eyes to find Sally standing over me with her fist pressed between my legs. Another burning drop touched my anus and I was coming, screaming out my pleasure as my body tensed against the hard iron bars of the grille. My pussy and bumhole clamped tight on the candles, hot wax spattering across my genitals as my climax arrived and I screamed with all my force.

It went on for a long time, with Sally using her fist on me and the others watching in awestruck silence. The instant I had finished another drop landed on my pussy, now producing only pain and no ecstasy. I squeaked and Sally quickly blew the candles out and pulled them from my aching holes. Steve and Paul immediately stepped forward to unstrap me, and a moment later I was sitting naked on the hard clinker and massaging my sore ankles.

'Get dressed, you little slut. Someone might have heard you screaming,' Lydia said, glancing back along the tunnel.

I realised that she was right and started to dress hastily, pulling my clothes on although still weak and sore from my experience.

'Good enough for you?' I asked, trying to sound brave and cool as I pulled my jacket shut over my boobs.

'Yeah, nice,' Steve admitted. 'Truth is we expected you to chicken out.'

'Would you have let me?' I asked.

'Sure, what do you take us for?' he demanded.

'I don't know,' I replied.

As we walked back along the tunnel I was wondering how I'd managed to do it. It had been an incredibly intense experience, and I was aware that if I hadn't let other people take control of me it could never have happened. Nor could it ever have happened in my normal life, but in ways I was living an adventure by being with them and that allowed me to behave in ways I wouldn't normally have been able to. I was glad I had done it though, and their attitude to me had changed even from what it had been that morning. The girls were a lot friendlier, even Lydia. who was plainly jealous and suspected that Steve and I had had sex. The men were a bit awestruck, as if they couldn't quite believe that I had let them have their wicked way.

There was still a lot of sexual tension, and I knew that I had turned them on. The trouble was that they were all in couples except for Darren, and while I had no specific objection to him, I didn't want to pair up. If any of them became a regular partner it would be Steve, and Lydia would have to make do with second best. Nevertheless, I was wondering if it wouldn't be possible to start something when Steve did it for me.

'How about blow-jobs all round then, girls?' he suggested as we emerged into the light and found that our game had definitely gone undetected.

In my frame of mind I was well up for sucking a yob off among the bushes and gave Steve a smile that made it quite clear that if it was my mouth he wanted to use then I was

50

more than willing. Lydia shot me a dirty look and immediately put her hand on his crotch, a possessive act that marked him firmly as hers but also meant that it was definitely going to happen. I knew that I'd end up with Darren but decided to put up with it, at least for the time being.

We took it in turns, using a brick hut that must originally have been something to do with the railway. Steve and Lydia went first, she leading him in by the hand with a possessive grin on her face. The rest of us stood around the hut, our mere presence more than enough to deter the occasional dog walkers and joggers who passed from investigating it. There was a small, dirty window at the rear of the hut, and I couldn't resist peeping, finding Lydia down on her knees with her cheeks sucked in as she worked on Steve's erection. The sight got me even more in the mood, and as I gave way to Sally's sister Chloë at the window I was thoroughly looking forward to my turn.

There was a definite pecking order among them, with Sally and Paul following Steve and Lydia. As we waited, Phil had his arm around his girlfriend, Lucy, and was fondling her bottom, while Teo and Chloë were looking in the window together, watching Sally suck Paul. That quite clearly left me with Darren, although he was looking a bit furtive, as if unsure whether I would be willing despite his having just helped torture me.

I wanted my share of cock and put my arm around him boldly, making it obvious that I wasn't going to leave him out. He grinned and kissed me, which I responded to. He was only a little taller than me, and skinny, but with hard wiry muscles that at least indicated a fair bit of strength. Taking heart from the warmth of my response, he put his hand up my skirt and began to knead my bottom.

We were last, and by the time Teo and Chloë emerged from the hut Darren had been feeling me up for the best part of half an hour. I was feeling pretty turned on, a feeling which became stronger as we entered the hut and I caught the rich scent of sex in the humid air.

Darren wasted no time, but tugged the zip of his leather

trousers down and was already pulling his balls and cock free as he sat down on the damp concrete floor. I had to kneel to get at his cock, with my bum in the air. As I went down he pulled my jacket zip open and took my boobs in his hands. His cock was right in front of my face, a thick, flaccid shaft that looked very pale against the black leather of his trousers. He started to knead my breasts as I gulped his cock into my mouth. I could see someone watching out of the corner of my eye as he began to stiffen in my mouth, possibly Sally, but I couldn't be sure.

The whole thing was extremely sordid, me kneeling on the floor of a disused railway hut with a yob's cock in my mouth while he pawed at my tits. It was perfect for my bit-of-rough fantasies though, and I was soon sucking eagerly on his rock-hard erection. Nor could I resist playing with myself, going down on to one arm and sliding a hand down my rubber panties to find my clit.

I was dizzy with pleasure as I masturbated and sucked cock at the same time, and reached my orgasm an instant before Darren filled my mouth with sperm. I was still coming and swallowed it down with an abandonment that drew a squeak of delight and disgust from whichever one of the girls was watching at the time. I was purring as I pulled back and even licked the last few drops of white fluid off his cock before getting up.

Afterwards I was in a contented, sleepy mood, satiated with sex after two orgasms and quite happy to let Darren put his arm around me as we walked. It was hot as well, and I didn't have a care in the world as we walked slowly along the path in a vaguely southerly direction.

Unfortunately I hadn't counted on Lydia's bitchiness and really thought they had accepted me. Otherwise I might have been a bit wary when she glanced at me and then started talking earnestly to Steve. He called a halt and disappeared up a track that led to a bridge, returning after a few minutes with a plastic bag. I had spent the time snogging with Darren and assumed that he had simply gone to get some food and perhaps some beers for lunch.

I was right, but only partly. We had reached what had

once been a skateboarding area and before that a station. Darren and I had climbed on to the top of the skateboard ramp, and were sitting there minding our own business. Steve distributed beers and cold meat pies, which were pretty disgusting. Only when we had nearly all finished did he stand up and turn to face the rest of us.

'Who says we tag Tasha?' he announced, using the name they had all called me from the start.

I had no idea what he was talking about and could only sit there looking puzzled as the others chorused agreement to whatever he was suggesting.

'On her bum!' Lydia called, then Steve pulled something out of his bag and I realised what they were going to do to me.

It was a can of spray paint, metallic turquoise as it goes. At the sight of it I remembered reading the word tag in a magazine article. It refers to those spray-painted slogans you always see on walls beside railways. Lydia obviously wasn't content with having seen my pussy tortured with hot wax, or maybe she felt I'd enjoyed it too much. In any case, this new torment had obviously been chosen to humiliate me. She didn't know that I had been getting off on humiliation, but they didn't give me a lot of say in the matter anyway.

I was grabbed and pulled into the woods at the side of the path. Steve and Darren held me while Lydia pulled my skirt up and took my pants off, ignoring my squeals and protests completely. The men then held me firmly in place while Lydia tagged my bottom, spraying something across my cheeks while the rest of the girls laughed at my plight. They then made me stand there with my skirt up and no panties until the paint was dry, all in all an utterly humiliating experience – although I like to think I took it pretty well.

It was only later, when I got home, that I realised the full extent of the defilement she had subjected me to. What she had sprayed across my bottom was her own name, as if I was her property!

To say that I was outraged would be an understatement,

but I couldn't deny that it also produced an oddly subservient feeling that really turned me on. Unable to resist my urges, I stripped and posed, putting the vibrator to my pussy while I looked at the tag on my naked bottom. It was a brilliant orgasm, but I was swearing revenge even as I came.

Six

In the clear light of Monday morning the previous day seemed like a dream. I could scarcely believe what I had done, not only in terms of being so wanton but in terms of surrendering myself to their will. The build-up of excitement during the week must have been even keener than I had realised, and the same was true of the strength of my new fantasies. Ironically, despite everything I had done, or rather had done to me, I still felt frustrated because I hadn't had my spanking.

I felt as if I had though, after taking over an hour to scrub the blue paint off my bottom. By the end my bum was as pink and sore as if they had put me over their knees one after the other. I could appreciate that Lydia was jealous of me, women often are, but there was something really cruel about what she had done. I resented it but couldn't help being turned on and knew that I would be going back for more.

Monday and Tuesday were easy days, while there was a tasting I wanted to attend on the Wednesday. It was being given by a group of cooperatives from south-west France and included things like the Basque wine, Iroulguy. It also gave me the chance to talk to the actual producers. So few people know anything about the area that attending would let me really show off, both in my articles and to my colleagues.

I got up around ten, which is one of the advantages of being clever and successful. I showered, dressed and set off for the hotel in Victoria where the tasting was being held.

It was everything I had hoped for and I spent a happy three hours tasting, making notes and flirting with the younger growers. I spat most of my samples, but was still fairly tipsy by mid-afternoon and was glad to take a freshening-up break. I was making some subtle adjustments to my eye make-up and wondering if it was a good idea to take my flirting any further, when the door banged open and one of my colleagues swept into the room.

'That bloody man!' she announced hotly.

I turned to find that the speaker was Sophie Carlisle, quite a senior female wine writer and someone who I had always regarded as calm and sensible. She was married to a successful wine merchant and wrote detailed reference books that were more suitable for the trade than for amateurs.

'What's the matter?' I asked, surprised at her vehemence.

'That bloody man Thurston,' she replied. 'He's obsessed with bottoms, particularly mine!'

'Sorry?' I queried.

'You must have noticed,' she went on. 'He's always staring at us and making remarks about the shape of my bottom. He's even propositioned me before now! I just overheard him talking to that ghastly man Ottershaw, and I distinctly heard him say he would like to see how I looked in just my knickers! The bloody pervert!'

My ears pricked up. Of all my male colleagues, John Thurston was the one who most often intruded into my spanking fantasies. While I made suitably placatory remarks to Sophie Carlisle I was wondering if his fascination with bottoms extended to spanking them. He had patted mine as he held doors for me more than once, while Sophie had an excellent figure for her age, with a trim waist and a round, well-fleshed behind which I could well see him appreciating. The idea of being over his knee put butterflies in my stomach.

'The dirty old bastard said it would take me down a peg or to be paraded in my knickers,' Sophie Carlisle continued. 'That's what he said, his actual words! Can you believe it! And I'm sure he knew I could hear!'

'That's dreadful!' I sympathised, thinking of her being made to strip to her panties.

He had obviously made the comment in order to humiliate her, presumably because she had turned him down. I also had no doubt that if she complained both he and Ottershaw would stoutly deny the accusations, leaving her even more shamefaced than if she swallowed his taunts.

It's not a big step from suggesting a girl be stripped to suggesting she be spanked, and her remarks had my heart fluttering. I could imagine nothing more humiliating than being told off by him, held down, having my skirt pulled up, feeling his dirty, intrusive hand on the seat of my panties, then down them . . .

I was trembling as I left the loos and wondering if I dared flirt with him and risk it actually happening. The idea filled me with self-disgust, but I just had to, and when I came back into the tasting room I headed not for the handsome young *vigneron* I had been talking to before, but for the big, ruddy faced figure of John Thurston.

He was talking to Percy Ottershaw and some others at a stand of wines from Madiran. He smiled ingratiatingly as I approached and handed me a glass along with a few remarks about the tannin structure of the wine. I accepted it and took a delicate sip. It was heavy and painfully young, although it certainly had potential.

'What do you think, my dear?' Thurston asked.

'A bit like you really, John,' I answered. 'Big, strong and dark.'

A bit corny I know, but there was no need for subtlety and vain though he might be I was sure he would take a bit of convincing that someone as young and attractive as me actually wanted him. Besides, if I'd said the wine resembled him because it was deep red and astringent, he might not have been best pleased. On the other hand he might have put me across his knee on the spot, which would have completely blown my mind.

As it was he smirked and gave Percy Ottershaw a knowing look which I suppose I wasn't supposed to see. The import of it was more or less: 'So, little Natasha's drunk; I wonder if I can make anything of the fact?' From then on it was plain sailing. All I had to do was respond to his compliments, which were even cornier than mine. In fact it was so easy that my qualms quickly faded to the point where I knew I could do it and was sure I was finally going to get what I needed so badly. Of course several glasses of old Madiran followed by several more of strong, sweet Jurançon may have helped.

It was inevitable that he suggest returning to his flat to compare tasting notes and equally inevitable that he chose a moment when Percy Ottershaw was out of earshot to do this. I accepted with a giggle while all my fantasies of humiliation and exposure boiled inside me. We left the tasting together and headed back towards his flat. This proved to be a smart studio off the King's Road and centred on a square room with a wonderful glass dome for a ceiling.

As I crossed towards the settee I dropped my notebook and bent to retrieve it, making a deliberate display of my legs and stockings and presenting him with a view of my cloth-covered bottom that I was sure he would find hard to resist. It had been a deliberate piece of flirtation, but I was still a bit surprised when he grabbed me and pushed his crotch against the taut seat of my skirt. I squealed in an alarm that was only half fake and stood up. An arm came around me, one hand cupping a breast while the other took a good handful of bum-cheek.

'You have the most beautiful bottom I've ever seen Natasha,' he breathed hotly in my ear. 'Forgive me, but I just have to touch it.'

I made a weak protest as he began to pull my skirt up and knead my breast, rubbing the nipple through my blouse. He was kissing my neck too, and I couldn't help responding despite my misgivings.

'That's right, give in to it,' he sighed as he hoisted my skirt up.

I sighed as he took hold of my breasts with both hands and started to rub his crotch against my panties. The bulge of his cock felt hard between my cheeks, pressing the silk down between them. He began to fumble with my blouse buttons, murmuring praise in my ear as he rubbed his cock on me. I put a hand on top of his, resisting more out of instinct than any desire for him to stop.

'Oh you're lovely, Natasha,' he said, almost begging. 'Come on, let me have those lovely big breasts out and those sweet little panties down.'

I took my hand away, thinking what a dirty bastard he was and how exquisite it would be to be spanked by him as he pulled my blouse open. He was clumsy and urgent, grabbing at my bra and pulling it roughly up so that my breasts fell out. For a moment I felt their unsupported weight and then his hands curled beneath them and his thumbs were on my nipples. I sighed and stuck my bottom out, eager for the feel of his prick in my crease as my nipples popped up under his rough caresses.

'That's it, my little one,' he breathed hoarsely, 'let yourself go. Now for your panties.'

He let go of my breasts and moved down until his face was level with my bum. I stuck it out, sure that at any moment he would reveal his true need, pull me down across his lap and give me a bottom-blistering spanking.

'Silk,' he murmured, rubbing his face against my panty seat. 'I might have guessed. You're so elegant, so refined.'

His hands went to my waistband and started to pull. I sighed deeply. This was one of the prime elements of my fantasies, the moment a dirty old man took my knickers down. It was bliss. They slid slowly down my cheeks, the silk tickling my skin; his red, lust-filled face no more than a couple of inches from my panty seat, then from my naked bottom. He was admiring my bottom, the naked pink cheeks bare for his lecherous eyes to cherish, probing every secret detail of my fresh, girlish rear.

'Bend a little, darling,' he said as he inverted my panties around my thighs. 'Stick it out.'

I did, although I knew that it would make my cheeks part and show off my pussy and anus. I felt the air on the rear of my vaginal pouch and knew that he could see it, every hair and wet pink fold of my sex, blatantly on display for him.

'I've got to touch it,' he sighed. An instant later a finger found my skin, but not on my pussy, on my anus.

I suppose it wasn't surprising that if he was obsessed with girls' bums then he would be obsessed with the tight little holes in the centre as well. He certainly was with mine, touching it and pulling the sides of my ring as if trying to see up my bottom. It was much the same treatment as Evan Dunstal had given Charlotte before he buggered her, and inevitably a sneaking suspicion entered my head.

'You're not putting your cock up it,' I told him, trying to sound firm.

'Oh but, Natasha, you're so pretty there,' he answered. 'Are you virgin?'

'Up my bottom, yes!' I replied, pulling away with the sharp realisation that while he might or might not intend to spank me, he was definitely after my anal virginity.

'I'll be very gentle,' he promised, still on his knees as I turned round. 'I'll open you slowly and use plenty of lubricant, and put my fingers in before my cock.'

He was pleading, and I couldn't find anything to say, being completely taken aback by the sheer crudeness of his words. I could feel myself melting though, remembering my fantasies of being buggered after a spanking and wondering how his cock would feel in my anal passage.

'Come on, Natasha,' he wheedled, 'let me do it. I can't resist you, you're too lovely.'

'You're a dirty old man, do you know that?' I responded, trying to sound cross but not really succeeding.

'Come on, you want to really,' he pleaded. 'I'll make you come while I'm in you, I promise. Come on, Natasha – do it for me.'

'I . . .' I started and then stopped. From that moment of hesitation I was lost.

'You know you want it,' he said. 'Look at me, look how you've excited me.'

He pulled his zip down and adjusted his underpants, releasing a big, brown cock, already more than half stiff. I swallowed at the sight, thinking of what he intended to do with it, thinking of my tight, virgin bumhole and how it would feel stretched around an intruding cock, just like Charlotte's had been.

'Please don't let me down,' he said, sensing my indecision.

I like to think that if it hadn't happened to Charlotte I would have backed out. After all, wanting to be sodomised by a man over twice my age is just one of those things I could never, ever have admitted to; any more than I could admit to wanting a bare-bottomed spanking. Yet I hate feeling less experienced than my friends, and Charlotte had let Evan Dunstal put it in her bottom and had obviously enjoyed it.

'Maybe ... maybe if you warm me up a little first,' I stammered, hearing my own words but hardly believing I was a saying them.

He got to his feet and came towards me, smiling now and holding out his hand. I let him take me by the arm, surrendering myself and hoping that he took the hint about warming me up.

Directly beneath the dome, in the centre of the polished wooden floor, was a big sheepskin, just the right size to kneel on. He steered me towards it and pushed me down. I went, and my knees sank into the soft wool. I felt cheated and dirty as I put my face into the rug and raised my naked bottom for his inspection, also tricked, as if he had promised me my spanking only to deny me and bugger me instead. I had the same feelings of being used and humiliated though, feelings which were added to by the idea of being tricked into a dirty sexual act.

He really brought the sensation of being dirty out as well, although I don't think it was intentional but simply that he was a bit tactless. First he made me cock my legs up one by one, like a dog pissing on a lamp-post. This was ostensibly so that he could pull my panties off, but doing it felt extraordinarily rude. Then he made a big deal of lubricating my anus. He used butter, which melted and dribbled down my pussy as he rubbed it in between my bum-cheeks. Then he put a finger in my bumhole, told

61

me how nice and tight I felt and then pulled it out, leaving my anus feeling open and sensitive.

I had my face in the wool and was shivering, torn between the physical pleasure of having my bottom greased and probed and self-disgust and humiliation at accepting it from him. He kept talking as well, which made it worse. His voice was thick with lust as he described how I looked with a big blob of butter melting in my anus and running down into my pussy.

'You're so pretty,' he sighed. 'Your anus is perfect, a little virgin rosebud for my cock. Oh you're so lovely, Natasha; your cunt's so pretty too. I'm going to fuck it while the butter melts.'

I opened my knees, anticipating his cock, only to feel something firm and cold against my bumhole. Thinking that I was about to be buggered, I gasped, only to realise that it was not his cock but a big pat of cold butter. He pushed it into my rectum while I gritted my teeth at the shame of it all, wiggled his finger about inside me and then withdrew. A moment later something hard and a lot warmer touched my pussy and I knew he was about to mount me.

A moan escaped my lips as his cock filled my vagina, easing into me until his pubic hair was touching the sensitive skin around my greasy, open anus. His hands gripped the waistband of my skirt and he began to ride me, slowly at first and then faster, making me pant and clutch at the sheepskin. He was soon grunting and moaning, pounding into me so hard that I was sure he was going to come up me and deprive me of my promised anal experience.

With any of the young men I've had sex with their control would have gone and they would have come inside me. One over-sexed student had even mumbled apologies at the same time as he filled my vagina with sperm and completely ignored my protests. John Thurston suffered from no such difficulties. He paused only to drop his trousers and pull his balls out over the top of his underpants and then carried on cheerfully working his cock inside me. Only when I was thoroughly on heat and panting my lust out into the rug did he calmly withdraw from my pussy and slide his erection up the buttery crease of my bottom.

I could feel the hard shaft between my cheeks, rigid yet slimy with butter and my juices. It was about to go up my bottom, and I didn't want to stop him. I was still dizzy from being fucked as the head of his cock nudged my anus. I could feel the butter squelching in my hole and hear it too; it was both delicious and obscene.

'Relax; push it out,' he instructed, 'as if you were on the loo.'

That really was the last straw. I mean, of all the filthy, dirty, depraved things to say to a girl. I did it though, and felt the tears start in my eyes as my bumhole everted to accept his cock. There was a disgusting squishy sound and a slight pain, then I felt my anal ring stretch and knew that the head of his erection was in my anus. I groaned loudly, clutching the thick wool of the rug as he forced his erection up my bottom, working it in inch by inch until my rectum was completely full of hard cock lubricated with molten butter. He gave a little shove and his balls slapped against my empty pussy.

Then he began to bugger me in earnest, using short, hard shoves each of which knocked the breath out of my lungs and smacked his dangling balls against my sopping vulva. It also made my breasts swing against the rough wool of the rug, the whole combining into an ecstasy quite different from that of being fucked.

I was out of control, but it didn't matter. In fact it was nice – surrendering myself totally to his perverted lust, allowing him to bugger me in the middle of his lounge. I mean, me, little miss perfect, with her skirt up, no panties and a big fat cock up her bottom. Not a handsome young stud's cock either, but that of a big, red-faced, ginger-haired man of at least fifty, a man I had allowed to butter my bottom and sodomise me with scarcely a squeak of protest.

There were tears in my eyes but I was sighing and

groaning as he rode me. I found the sensation of having my bottom full of his shaft almost unbearable, and the pushes even more so. After a while he put his hand under my belly and began to frig me, using his finger tips to rub my clitty. I groaned in pleasure, the final act of acceptance, allowing him to masturbate me to orgasm while he buggered me.

I'm sure he had done it before, because he had a precise knack of bumping his finger tips on my clitoris, yet the motion of his cock in my bumhole never stopped. I was soon whimpering with pleasure, and then my muscles started to spasm with the approach of orgasm. It was really happening, the filthy moment I had masturbated over so often, the moment when my anus started to contract in orgasm, not around a finger or the handle of my hairbrush, but around a man's erection.

I screamed and then bit the rug, bucking my hips up and down and kicking my feet in helpless, overwhelming ecstasy. He carried on, maintaining exact control of my body until I was shaking and whimpering for him to stop because I was sure I would pass out if he didn't.

My vision was red before it was over, only for him to take a firmer grip on my hips and start to slam into me, much harder than before. Now it hurt, with his cock going deep into me and his front slapping against my buttocks with each heavy push. I gave a gasp of protest but he took no notice and as his balls hit my pussy I realised that I was going to come again if I so much as touched my clit.

I put a hand back, squashing one of my breasts against my chest with the other and burying my face in the rug. He was grunting even more loudly than before as my fingers found my burning clitty, all sticky with pussy juice and butter. Then he was coming, right up my aching, agonised bottom, calling my name as I screamed, telling me I was beautiful as his penis erupted in my rectum. I was yelling and clutching at the rug as I came for the second time, aware of the burning pain in my bottom and thoroughly delighted by it. He gave one last, vigorous shove that pushed my open mouth into the rug and then stopped, leaving me to tease the last drops of ecstasy from my clit and then slump down as he started to withdraw from my bumhole.

Exhausted and dizzy with drink, sex and pain, I collapsed on my side. I was vaguely aware of his getting up and walking rather unsteadily into the kitchen, but I had no desire to move. He made coffee while I lay on my side, dribbling sticky fluid on to his rug. I was indifferent to my exposed breasts and sex, my thoughts running only on the experience he had just put me through.

Only when he came back with a mug of coffee did I finally manage to rouse myself. Even then all I could do was sit there cross-legged in a patch of my own wetness until I had taken in enough coffee to restore myself. He made no objection, even though I imagine it must have been the end of his fine sheepskin. Instead he just sat there, grinning at me and sipping coffee until I finally started to feel self-conscious about my bare boobs and pussy.

He cooked while I tidied up, preparing a dish of scallops and crab meat in a faintly hot sauce. I felt used, but had the sense to realise that I had made my own choices and that is was pointless to be cross. His efforts with the coffee and the meal destroyed any lingering intentions of restoring my pride by being nasty to him. I was desperate to be alone with my thoughts though, and so I left as soon as was politely possible, declining his offer of sleeping together. He was clearly disappointed but took it well, perhaps realising that he had been incredibly lucky to have me at all, never mind to have me surrender so absolutely.

I went home with a sore bottom-hole and extremely mixed emotions. The orgasm had been wonderful, and I was actually quite glad to have lost my anal virginity. I didn't feel scared of men putting their cocks in my bottom any more, because I knew that it didn't hurt as much as I'd anticipated. I was even looking forward to doing it again, because the combination of the breathless, stretched physical sensation and the mental feelings of dirtiness and humiliation had been simply exquisite. On the other hand, the next man who I accepted in my anus was not going to be John Thurston. Had he spanked me first it would have been different, but if I was going to have regular sex with a dirty old man I wanted it perfectly in accord with my fantasy and nothing less.

Seven

The next morning I awoke to the realisation that the flesh around my anus was slightly bruised. This made me feel more than a little sorry for myself, and I began to realise why people used the word 'buggered' for something that had been put out of action. The dull ache between my bottom cheeks made it uncomfortable to sit down, rather as if I had been beaten. This made it hard to concentrate on work and also meant that memories of the day before kept coming back to me. The result was that I spent the day alternating periods of work with periods of really self-indulgent masturbation. This involved a lot of cold cream and wriggling around on my bed with my bottom uppermost. It also involved thinking of how nice it would have been if John Thurston had given me a really sound spanking before sodomising me.

By Saturday I was back to my usual self and looking forward to the party that was being held at Steve's flat that evening. All week I had been struggling with my reaction to Lydia's desire to make me accept an inferior social position to her. On the one hand, it raised a strong sense of indignation in me and made me determined to revenge myself on her, especially for tagging my bottom. On the other hand, there was definitely something sexy about a girl wanting to make me crawl to her, just so long as it involved her doing rude things to me. I found the discovery that the idea of being bullied by a girl excited me more than a little disturbing. I am used to being popular and freely admit to having occasionally tormented other girls and thoroughly enjoying it. Being on the receiving end was a new experience for me, yet I couldn't deny I rather liked the idea.

Feeling in need of some new clothes, I spent the day shopping. My previous tarty outfit had seemed so good when I bought it and I had felt so naughty when I first put it on. Steve and the others had liked it, but it didn't make me stand out from the other girls, Lydia in particular, with her outrageous hairstyle, pierced tongue and the tiny black cat tattooed on one cheek. As I have a respectable job I couldn't outdo her on the body decoration front and so had to try and do it with clothes. As she regularly went around in a mini-skirt with no panties underneath this was not too easy. I had a better figure, of course, and decent sized boobs; hers were tiny. The knack then was clearly to show my natural advantages off in a way that she couldn't compete with, and if she made me take some humiliating punishment for outshining her then so much the better.

Not that it was easy. I spent ages in Camden, where there was plenty of choice but nothing that really stood out. I wanted to be the centre of attention, and while I was confident in my looks, I had to admit that for once I had some serious competition. Lydia was strikingly pretty: small, pert and firm with small, high breasts, a tight waist and a round, somehow boyish bottom. Sally was more my height, lean and athletic but moderately busty. Her sister Chloë had a similar face and body, but with a bit of puppy fat, especially on her bottom. Lucy was a tiny natural blonde with plenty of curves and a vivacious manner. So while I did have my usual natural advantage in looks, it wasn't by much; I needed something daring to get their attention, particularly Steve's.

Just as I had done on my first trip to buy outrageous clothes, I spent a while looking at piercing booths, but once more failed to actually do anything about it. Only when I was staring morosely at the hundredth leather mini-skirt did I realise that I was approaching the thing from entirely the wrong angle. The first time I had seen them their antagonistic reaction to me had been born of jealousy. Now that I had made it clear that I didn't consider myself above them they were no longer antagonistic, but they would still be impressed by an image that they normally regarded as unobtainable. Of course they didn't know that I could afford that sort of thing, so I would pretend I had stolen it, thus reinforcing my credibility.

Half an hour later I was in Bond Street, putting one of my credit cards to the use for which it was intended. My choice was simple, a beautifully cut dress in deep blue velvet and a new pair of heavy silk panties, nothing more. I then brought some more make-up and headed home, sure that I would be a hit.

I was. The men were impressed to say the least, and although there was a measure of feeling that Darren had at least some claim on me, the others were not lacking in attention. My shoplifting story also went down well, with not one of them doubting my word. After all, I had a dress that was plainly expensive and, as I was supposedly unemployed, how else could I have come by it?

Lydia and Chloë were jealous and didn't make much effort to hide it, while Sally, who didn't seem to see me as a threat, was more admiring than anything. Lucy was the hardest one to handle, because she admitted frankly that she loved the dress but would never have the courage to shoplift. The implication was that I might do it for her, which I knew I would never be able to do.

Not that that was an immediate problem, and the party progressed with me basking in male adulation and female jealousy, something which I have always enjoyed. I was also getting rapidly drunk, having brought two bottles of respectable port, also supposedly shoplifted. Curled up next to Darren, who had one hand stroking a velvet covered breast, I was feeling thoroughly relaxed and in the mood for the rough sex that was sure to come later.

The conversation had turned to piercings, and the girls were showing theirs off to one another. Both Lydia and Chloë had already lifted their tops up over their breasts to show their nipple piercings and had stayed like that to allow their boyfriends to fondle them more easily. The display of bare female flesh was making me feel distinctly warm, especially with Darren doing his best to keep my nipples erect.

Sally had had her tongue pierced to improve her striptease act and stood up to show us, sticking her tongue out and wiggling the tip suggestively. The piercing was a metal bar with a ring on the underside, to which a tiny key was attached. This worked a diminutive padlock that joined the rings she had through her pussy lips. The idea made me wince a bit but also thrilled me, and I was wondering whether she would mind me asking to see her pussy piercing when Lucy beat me to it.

'Let's see your pussy rings, then, Sally,' she said eagerly, without a trace of the embarrassment I felt at asking to see another girl's sex.

Sally laughed and put her hand straight to the zip of her tight PVC shorts. I found a lump in my throat as I realised that she was going to do it and stared entranced as she peeled them down over her slim hips, displaying her pussy to Lucy and her sweet little bottom to me. She had no panties underneath, and her bum was stuck out bare, sending a shock of guilty lust right through me.

'Let's see,' Steve called out from where he was sprawled on the bed with his hand up Lydia's skirt.

Sally turned, managing to make the movement look graceful despite having her shorts around her thighs. Her new position gave me as good a view as it did Steve, and I felt a hot flush as she quite blatantly stuck her hips forward and spread her pussy with two fingers. I could see everything. He pubic hair was trimmed short and shaved into a love-heart. Beneath, her vulva was pink and moist, the clitoris showing as a little shiny dome beneath its fleshy hood. Neat inner labia curved down, both pierced with rings and joined by the tiny padlock.

'Didn't it hurt?' I asked, aware of the tremor in my own voice.

'No, it was done with a local anaesthetic,' she answered,

still casually holding her pussy open for our inspection. 'You don't have any, do you?'

They had seen me nude, so they knew the answer, but from the moment I shook my head I knew I was lost.

'You should get one,' Sally answered.

'I was thinking about it today actually,' I answered uncertainly. 'There are lots of stalls that do it in Camden Market.'

'You don't want to waste money,' Chloë put in. 'Except for really tricky ones you can do it at home. I'll do it for you if you like.'

I swallowed, not at all sure of myself but knowing that to refuse would be to lose a lot of face.

'Come on,' Lydia continued when I didn't answer. 'I'll do your tummy button, that's not hard.'

'But what about anaesthetic and sterilisation?' I queried.

'Don't worry,' she insisted. 'Pour some more port down yourself and we'll use ice to numb your skin. The needle can be sterilised with a candle flame.'

'Needle?' I asked.

'Sure,' she answered. 'We need to make a hole. Mine stays open now, so you can even borrow my tummy-button ring to keep it open.'

As she still had her top pulled up over her tits I could see her piercing, which was a ring with a tag attached made of silver letters that spelt out her name. If I accepted her offer I would be going around with her name on a ring through my tummy button, an idea that sent a thrill of subservient pleasure through me, just as having her tag my bottom had done. I couldn't resist it and was agreeing even as I realised that she had once more marked me as her inferior, even her property. That would have had me shivering even without the prospect of a needle being pushed through the flesh of my tummy, but a part of me still managed to feel outraged at her assumption of power over me.

'Why not tie her down to do it?' Paul suggested. 'She likes that.'

'Yeah, nice,' Steve agreed as Darren arm's tightened around me.

I squeaked in a protest that was only half fake. I was once more firmly the centre of attention, and that was nice, come what might.

'Slowly, slowly,' Lydia interjected. 'You can't just stick it through.'

I had been wriggling in Darren's grip but relaxed at her words, at least physically. For all my drunkenness and delight at the prospect I was determined to have it done safely; the men's attitude suggested indifference to such details. Lydia, in contrast, was cool, even scientific, in her approach and evidently knew what she was doing.

'First we need to make a biro mark where we're going to make the hole,' she continued. 'And we need her standing up for that, because tummy flesh changes shape when you sit down and it needs to look right.'

Darren let go, rather reluctantly, and I stood up. I was shaking as they found a mirror and got me to make a biro mark where I wanted the ring to go through. I chose the taut piece of skin at the top of my tummy button, already imagining how it would look with Lydia's name tag hung from it.

The idea of tying me up obviously excited Steve, because he insisted on it. I complied, keen to get the most out of the experience. The men did the work, strapping me firmly to the bed with my limbs tied to the corner posts. Spread-eagled and helpless, I watched Lydia take out her piercing and sterilise it while Darren pulled up my dress again. Inevitably he pulled it right up over my breasts, rucking the material around my upper chest and leaving my erect nipples poking up expectantly. My panties, no more than a scrap of silk, were all that hid my sex, and I felt immensely vulnerable. This was made worse by my legs being far enough apart for a man to mount me and slide his cock inside me, about which I could have done absolutely nothing.

Once I was firmly strapped in place they stood back, looking down at me with lust in their eyes. Only when Lydia returned with a tray of ice did they move apart. She climbed on the bed and knelt between my open thighs, just

72

as a man would have done were he about to enter me. She took an ice cube from the tray and placed it on my tummy, the cold sensation making me squirm inside. Beyond her I could see Sally preparing things. She was heating a needle and had put one of the port corks in a glass of vodka. Leaving the needle in the flame, she dipped a tissue into the vodka and passed it to Lydia, who used it as a swab to sterilise the skin they intended to puncture. My trembling was becoming stronger as they worked, their cool, nurse-like efficiency making me feel even more sensitive and vulnerable.

'The cork is to stretch your skin out, otherwise it might tear,' Lydia explained, taking it from Sally. 'Now hold still; just relax.'

I was trying but it wasn't easy. Lying tied to the bed in a ring of excited faces, I felt anything but relaxed. Lydia put the cork into my tummy button, stretching the skin taut around it. Then she reached back for Sally to pour some vodka on to her hands. Wiping them, she took the sterilised needle, through which a vodka soaked thread had been run. I was leaning up, and could see the skin of my belly giving little involuntary spasms. My teeth were set as Lydia bent down, took a firm hold of the cork, placed the needle against the mark I had made and then pushed.

There was a sudden sharp pain, no worse than having an injection. Also like an injection, the anticipation of pain had been worse than the actuality. My breathing was still coming deep and even as she pulled the needle through. The vodka was stinging the puncture, and I could feel the thread running through my skin despite the effect of the ice.

Their eyes were riveted on my tummy as Lydia completed the work, pulling the hole open with the thread and slipping the slim pin of her name tag through the hole. I heard the minute catch click and knew I had been marked; knowledge that put a hard lump of passion in my throat.

'She's soaking,' Chloë remarked, glancing down at the crotch of my panties as Lydia stood back with a look of delight and triumph on her face.

Chloë was right. I could feel the dampness of my panties and knew just how aroused I was. The piercing hurt, a little, and was giving me an endorphin rush, but more important were the delicious feelings of naughtiness for doing something my parents and others would have disapproved of and because the little silver letters attached to the tummy-button ring spelt out Lydia.

'I've got to fuck her,' Darren said hoarsely.

At that instant I would rather have had Lydia mount me or even sit on my face and make me lick her just as I liked to make men lick me. Yet I was helpless and it was their decision who had me and not mine. I sighed and closed my eyes, waiting to be mounted and given the rough, hard entry that was being offered.

'Careful of her piercing,' Lydia warned as I heard the bed springs creak and felt the smooth leather of his trousers touch my thighs.

I opened my eyes again, unable to resist watching him prepare himself to enter me. He was unbuttoning his trousers, his expression one of glee mixed with just a little guilt. Not much though, nowhere near enough to make him hesitate as he peeled his zip open and pulled his cock and balls over the rim of his underpants. The thick, half-stiff shaft squirmed under the skin, swelling quickly at the prospect of my defenceless vagina. He put a hand to his cock, using short, quick jerks to excite himself as the other hand closed firmly on my panties.

Too late I realised his intention and could only squeak in helpless protest as he wrenched at my beautiful new silk panties. They had never been designed for such abuse and tore, leaving my vulva exposed before him. The shock of having my panties ripped off increased my vulnerability to an agonising peak, compounded by the indignity of having my expensive underwear ruined to allow him to get at my sex.

As he knelt forward and pressed his now fully erect penis to my vulva I lifted my bottom to let him in. For a moment his cock touched my clitty then it was against my vagina, stretching me, opening me, filling me, as he slid it in to the

74

hilt. I groaned as he began to fuck me. His hands were under my buttocks, lifting me into his lap in a rather awkward position. I didn't care. My vagina was full of penis and my brain was full of the pleasure of being thoroughly used.

The position may have been uncomfortable for him, but that didn't stop him coming just as quickly as he had when I had sucked his cock in the railway hut. Just as I was getting nicely into the rhythm of his pushes, he pulled out, grabbing his cock even as the sperm erupted from the tip. It splashed over my pubic hair and on to my vulva, adding the feeling of being soiled to my ecstasy.

I was desperate for someone else to take over and looked up, pleading with my eyes. The men returned looks that made it quite clear what they had in mind for me, and from the girls' expressions I knew that I was going to get at least one more cock. Paul's was already out of his trousers, Sally nursing it in her hand to keep it ready, not for her pussy, but for mine.

He stepped forward, his erection jutting up from his fly and aiming directly between my legs. I stuck my tongue out, making a licking motion to show just how willing I was.

'Why not put yours in her mouth, Phil?' Lucy said quietly but with real passion, perhaps judging my tongue gesture to indicate willingness to suck on a cock or two.

Phil needed no further prompting, and was easing his fly down even as he stepped towards the upper end of the bed. I opened my mouth and let him feed his flaccid cock in, sucking as he took hold of one of my breasts and began to knead. He started to stiffen in my mouth as Paul climbed up between my legs. Like Darren he put his hands under my bottom and lifted me up to his cock. It went in easily, making me moan around my mouthful of cock as my pussy filled.

I was in heaven, with one cock in my pussy and another in my mouth, sucking eagerly while Paul rode me into a state of dizzy happiness. I suppose the girls felt that they were giving me to their boyfriends rather than their boyfriends going behind their backs; after all, I was helpless. In any case, they seemed quite happy about me being had. Lucy even joined Phil in fondling my breasts, her delicate fingers working on my nipples and her eyes locked on the junction between her boyfriend's penis and my mouth.

I was high enough to be looking forward to a mouthful of sperm, but Phil had other ideas, taking his time in my mouth so that he could keep his erection for my pussy. Unlike Darren, they really gave me my fill, Paul pumping away until my pussy was starting to feel sore, and Phil really taking his time in my mouth despite my best efforts to make him come. Finally it happened, Paul grunting and giving a last, hard shove even as Phil lost control and filled my mouth with salty, male-tasting sperm. To my surprise he pulled back and scrabbled round to get between my legs even as Paul was draining his cock over my pubes. Obviously determined to fuck me, Phil managed to get himself inside, filling my vagina with a cock already wet with my saliva and his sperm.

It was useless to protest; Paul had come inside me anyway, so my vagina was already full of semen. Somehow that added to it, making me feel even more helpless and abused as Phil began to hump me with desperate pushes. Behind him Sally was on her knees, licking a mixture of come and my juices from Paul's cock. Phil was deep in my pussy and I realised that he wasn't going to lose his erection and might even be able to come inside me.

He did, by which time I was sore and dizzy, covered in sweat and come and totally abandoned to their lust. Teo, Chloë's muscular black boyfriend, had put his cock in my mouth and come all over my face and breasts. She and Lucy had rubbed his come in, giggling at the feel of my erect nipples under their coating of sperm. Once Phil had had his orgasm inside me I was left gasping and shaking on the bed, soiled and near naked, with my torn panties around one thigh and my beautiful blue velvet dress smeared with semen. Only Steve hadn't had me, and from the way he was looking I knew he wanted to.

I saw him exchange glances with Lydia; a wicked smile crossed her face. He was very much the leader of the group and couldn't very well not have me when all the others had. On the other hand it simply wasn't going to be practical unless Lydia let him. I shot her a pleading glance and her smile broadened into a sadistic leer.

'Beg me to let him fuck you, you little slut,' she sneered, then turned to Sally. 'Rub her clit Sal, keep her high.'

'Please, Lydia, let Steve fuck me,' I responded immediately, far too far gone to care about my dignity.

'Say how much you want it,' she demanded.

'I want it a lot, I really do,' I answered as Sally's knuckles found my vulva and started to rub.

'Say where,' she ordered.

'In my pussy, please . . . please,' I begged.

'Talk dirty, you stuck-up little tart,' she snapped back. 'Come on, call it a cunt.'

'OK,' I gasped, full of humiliation at what she was making me do but eager for it all the same. 'I want Steve to fuck me, to put his lovely cock in my cunt, my wet, eager cunt. Please, Lydia, let him fuck me!'

My voice had risen in pitch, almost to a scream. I was rapidly loosing my last vestiges of control, but she just laughed and reached out her hand to pull down Steve's zip.

'Is this what you want?' she teased as she pulled his cock out. 'This nice fat cock in your dirty little cunt.'

'Yes,' I managed.

'Then tell me who owns you,' she answered. 'Who it was who tagged your fat bottom and whose name you're wearing in your belly button.'

I was close to orgasm, my resistance completely gone as Sally worked on my clitoris and Lydia pushed my mental buttons.

'Tell me,' Lydia said coolly as she leant over me and gave one of my straining nipples a contemptuous flick.

'You, Lydia. You,' I mewled.

'Go on, then, fuck the little tart,' Lydia laughed, drawing back.

One instant more and I would have asked to lick her

with her sat on my face, even offering to tongue her bottom. As it was I was left stammering out my thanks as Steve climbed on to the bed and got down between my thighs. Sally had had me on the edge of orgasm and kept her fingers on my pussy as Steve pushed himself into my vagina. Once more I had the blissful sensation of being stretched around a fat penis, only with a set of skilled fingers working on my pussy as well.

It didn't take long to come. My muscles started to contract as Steve pulled my cheeks open and touched a finger to my anus. My limbs were tense against my bonds and I was acutely aware of my every sense: the cock inside me; the fingers on my clitty, the hands working my breasts and the sharp tingle of my new piercing, the piercing that bore the name of the girl who had just made me declare myself her property. I called her name as I hit my climax, not quietly but aloud so that everyone heard. My shame burst like a bubble inside me but I was far past resistance and could only slump down into a sweaty heap, mumbling Lydia's name over and over as my orgasm subsided.

Eight

The following morning, as I sat in casualty waiting to collect my morning-after pill, my thoughts ran through the way I had been treated. I knew they were using me, but it was so nice that I didn't care, especially when at bottom I felt confident that I could handle whatever they chose to do. They knew that my background wasn't really like theirs, and Steve at least saw me as a spoilt rich girl deliberately slumming it. Lydia of course was no better, but they were much more accepting of her than me. Lucy at least genuinely liked me, and Sally and Darren certainly had at least some feelings for me. Chloë was friendly enough, if a little jealous, while the other men really just saw me as a way to some easy sex. Lydia's attitude alone was unusual and intensely aphrodisiac, whether I liked it or not.

It was more than a little embarrassing collecting the pill from the hospital's casualty department, but it was a Sunday and so I had little option. Once done, I set off for Evan Dunstal's church, theoretically to lend my excellent voice to the choir, but in practice to try and put a spoke in the works between him and Charlotte.

For all Evan Dunstal's bizarre sexual habits, he had struck me as a bit of a prude, especially where his precious church was concerned. Like most self-important men, he was sensitive to anything that trivialised him, which undoubtedly would include any show of disrespect in his church. My first move then would be to outrage him and try to make him lose what I was sure was a rather fragile temper.

79

So I changed into a pair of tatty jeans with rips that left a good slice of bum cheek on view and a crop top that left my piercing showing, ordinary enough street wear, but hardly what he would expect for church. Charlotte accepted my dress without comment, but was fascinated by the piercing and insisted that I explain how I had come by it. I bent the truth a little, telling her that a girl called Lydia had done it and had put her name tag in because she had nothing else to hand. The details of how it had been done I left out.

We drove to the church, chatting cheerfully as we went. Charlotte wanted to know how it felt to have a ring through my tummy button and I admitted that it made me feel naughty. This was true, the slight ache serving as a constant reminder of the previous night's excesses and keeping me sexually aware. It reminded me of how I had felt after altering the hem of my school skirt by several inches to make a better display of my legs. That had worn off after a while, the sensation simply becoming too familiar to be exciting. I suspected that the same would be true of the piercing, but was keen to enjoy the thrill while it lasted. The effect of it being Lydia's name tag was less strong than it had been when I was coming – a lot less. Nevertheless, it was there, and I got a hot flush every time I thought of how she had made me declare myself her property in front of everybody.

Evan Dunstal, as handsome and sanctimonious as ever, greeted us at the church. The look he turned to my bare midriff told me that I had been right in my assumption that he would disapprove, and as we walked into the building I was steeling myself to carry out my scheme. The congregation were a pretty sorry lot, and I got several more disapproving looks as we passed down the aisle. I had been expecting to go straight to the choir stalls and was surprised when Evan and Charlotte turned towards a door near the end of the church. As we went through I realised that we were in the room in which they had had sex.

'You'll want to change, Natasha,' Evan said, a statement

80

of fact, not a question. 'Any of the spare surplices should fit you.'

'I'm quite happy as I am,' I replied.

'I'm sorry, but you'll have to change,' he said firmly.

'Why?' I asked. 'Do you think I'm indecent?'

'Frankly, yes,' he answered, his voice showing touches of both embarrassment and indignation.

'Why?' I demanded.

'Look,' he answered, 'I realise that body jewellery is the fashion nowadays, but it is hardly appropriate for the house of God.'

'Do you want me to take my earrings out then?' I asked. 'Charlotte's wearing them too for that matter, and I'm sure some of the congregation are.'

'Earrings are hardly the same as a belly stud,' he answered. 'And in any case, if you wish to sing in the choir, you must wear a surplice.'

'I'm not wearing somebody else's dirty old clothes,' I protested.

'They have all been freshly laundered,' he retorted, now distinctly cross.

'Please, Natasha,' Charlotte put in.

'Very well,' I answered, and peeled my crop top up over my bra-less breasts.

His face was a picture, red and pop-eyed, horribly embarrassed yet unable to tear his gaze away from my naked boobs.

'Don't stare then!' I snapped, adding perturbation to his emotions.

He turned quickly away. Charlotte was looking at me in surprise but said nothing, reluctant as always to criticise my behaviour. I peeled my jeans off, kicked my feet free and walked boldly over to the line of surplices, making sure that Evan got a good view of my panties.

'Stop staring, you dirty old man!' I snapped, conveniently ignoring the fact that he had very little choice.

That was the point that three other choir members walked in, an old couple and a middle-aged woman. They heard what I said and saw me in just my panties but of

81

course knew nothing of what had happened before. I changed character on the instant, grabbing a surplice and pulling it hurriedly over my head, hopefully giving the implication that Evan had forced me to strip to my knickers. It worked at least partially, because the middle-aged woman gave him a look of shocked incredulity and me one of concern.

'The patronising bastard!' I said to Charlotte as we left the vestry.

'You were a bit unfair,' she answered softly.

'No I wasn't,' I responded. 'He's got no right to tell me what to wear or that I look indecent. I mean, you say he preaches tolerance and mutual respect and meekness, but he certainly doesn't practise it! No, what the paternalistic hypocrite wants is for everyone else to be tolerant and respectful and meek while he bosses them around!'

She didn't reply because we had come out into the main body of the church and fifty assorted pairs of ears had been flapping in our direction. I was sure I was having some effect though, especially as what I had said was true.

The service went well enough. I sing well and enjoy doing it and wasn't too bothered by the incompetence of most of the other choristers. The rest was simply boring, the usual drivel but fancied up to convey his message of the need for tolerance and morality to combat modern social decay. How you have tolerance and a strict moral code simultaneously beats me, so I turned off and thought about being gang-banged by five yobs instead. My pussy was still sore from the experience, but I would have been more than willing to take a repeat performance.

When it eventually finished we returned to the vestry. Evan Dunstal gave me a look of warning, as if to make it very clear that I was not to remove my surplice until the other choristers had gone. It was as if I was being dared, and that always brings out the devil in me. I seriously considered peeling off the surplice and just strolling around in front of them all wearing nothing but a diminutive pair of blue silk panties. He would have been furious, but it would have been too blatantly provocative when what I needed to do was put Charlotte off him. Instead I waited, sitting demurely to the side and pretending not to realise that my surplice was stretched taught over breasts that were obviously bare underneath. I then asked Charlotte if she could check on my car while I changed. Only when she was gone did I speak up.

'You mentioned the need for people to love and tolerate one another in your sermon,' I began. 'That's very nice, but isn't it a bit hypocritical to say that after ordering me to dress in the way you expect?'

'There are certain natural morals laws that we must all follow,' he replied, no longer flustered but once more the wise priest talking down to the silly and misguided little girl.

'There are no such things as natural moral laws,' I replied, laughing because I knew it would annoy him more than anything I could say.

'Nonsense,' he answered, only not quite as coolly as before. 'The bible teaches us –'

'Oh come on,' I interrupted, 'that lot in the Old Testament were always slaughtering each other. Look at David and Goliath. "Thou shalt not kill"? More like "Though shalt not kill except when it happens to be convenient".'

'That's simply not –' he began, his face once more beginning to colour.

'And you're no better yourself,' I continued. 'You have the nerve to object to my tummy piercing yet you don't mind earrings. What's the difference? The difference is that one offends your moral values! But they're not "natural morals", are they? No, they're just a mixture of your upbringing and what's convenient for you. And you're a hypocrite in any case, aren't you? You object to girls showing a little flesh, but you're quite happy to seduce Charlotte, aren't you?'

'How dare you!' he thundered, his face now crimson.

'And as for this farce,' I went on without a break, waving my arm in a gesture that took in the church as a whole, 'it's just an excuse to con money out of gullible,

83

insecure idiots, isn't it? And to get infatuated girls to drop their knickers for you as well!'

That did it. The whole idea was for him to strike out at me so that Charlotte would find me in tears with a convincing bruise. As it was he grabbed at me with astonishing speed and caught me by the collar of my surplice. Before I knew what was happening he had pulled me hard down across a table. His hand twisted into my hair, pushing my face against the rough wood. I squeaked and swore at him, then saw that he was struggling to get his belt free of his trousers. It had finally happened. He was going to beat me.

I was full of rage and consternation, unable to move and hypnotised by his actions as he pulled the thick leather belt out and doubled it up. There was a lump in my throat and my breathing was coming fast – terror, lust, shame, yearning and a dozen other emotions swirling in my head as he lifted the belt. I saw his face, the teeth gritted in fury and determination, the eyes glittering maniacally. Then the belt came down, hard, smack across the fullest part of my bottom.

It hurt, a heavy pain that both ached and stung. I squealed and called him a bastard, ordering him to let me go. His grip in my hair only tightened, his hand twisting to draw my head up and force me to pull my back in and bring my bottom into prominence. The belt smacked down again, harder, creating a burning pain in my poor bottom. I squealed again, a sob rising in my throat only to be cut off by my scream as the third blow landed hard across the back of my thighs.

He stopped; relief and disappointment welled up in me simultaneously but only for an instant before I realised that the beating was far from over. Instead he had gripped the back of my surplice and was hauling it up, exposing my calves, my thighs and then my bum, vulnerable under taut blue silk panties.

'Insolent little bitch!' he exclaimed and then took the belt to me again.

If it had hurt on my surplice, then it was agony on the seat of my panties, the blow making me kick and yell out in pain. He took no notice, planting another across my buttocks and then another right under the tuck of my cheeks. I lost control completely, screaming and kicking as he beat me mercilessly even as I could feel my pussy coming on heat. I had begun to whimper, begging him to stop even while hoping he wouldn't do anything of the sort. He just carried on, whipping my bottom into a hot ball of pain while I struggled and swore futilely in his grip. I was soon crying, not quiet, restrained tears, but hot, angry ones, full of shame and dismay at my punishment.

Finally it stopped and I was lying limp over the table, mewling pathetically with the tears running hot down my cheeks. My buttocks were throbbing with pain, a pain that centred on my wet, gaping vagina. I was breathing hard, my head dizzy with sensations – pain, humiliation, self-pity, but above all a desperate need to have his cock inside me. I reached back, my hand shaking violently as I took hold of the waistband of my panties. He had stood back and I looked up at him, pleading with my tear-stained eyes as I took my panties down to offer him my willing vagina.

'Do it some more on the bare, you bastard,' I gasped. 'Then fuck me, hard, or put it in my bum if that's what you need, you dirty pervert.'

He stopped, his eyes locked on my naked bottom and my flaunted vagina and anus. I thought he was going to do it and let out a long sigh of anticipation, only for him to go completely berserk. He grabbed me by the hair and pulled me sharply upright, called me a whore and a pervert and several other things as he tore the surplice off and threw my shoes, jeans and top at me. I caught them and ran, genuinely afraid of what he might do if I put up any resistance.

His furious tirade followed me into the church as I staggered down the aisle, frantically trying to dress and run at the same time. Only when I realised that he was not coming after me did I pause, preferring to take my chances that he wasn't going to follow against the alternative of running out into the street in just my panties, and those half down over my reddened bottom.

What I should have done, of course, was go to the car and tell Charlotte what had happened. Once back at the flat she could have seen my belt marks and I'm sure that that would have been the end of her relationship with Evan Dunstal. I couldn't do it. He had beaten me, bringing out all the sexual tension that had been building up in me since the first spark that had given me the need to be spanked. Only he hadn't completed it, instead leaving me with my bottom burning and my pussy desperately in need of attention. I didn't know what I wanted and felt fragile and vulnerable, not at all the right mood for bringing the scheme I had set out with to fruition.

Instead of telling her I mumbled some excuse about having argued with him and drove rapidly home, twice nearly hitting other cars. She was deeply concerned, clearly aware that I was flustered but not knowing why. She could also see that I'd been crying and wanted to be sympathetic, but I was simply too bewildered to find the words I needed for any sort of explanation. She was actually very good about it, leaving me in peace as soon as she realised I didn't want to talk.

I was absolutely seething with lust, all the complex and contradictory emotions that contributed to my spanking fantasy swirling in my head, leaving no room for anything else. Only by making a hasty excuse did I stop myself from trying to seduce Charlotte on the spot, and once in my flat I slammed the door and locked it. Collapsing on the bed I lay staring at the ceiling and let my mind run.

It had happened. A man had lost his temper with me and beaten my bottom. He had even pulled my surplice up and done it across the seat of my panties. My intention had been quite different, at least consciously, but he'd done it and my bottom was a mass of hot, throbbing flesh.

I turned with a single motion, struggling with the popper on my jeans even as I hunched myself up into a kneeling position. The mirror showed my jeans, the seat taught and full of cheeky, girlish bottom; two slices of suspiciously red flesh showed where the carefully positioned rips exposed me. Down they came, taking my panties with them to reveal a sight so erotic that it made me groan out loud. My bare bottom was covered in thick red wheals, the skin flushed every colour from blush pink, through angry crimson to a sullen, bruised purple. In the middle my vagina was a wet, gaping hole, clearly ready for entry. Above it my anus showed clearly, just as it must have done when I pulled my panties down for him. Given that he liked girls' bumholes, I couldn't imagine how he had resisted stuffing his cock up mine.

With my jeans and panties in a tangle around my thighs and my eyes locked on my beautiful, punished bottom, I began to masturbate. I was in just the same position I had used the first time I had come over the thought of being spanked. Then my bum had been a smooth, even pinky white, rude but pretty, salacious but still somehow innocent. Now it was very different, discoloured with the marks of a man's belt, a man who had forced me down, stripped me to my panties and taken his belt to my naughty, impudent, brattish little backside. I had offered him the prize of my submission, pulling down my own panties to display my pussy and offering it to him, even offering him my anus to make a tight, dirty slide for his cock. He should have taken me as a prize, accepting what was offered, perhaps first in my vagina and then up my bum, perhaps applying the hard correction of his belt to my naked flesh while he sodomised me.

Instead he had rejected me, turned down the most precious, intimate thing I had to offer. Then he had thrown me out, all but naked – a rejected, beaten slut with her red buttocks on show so that people could look at her and know that she had been chastised. That had been me, red bottomed in a church with nothing but a pair of skimpy panties to hide my shame. I had been well beaten, truly punished for my insolence and lack of respect.

I was rubbing hard at my clitty, almost at orgasm. Staring fixedly at my reflected bottom, I reached back and found my anus with a finger, popping the top joint in. I pulled it out and did it again, watching the dirty little hole open and let my finger in as I rode at the very edge of orgasm. I had been whipped and now I was masturbating my vagina and anus over the memory, loving every instant of the degradation I had been put through. That was the final point, the sheer, absolute, unbearable shame of having had my bottom exposed and beaten – beaten until I was blubbering and kicking and begging to feel my persecutor's penis inside me, be it inside my vagina or my rectum.

I screamed as I came, not just a little cry of ecstasy but a full-blooded screech. My whole body seemed to contract and then explode, not once but again and again until I was left lying on the bed in a sweaty, half-naked heap, one finger still pushed well up my bottom-hole.

For a long moment I lay still, listening in case any of my neighbours had heard my scream. They could scarcely not have done, and a moment later I heard a thud that I was sure was Charlotte's door. Pulling my finger out of my bottom with a sticky pop, I scampered for the bathroom, only to trip over my jeans and panties and end up in a kneeling position with my bare red bum stuck up in the air.

It was just as well I had locked the door, because that was the moment Charlotte tried the handle; if it had been unlocked she would have caught me like that. As it was I responded to her concerned question with an assurance that I was all right and promised to open the door in a moment. Hastily washing my hands and adjusting myself, I tried desperately to regain some semblance of being in control and went to answer the door.

Charlotte was standing outside, looking worried. I smiled and motioned her into the flat, only then realising that the scent of sex was strong in the air. She gave me a curious look and I found myself blushing and for once in my life quite unable to say anything. Then she smiled and gave me a knowing look to which I responded with an embarrassed grin.

I put coffee on and we made small talk for a while, each uncertain of what to say. Only when I had sunk two cups of strong coffee did my natural strength of character begin to reassert itself; by three I had decided to tell Charlotte everything. Not, however, until I had treated her to a long and alcoholic lunch while I concocted the best story to ensure that she never wanted to see Evan Dunstal again.

Nine

Rather than visit a restaurant where we could be overheard, I put a couple of bottles of Tokay d'Alsace in the fridge and left them to chill while we visited a delicatessen. It was a sultry day and Primrose Hill itself was crowded with people sunning themselves, walking dogs and so forth. We chose as empty a spot as we could and spread out our picnic. Only when we had eaten and drunk nearly half of the second bottle did she ask the question which I knew she had been holding in since we had left the church.

'So what's the matter?' she asked.

She was kneeling up, her knees together and her feet splayed out behind. She still had on the plain white dress which she had worn to church, which made her look demure yet clung to her breasts, hinting at hidden treasures. She was obviously wearing a sports bra underneath it, as usual, because her boobs looked high and round. It was such an innocent picture, so sweet and caring that I suddenly didn't want to play the hurt and abused friend. I had been planning to paint Evan Dunstal as a sort of fiend in human shape, saying that he had refused to leave the room while I changed, waited until I was in just my panties, pushed me over the desk, beaten me and then fucked me.

It would certainly have put her off him, especially as I could show the marks on my bottom to prove my story. She knew I had masturbated, which might take a bit of explaining after such a supposedly terrible experience, but

90

I was sure that with the right measures of mock confusion and embarrassment I could do it. The trouble was that all I would elicit from her was sympathy, and my urge was for a very different reaction.

I took a sip of Tokay, suddenly very unsure of myself. Being molested by Lydia was one thing; she liked to take charge and all I had to do was enjoy it. Seducing Charlotte was quite another – a prospect that made me tremble with guilty desire just to think about. No, he could wait. What I wanted was Charlotte. She was waiting patiently for my answer, her pretty face full of concern and sympathy.

'Are you really upset? About Evan?' she managed at last.

'No . . . I mean . . . oh I'm sorry, Charlotte,' I replied, judging both my words and hesitations exactly. 'I suppose I was a bit of a bitch really, but –'

'No you weren't,' she broke in, putting a reassuring hand on my shoulder. 'He can be a bit strict, but it's only because he believes so strongly.'

'Oh it's not that,' I carried on. 'It just that I'm a bit tense . . . and confused and . . . jealous I suppose.'

'Jealous?' she queried.

'Oh it's really silly,' I answered. 'You're going to think I'm really silly.'

'No,' she assured me.

'I'm just jealous because we used to get on so well, and now you're giving him all your attention, and, and . . . and it just feels really bad.' My words came out in a rush.

'I'm sorry,' she said, so sweetly that I could have taken her in my arms then and there, onlookers or no onlookers.

It wasn't the first time I'd talked a girl round to sex, and there's a time to speak and a time to stay silent. Now I stayed silent, turning my face a little away and toying with a blade of grass in an embarrassed, distracted manner. I was the very picture of coy, sexual uncertainty, the innocent girl embarrassed by her sexual feelings towards a friend. What I was actually thinking was how I was going to explain the state of my bottom to her if, or rather, when, we did end up in bed.

I waited perhaps a minute, decided on my story and then

gave her the line that would either see us in bed together or have her running away with her cheeks red with blushes.

'Charlotte . . .' I began, speaking quietly and with a deliberate catch in my voice. 'I . . . I mean when I was – you know, playing with myself earlier, I was thinking of you.'

I'd been pretty well certain of success, but one glance at her expression was enough to remove the final doubt. She had a little mischievous smile at her lips, a smile that told me that she was willing.

We said nothing, simply drained the bottle, picked up the remains of the picnic and set off down the slope together, hand in hand. I kissed her as soon as the door of my flat closed behind us, not just because I knew that it was necessary to break down the final barrier of actual sexual contact, but because I needed to, badly. She sighed and let her mouth open under mine, our tongues meeting as my hands slid up her back. My fingers found the nape of her neck, tickling her gently in among the short stubble of her hair. The touch increased her passion and she returned it, one hand going to my own neck, the other coming forward to cup one of my breasts. She squeezed it gently and curled her hand beneath it, as if to test its weight, something that I've known other girls to do to larger breasted friends before. At that touch I knew that she was not merely willing but eager and that I no longer needed to play a game.

I shivered as her thumb brushed over my nipple; I put my arm firmly around her waist and began to guide her to my bedroom. We began to kiss again as we sank down on to the bed and once more she touched my breasts, both of them this time, one in each hand with her thumbs stroking my nipples through my top. I pulled it up, baring them to her. I could feel her fingers trembling as she cupped them, naked in her hands, once again with her thumbs to the nipples. Her kisses left my mouth, moved slowly down to find my neck, on to my breasts and to a nipple. I moaned as her teeth nipped the hard bud, then her tongue began to lap at it, gently, teasing me and filling me with a delicious sensation.

She came down on top of me as I lay back, still suckling my breasts and mumbling sweet things through her mouthful. One of her hands was on the breast she was sucking, the other moving down, stroking my belly, touching the piercing, tracing the shape of my tummy button and then sliding down to find the button of my jeans. I arched my back, stretching luxuriantly in utter bliss. Concentrating on the sensations from her agile fingers and tongue, I could feel my nipple in her mouth and the slight tension as she tugged at the button that would open the way to even more sensitive areas. It popped open and her hand was gliding down the front of my jeans, fumbling urgently at my panties to get at my pussy. She missed, and cupped my silk-covered pubic mound, a finger pushing the soft material down between my pussy lips. For just an instant she made contact with my clitty, making me start and grunt at the shock of pleasure.

Then her hand was out and peeling down my zip. I put a hand behind her head, stroking the fine, short cropped hair as she suckled on me. My jeans were open, her hand burrowing back down, once more to cup my pussy and rub my panties in between my sex-lips. I pulled my legs up and opened them, offering her my sex unreservedly. She responded by cocking her leg over mine and pushing her thigh against me. I squeezed my legs together around it, feeling the sleek yet muscular leg. Her dress had ridden up and my legs were clamped around her bare flesh. My thigh was pressed against her panty crotch, just as hers was pressed against me. She shoved with her legs, almost a kick, hard against my pussy and producing that blissful push sensation, like being fucked or bounced on a man's lap.

'Let's rub pussies,' I suggested, now aware, from the skill with which she had been touching me, that she was no newcomer to sharing her body with another woman. 'I want to come with you.'

She giggled and pulled back, putting her hands straight to the hem of her dress. I watched as she untangled it from under her bottom and pulled it up, revealing white cotton panties with a single bow of pink ribbon at the front above the neat bulge of her pussy, then her sports bra, her breasts held high and enticing within it. She giggled and I realised just how lustfully I must have been staring at her. In response I sat forward and grabbed her bra, pulling it hard up over her breasts. She squeaked at the rough treatment and grabbed at my legs, throwing me back on to the bed. I tried to resist as she took hold of my jeans but I was laughing too much. Besides, she wasn't a fitness teacher for nothing and quickly had me rolled up for my jeans and panties to be pulled off at her leisure. Down they came, Charlotte lifting my bottom easily and tugging the lot over my hips. Of course as my thighs and the tuck of my bottom were exposed she got a prime view of the red welts that Evan had put across me earlier.

I had meant to tell her that it had happened at the party the previous night but had got too carried away. Now it was all on show, along with my pussy and bumhole; Charlotte was staring open mouthed at my reddened buttocks.

'What happened?' she asked, sounding shocked and still holding my legs up by my jeans and panties.

'Don't worry; I've just been spanked,' I answered hastily.

'Spanked?' she echoed, her pretty mouth open in an O of disbelief at the revelation that someone had beaten me.

'Spanked,' I confirmed, suddenly realising that I had an opportunity to really build on my fantasy.

'Why?' she asked. 'I mean, what happened?'

'One of the guys at the party did it,' I explained, excited simply by the way she had first said 'Why?'– as if to imply that spanking my bare bottom was a reasonable thing to do as long as I deserved it.

'You let him?' she asked incredulously.

'He said I'd been naughty,' I continued, ignoring her tone. 'He said I was a brat because I'd flirted with him and then turned him down. He said I needed a spanking. Then he just did it. There was nothing I could do. He was really strong. He just pulled me down over his lap, in front of everyone. He twisted my arm behind my back. I was kicking and struggling but I couldn't get up. I was helpless. Then he pulled my dress up and showed them all my panties, calling out to tell everyone to come and watch what happened to naughty girls. They all started clapping as he took hold of my panties. I struggled like mad but he just twisted my arm harder. Then he took down my panties, really slowly. I couldn't stop him. It was so humiliating – my bum stuck up bare in front of about twenty people, all laughing and clapping because I was about to be spanked. Imagine it, a bare bottom in front of all those leering eyes and the indignity of being punished on it while they all watched. He waited a bit while they all had a good stare. I'm sure they could see everything, my pussy, my bumhole, everything. Then he started to spank me with his hand. They clapped in time to the smacks. I tried not to make a fuss but I couldn't help it, it really stung. I started to kick my legs about, which made them laugh even louder, especially the girls. Someone gave him a belt and he used that on me, which made me lose control completely. That was what made the marks, mostly. By the end I just didn't care anymore, my bottom hurt and I was crying with shame but all I could do was lie there while they made a big joke of it.'

'You enjoyed it, didn't you?' she asked quietly.

I nodded. After all, from the way I had described it it was pretty obvious. She said nothing, but just looked at me. Her legs were apart and I could see the front of her panties, with a tell-tale damp patch where the material was stretched over her swollen vulva.

'May I see ... properly?' she asked, her lip trembling and her eyes huge and moist.

'Better still,' I answered. 'Rub some cream in for me.'

She nodded and I got up, fumbling my jeans and panties off as I climbed from the bed. My heart was hammering as I ran into the bathroom for my massage cream; I was naked but for shoes and the top that I had lifted over my breasts. I stripped quickly, returning to the bedroom to find Charlotte sitting on the bed in just her white panties.

She looked up at me, clearly expectant, and held out her hand for the cream. I gave it to her, took a pillow and lay face down on the bed with the pillow under my hips so that my bottom was lifted.

'That looks so sore,' she said, as her fingers brushed ever so gently across my welted rear cheeks.

'It is,' I sighed, 'and it needs soothing. Cream me, Charlotte, rub it in all over, touch anywhere you like.'

I lifted my bum a bit more, hinting that the cream would be as welcome down between my bottom cheeks as well as on top of them. She giggled and a sudden cold sensation told me that she had squeezed the cream out on to my bottom. I sighed more deeply as her hands found the crests of my cheeks and began to rub the cream in. It was cool and soothing, a truly blissful sensation on my still-hot, bruised buttocks. She had her fingers spread out, not kneading in the way that men tend to fondle girl's bottoms, but stroking softly in little circles.

I was in heaven, content to lie there with her massaging my poor beaten bottom for as long as she wanted to do it. She was in no hurry either, rubbing the cream well in, then applying more and smoothing it over my bottom and the parts of my thighs that had been whipped; round and round, easing away my pain and bringing my whole awareness to centre on my bottom. She carried on for what seemed an age, showing no impatience whatsoever but apparently happy just to caress my bottom, only pausing to add more cream. The fifth lot of cream was put on more liberally; a dollop of it landed in between my cheeks and ran slowly down to come to rest in the dimple of my bumhole, cold and moist against my sensitive anal skin.

Charlotte put her hand back to my cheeks, rubbing more firmly and pulling them open. I groaned in delight and lifted my bum still further, making my cheeks part in the hope of getting some attention to my pussy and anus. Charlotte giggled and climbed in between my legs, using her knees to push them apart and make an even more open display of my sex. I knew she was going to do it but still gasped when a creamy hand slid beneath me to cup my pussy mound. My clit was caught between her two middle fingers, which she moved like scissors, producing a sharp almost unbearably exciting sensation. Then her thumb was opening my vagina, sliding inside to fill me and draw a new moan of ecstasy from deep inside me.

'Touch my bumhole, too,' I begged, knowing that I would come if she kept on playing with my clit and desperate for every part of me to be stimulated.

She seemed to hesitate but then I felt a finger squash down into the blob of cream on my bumhole. I reached back and pulled my slippery buttocks apart as she started to rub my anus, making little circles around the hole with her finger.

'Put it in,' I pleaded as I felt the muscles of my sex give the first twinge of approaching orgasm.

Again, she hesitated, and then her finger was opening my anus and sliding inside me even as she squeezed my clitty and pressed the flesh of my vulva between it and the thumb that was in my vagina. I could feel the cream in my bottom-hole and the heat of my clitty. My vagina was contracting around her thumb, my anus around her finger. My back was arched and my mouth open, my eyes shut as I came in one long, shuddering climax. I screamed, only to have my mouth blocked by Charlotte's as she came forward, her fingers slipping from my juice- and cream-soaked holes in her eagerness to kiss me as I came.

Our tongues met in a long, sensual kiss as my orgasm slowly subsided to leave me trembling in her arms. Then she was holding me and whispering soft words in my ear, cuddling me as if she never wanted to let go.

If there's one rule I try to keep with men, it's to make sure I come first. Most men lose interest once they've reached a climax and a good few assume that a girl's satisfaction comes entirely from pleasuring them. My brief fling with the shoe fetishist had been the worst example of such lack of consideration, but a lot of others had simply assumed that having a cock inside me for five minutes was enough to leave me in a state of sleepy satisfaction. It's not, and I have had more than one argument about needing my pussy licked, something that many men seem to see as an insult to their virility.

Girls are different, and a lot less selfish. Charlotte had taken me to heaven and I had no intention of not returning the favour, only now that I had come I could be a lot cooler about doing it. We hugged for a long while, with me running my nails gently up and down her bare back just to show her that I was still up for giving her an orgasm. She purred and clung tighter, evidently content to let me do as I pleased, so I rolled her on to her back and simply took control.

What I'd originally wanted to do was rub our pussies together until we both came and I still had a lingering desire for it. So I pulled off her panties and peeled my own top off to leave us both stark naked before climbing in between her thighs and getting myself into position. She acquiesced, following my movements with a skill that suggested it wasn't the first time. With our legs scissored together and our hot pussies in direct contact I began to rub at her, moving my hips back and forth to keep my lips grinding against hers.

She quickly started to moan and play with her breasts, leaving me to do most of the work. I was hardly unaffected myself, with my clitty rubbing right against her, but tried to stay firmly in control so that she could get the most out of what we were doing. I knew she was going to come when she started to clutch at her breasts and murmur my name in between pants. I rubbed harder, squeezing her bottom and belly between my thighs as her pants turned to gasps and then little cries. These went on and on, dying only slowly to become whimpers and then simply hard breathing – a style of orgasm very different to my own.

Once more we cuddled for a while and then slowly began to explore each other's bodies in detail. The rest of the afternoon was a welter of sex and cuddles, becoming increasingly naughty as our intimacy grew. We made each other come again, in a sixty-nine with me on top and her lovely long legs wrapped around my head while I licked her pussy. After that we fell to talking, Charlotte demanding every detail of what it felt like to be spanked. It was obvious that she was getting turned on by talking about it, so I asked to spank her. She agreed cheerfully and draped herself naked across my lap.

Instead of simply wading in and pinking her bottom I gave her two little smacks to give her a foretaste of what was coming; then I made her dress and go upstairs to her flat to fetch the pleated white skirt she used to play tennis in and various other bits and pieces.

When she came back I explained that spanking was a lot more fun if the victim felt the full humiliation of her position. I then sat on the bed and watched her dress up in full tennis gear; only then did I put her across my knee. She looked really sweet in her pleated white skirt and I started talking to her as I pulled it up, describing how she looked with her big white tennis pants on show and how tight they were across her bottom. With her skirt fully raised I began to make slow circling motions on the seat of her panties with my hand, feeling the firm hemispheres of her bum beneath the white cotton. I was enjoying myself and made an effort to thoroughly humiliate her, holding her panties tight up so that they pulled at her pussy and made her bum-cheeks bulge out at the sides, then telling her how she looked. I could feel her trembling and knew that my subtle, calculated sadism was having the desired effect.

I told her she was a slut and a dirty little tart as I rubbed my hand on the wet bulge of cotton that contained her pussy; I kept it taut by holding the back of her panties tight up. She moaned in rapture and I decided she was ready; I let go of her panties and pulled them down with a swift, unceremonious tug. Before she could ready herself I planted the first smack on her delightful bottom, making her cheeks bounce and resulting in a satisfying squeal. From the moment I had first decided I liked the idea of spanking I had known that it would turn me on, but I had never realised that it would be so much fun. I was enjoying myself enormously as Charlotte's tight little bottom began to turn pink under my slaps: I laughed at her pathetic squeals and the way her legs kicked and her bottom parted to show off her wrinkled brown anus as the punishment started to get painful.

After a while I grabbed her wrist and twisted her arm into the small of her back, which was always a detail of my own spanking fantasies and helped to keep her still while I beat her. Her bottom was very red and she was breathing heavily, but making no effort to get down despite the state I had put her in. She started to whimper and moan as I set to work again, and then to beg for another orgasm. I ignored her but took my hairbrush from the bedside table and brought it down hard across her defenceless bottom. That really made her yell and I set to work with a delicious sadistic glee, beating her until she was writhing and squirming across my lap with her legs kicking like anything. Finally I stopped, leaving her gasping for breath with her thighs wide apart and her panties stretched taut between them.

She was begging to be made to come and I slid a merciful hand under her belly, cupping her pussy so that she could squirm her clitty against my hand while I put my thumb in her vagina. It took no time at all, but I kept masturbating her even when she had climaxed, taking a delight of mixed eroticism and sheer cruelty in her whimpering, shivering response.

Inevitably she wanted to do me after that and I really had to let her, going across her lap for a gentle spanking. It was nice and would have been nicer if she could have been firmer with me, but I was already bruised and in no condition to be properly punished. In any case, although I enjoyed the feeling of lying across her knee in the nude, it wasn't close to the sensation of being forced to take a strapping by an angry man. I came again though, with her fingers on my clitty and the handle of my hairbrush stuck up my pussy to humiliate me.

When we had eventually both had our fill and were lying together on the carpet with a big plate of buttered toast and glasses of orange juice, I told her everything: all about my spanking fantasy, and Antoine, and Lydia and Steve, and even John Thurston, everything except the truth about Evan Dunstal.

In return she admitted to having had several other sexual experiences with girls, and to having always liked the idea of taking me to bed. She also knew Antoine from the college and agreed that he seemed the sort to think that girls ought to be disciplined. The only question seemed to be how to make him give me a spanking without realising that he had been goaded into it.

Ten

Antoine had obviously decided that I was his girlfriend. This was fine as long as he didn't actually expect to move in with me, which would have made things more than a little difficult. When we had sobered up and come down from our sexual highs, Charlotte and I had both felt a little embarrassed, but not too much; I was sure we'd be back in bed together in due course. It was Antoine ringing that finally broke the spell on Sunday, otherwise I'm sure we would have shared a bed that night. As it was we didn't, and I accepted a date with Antoine for the Thursday evening.

By Thursday, I hoped, the belt marks on my bottom would have faded. They did, and as it happened the satisfaction of having been beaten faded too. On Monday the red had gone down, leaving only a few curiously shaped bruises. These produced a dull ache, which, in conjunction with my tummy button, served to keep me in a dirty frame of mind all day. I knew I'd been punished, and even while networking in a café with a group of the girls I was aware that I was sitting on a smacked bottom. By the evening my state of sexual tension was so high that I wanted to pull my panties down in the street and show everyone. Not that I did. Once back at the flat my bum was bare and the vibrator was on my clitty before I'd even had a coffee. Had Charlotte not been out teaching I would have gone upstairs and had her too, but as it was I had to content myself with two orgasms in my now familiar kneeling pose with my bare bottom on show in the mirror.

Tuesday was less fun, with the intensity of the memory fading with the bruises. I still had the delicious feeling of knowing that I had been punished, but it required effort to sustain it and my evening's masturbation was a lot less spontaneous and not nearly as satisfying. Wednesday was busy, with an article needing to be finished and teaching in the evening. I gave Charlotte a lift home, and while we had a kiss and a cuddle neither of us seemed inspired to take it any further. For my part this was at least partially because she admitted to me that she was still seeing Evan Dunstal. I went to bed feeling put out and curiously nostalgic. It was strange feeling, rather like those which I had always had when returning to school after the holidays, particularly summer holidays – a bitter-sweet combination of melancholy and memories.

I tried to tell myself not to be silly, but the feeling wouldn't go away and I spent a long evening lying face down on my bed, feeling sorry for myself. I was almost in tears at one point, which was ridiculous. Girls are supposed to cry because they've been spanked, not because they haven't. After a while I got up and made a coffee, but for all my efforts I still felt bad. The experience with Evan Dunstal had been good, but it had not dissipated my need for bare-bottom discipline. Instead it had strengthened it. Unfortunately it was hardly likely that I could get a repeat performance. I had enjoyed being across Charlotte's lap too, but that simply wasn't the same thing. In her case I had enjoyed dishing out the spanking more than taking it. She was made to be spanked by me, to kick and wriggle over my lap in her pain and humiliation just for my amusement and erotic pleasure. By contrast she was too gentle and playful to really make me feel punished.

On Thursday morning I was thoroughly looking forward to my date with Antoine. Forever the optimist, I had forgotten his drawbacks as a lover and was quietly confident that if I pushed the right buttons I would end up the next morning with a smarting bottom and the prospect of regular discipline in the future.

As soon as we met I sensed a change in him that both

worried me and increased my hopes of having found a man who felt I needed regular spankings. He was far more possessive than he had been before, very much the assertive, dominant male. Before, he had given me the full seduction routine as a prelude to anything physical. Now he was full of confidence, arrogance even – kissing me firmly, putting his arm around my waist and telling me exactly how the evening was planned. He had already selected a restaurant and, as before, he chose the wine, despite having only a fraction of my knowledge and experience.

I played along, making all the right responses and massaging his ego as necessary. By the time we left the restaurant he was completely full of himself and completely sure that I was putty in his hands. Rather than go straight back he took me to a wine bar that belonged to a friend of his, assuring me that there we would be served French wine chosen by Frenchmen, which was in some mysterious way supposed to be the best. He also assured me that the atmosphere would help to allow me to see things the French way, the implication being that I was sexually and emotionally a beginner and needed him to coach me.

He really was supremely arrogant. As we sipped a moderately drinkable Coteaux Auxerrois he explained how I could reach levels of pleasure that had previously been barred to me by my repressed background. My version of sex, with lots of changing positions and lots of attention to my clitty, was, he explained, the result of me being unable to truly give in to my feelings. True rapture, apparently, could only be achieved by total surrender to him, this being simple nature for women. This included letting him come in me and reaching my own orgasm purely from the sensation of having his cock inside me. I knew I wouldn't. I need my clitty played with and have had enough lovers to know what I'm talking about.

I didn't contradict him; in fact I wasn't even paying attention. More important to me was converting all that macho energy into a rosy, smarting bottom. Rejection didn't work, he would merely sulk, as he had before. I also suspected that flirting with his friends would merely annoy him, and not in the right way. Embarrassing him, though, seemed an excellent idea as, while it would wind him up, his ego wouldn't be bruised if his friends saw what a little trollop he was going out with.

So I ordered another bottle, signalling the waiter with an imperious click of my fingers. I even managed to order Tokay without Antoine sticking his oar in and was presently filling my glass from the tall, elegant and distinctly phallic bottle. For all his conversation I was genuinely horny and began to stroke the bottle neck as he continued his spiel about the natural roles of man and woman. The glass felt smooth and hard under my fingers, like an impossibly stiff cock, and as he wittered on my mind drifted back to my first experience of pleasuring myself with a bottle.

It had been in a wood in Surrey near my parents' house, on the sort of baking hot day that always makes me want to strip and just walk around in the nude. I had pinched a bottle of Hock from my dad's cellar and sneaked off into the woods to drink it. Drunk and sheltered by the overhang of a big holly, I had felt secure enough and naughty enough to give in to the desire to find out what the smooth, hard neck would feel like inside me. I had slipped my panties aside and pushed it up my vagina. With the bottle inside me I had begun to play with myself, becoming increasingly bold as my excitement rose. After a while I had taken off my panties under my skirt, then my bra. I sat on the branch with my boobs and bum bare while I worked the bottle in and out and tickled my clit. Finally I had stripped completely naked and come on my back among the decaying holly leaves, delighting in the prickling sensation on my back, bum and thighs and the feel of the bottle in my vagina. I had felt wonderfully rude and also vulnerable – naked in a place were any passer-by might catch me being dirty with myself. I've always had an exhibitionist streak in me, and it was coming strongly to the front as Antoine talked to me, fondly imagining that it was his conversation that was turning me on.

'Don't you think girls' pussies are pretty then, Antoine?'
I asked as he once more expounded his philosophy of how
a woman should take her pleasure only from the male.

'*Mais bien sûr . . .*' he began, using French as he had
increasingly done since we had entered the wine bar.

He didn't expand on his statement, but stopped dead,
staring at me. This was because I had slid into the corner
of the alcove, cocked a leg up on the bench so that my
panties showed under my little skirt and was now stroking
myself through the gusset.

'Natasha!' he said urgently as he glanced wildly around
to see if anyone else had noticed.

The alcove gave quite a lot of privacy and I didn't know
anyone in the bar, otherwise I would never have done it.
He knew them though, or at least most of them, the great
majority being fellow Frenchmen.

'Don't you think my pussy's pretty, Antoine?' I
breathed, pulling my gusset aside to give him a prime view
of moist, excited vulva.

All a waiter or guest had to do was walk past the alcove
and they'd have seen everything. Antoine knew this and
was intensely embarrassed, but I found the idea titillating.

'Don't tell me you really don't like to watch girls play
with their pussies?' I asked as he tried frantically to get
round the table.

'Antoine!' I squeaked, pretending to misinterpret his
actions as he reached me and grabbed at the hand that was
holding my panties open. 'Not so urgent! You can fuck me,
but not here, not in front of all your friends!'

Nobody could see us, but I was sure several of them
could hear us. I pulled away from him into the opposite
corner and once more pulled my panties aside for him.

'Patience, darling,' I breathed. 'All that can come later.
For now, why not watch me fuck my pussy with the
bottle?'

'Natasha!' he hissed, once more making a grab for me.

He was actually drunker than I was and I easily
managed to dodge him and move to the end of the table.
My skirt was still up, and now my bottom was stuck out

towards the restaurant, covered only by the rear pouch of a pair of diminutive, lacy black panties. Someone laughed at the sight and I hastily covered myself, wriggling my skirt down over my hips and turning a smile to them.

'I'm sorry,' I said, trying to look mischievous and contrite at the same time. 'We got a little carried away.'

I turned and sat back down, giggling, to find Antoine standing red-faced and furious.

'You're drunk; we're going home,' he said angrily.

It was so nice to hear that rough commanding voice, to which he would have only have had to add the words 'and I'm going to have to spank you' to make my evening perfect. As it was he grabbed me by the wrist and pulled me out of the alcove, just the sort of crude gesture I had always wanted to precede a spanking.

I tripped and slumped, judging it carefully so that he managed to catch me. With little option, he picked me up and put me over his shoulder with my bum stuck up, a deliciously undignified position.

'Fuck me, Antoine,' I begged as he carried me towards the door. 'Fuck my little pussy.'

'She's drunk, I'm afraid,' he managed, drawing laughter and a few ribald comments from his friends.

'Fuck me, Antoine,' I repeated. 'Come on, do it in front of your friends and make me suck your big cock first.'

We were outside and I shut up, undoubtedly to his relief.

'You are a disgrace, Natasha; I am taking you home,' he informed me as he set me down on the pavement.

'I'm sorry,' I mumbled drunkenly. 'I'm bad. I know I'm bad. You should punish me.'

He didn't reply, having managed to signal a taxi which was already coming to a stop beside us. I nestled into his arm on the journey back, biding my time until we were actually outside my flat.

'If you haven't any money I'll suck his cock,' I offered as the driver opened the door for us. 'Would you like your cock sucked, Mr Taxidriver? I bet you've got a nice thick one, haven't you? I like them thick.'

The driver didn't answer, although I suspect he might

have taken me up on my offer if Antoine hadn't been there glaring and fuming while he tried to pay as fast as possible. I conveniently managed to regain my feet while we got up to my flat, just in case any neighbours were looking. Once there though I slumped on to the sofa and rolled on to my front.

'I've been really naughty. Haven't I, Antoine?' I said pushing my bottom up. 'I'm sorry, Antoine. I don't mind if you want to punish me.'

It couldn't have been a clearer invitation unless I had actually asked for it. Doing so would have spoilt everything, but as it was I still felt that the actual decision to use physical discipline on my bottom would be his choice. It was offered, though – a firm, girlish peach surely irresistible to any red-blooded male.

'Maybe I will,' he said gruffly. 'Maybe I will.'

'OK,' I answered in my smallest, most pathetic voice as I began to shiver in anticipation of the coming exposure and pain.

'Get off the settee and strip,' he ordered.

'Yes, Antoine,' I replied quickly, melting to the note of angry command in his voice.

I sat up, my fingers trembling as they went to the zip at the back of my dress. It slid down from my chest and I looked up at him, my mouth slightly open as I reached back for my bra catch. He was looking down at me, his expression changing from anger to satisfaction as I peeled the bra away and revealed my bare breasts to him. Men often find something very vulnerable about a woman offering her breasts to them, and Antoine was no exception. I looked down, trying to seem repentant and a little shy as I peeled my dress down over my hips and off my legs. My shoes went with it, leaving me in stockings, a suspender belt and panties.

'Dance for me,' he ordered, his tone now both possessive and excited. 'A striptease.'

I stood up as he lowered himself into a chair. He still looked flushed but was clearly enjoying my combined excitement and contrition, a situation that I was sure could only end in me getting a good beating on my naked bottom. I dance well and gave him my best, wriggling, pouting and teasing as I stripped slowly. He pulled his cock out when I was taking off my second stocking and had it erect in his hand by the time I had started to tease with my panties. I have always enjoyed teasing men, especially promising the full exposure of my body only to withhold it. When Antoine ordered me to pull off my pants I did it though, without hesitation. I had had my back to him and had been wiggling my bum with my panties pulled tight in between my cheeks. On his order I bent forward, set my legs apart and eased them down.

There aren't many men who can resist a girl bent over with long, bare legs rising to a pert, equally naked bottom with her panties set just low enough to provide a full rear view of her pussy. Antoine was cool; he simply sat there nursing his erection as I dropped my panties to the floor and turned, completely naked and completely laid open to him. Not content with my exposure he made me dance again, wantonly, displaying every detail of my body for his pleasure. It is very humiliating for a girl to dance naked for a fully dressed man, the more so when his erect cock is sticking out of his trousers, ready for her pussy.

He was enjoying himself immensely, and when he had finally tired of watching me squirm on the floor with my bum up and open in the hope that he would beat me, he ordered me to fetch him a drink.

'Crawling,' he added as I started to get up.

I obeyed, my body trembling hard as I crossed to the drinks cabinet on my hands and knees without a stitch on. I was acutely conscious of my bare tits swinging under my chest and the air on my exposed pussy and anus. His cock was hard and he could mount me at any time he chose, or perhaps put a foot on my back, force me to the carpet and whip my bare buttocks before sodomising me.

I was really flustered and ready for just about anything, but he was enjoying himself far too much to hurry. He had me pour him cognac and crawl over to him with it. I was imagining the fantasy of lying across his lap while he

109

warmed my bum and sipped his drink. He wanted to sip his drink while we had sex but had something else in mind. As I leant forward he took me roughly by the hair. I really thought I was going over his knee and heard myself whimper in alarm and delight, only to have my face pulled against his erection.

'Kiss it,' he ordered. I obeyed, my nose full of the scent of aroused male as I puckered my lips and kissed the shaft of his penis.

'Now suck,' he said, pulling me further forward so that I was forced to take his erection into my mouth.

I began to suck, gently and lovingly while he held me by the hair and sipped casually at his cognac. It felt blissfully rude and subservient, to be nude with his erection in my mouth and my breasts squashed against the rough material of his trousers. The contrast of him being fully clothed and sipping at a drink which I had brought him on my knees made it even better; yet I was acutely conscious of my naked, out-thrust bottom and that it should have been hot and tingling from spanking. The idea of sucking a man who had beaten me really appealed, and just the thought was making me hotter and wetter as I sucked obediently on his penis.

Rather than say anything I stayed in place, meek and compliant to his will, praying that he would take the game a step further. When he pulled his cock out of my mouth I really thought my moment had come, only to be ordered to crawl to the kitchen and fetch a bowl. I did as I was told, although curious and a little apprehensive as to what he intended to make me do.

I chose a plain bowl and brought it back in my teeth, just to be even more puppy-like in my sexual devotion. He took the bowl and came forward on the chair, once more pulling my mouth on to his erection. He held me by the head and began to masturbate into my mouth, jerking at the base of his erection with real urgency while I suckled on and kissed the tip. As his cock jerked he pulled my head sharply back, surprising me as I had expected to be made to swallow his sperm. Instead he grabbed the bowl and got

110

it under his erection just in time for his come to splash into it. A second jet followed and a third, more feeble than the first two. The next gush was only a dribble, which he wiped off on the edge of the bowl even as he groaned out the dying pleasure of his orgasm.

It was obvious what he was going to make me do. A lot of men like the idea of girls eating their come, perhaps because it makes them feel powerful to watch a woman swallow their sperm. Antoine clearly intended to make me lick it up from the bowl; but not immediately, only when he had recovered enough to fully enjoy the sight. He had put me in a deeply subservient frame of mind and I was sure he was only waiting to give me my beating in order to further torment me. So I played along, feeling intensely humiliated by the prospect of being made to eat his sperm from a bowl on the floor but too excited to spoil things. His habit of going off in a sulk if I didn't do as I was told really had me caught; I hate being left cold when I'm turned on and so it was best to be obedient.

For a whole hour he tormented me, actually making me clean my own flat in the nude. He even made me do the lavatory bowl, kneeling naked over it in a pose that left me fully available for penetration or whipping. He wouldn't let me touch myself though, and when I tried in the hope that the action would lead to punishment I very nearly sent him off into the sulks again.

By the time he decided I was ready for my supper I was running with sweat and my pussy was so wet that the juice was trickling down the inside of my thighs. I had been polishing a glass-topped table when he suddenly got up and grabbed me by the hair. I took a quick breath as he stuffed his cock into my mouth and held me their to suck it, only letting go when he was half stiff. He then pulled me roughly away and dragged me across the floor by my hair to hold my face inches above the bowl of sperm. I was breathing hard, with my eyes focused on the pool of sticky fluid I was about to be made to eat. For a long moment he held me, his hand twisted hard in my hair as my breathing quickened and my expectation rose. Then without warning he pushed my head abruptly down, straight into the sperm. I didn't quite get my mouth open in time and it smeared over my nose and cheeks. I was whimpering deep in my throat as he began to rub my face in it, taking immense pleasure in my degradation.

After making sure that my whole face was liberally smeared with come he pulled my head back two inches and ordered me to lick the rest up. I poked my tongue out and tasted the strong, salty, masculine flavour then began to lap at it. I was snivelling in my shame, hoping that the unspeakable dirty act he was putting me through was the prelude to having my bottom beaten. He made me lick the bowl clean and then lap up what I could reach from around my mouth, cleaning the rest off with a piece of tissue that he then made me swallow. Finally he told me I was disgusting and sent me into the bathroom with the instruction that he would be waiting for me in bed.

I couldn't keep my hands off myself in the bathroom. I looked a real state in the mirror. My face still showed sperm marks and my mouth was full of the taste of it. I began to masturbate, making no secret of it. I was determined that he would hear my cries and beat me for doing it. I was bent over the sink, bum stuck out as my fingers worked on my clitty, groaning and panting in my ecstasy. Then Antoine was in the doorway, a belt in his hands.

'No, please not that,' I said hopefully.

'I've caught you,' he said. 'Can't you keep your hands to yourself?'

'No,' I admitted.

'Well I know what to do about that,' he said and strode towards me, the belt taut between his hands.

'Oh God, if you must,' I whimpered and stuck my bottom out, terrified and in ecstasy at the same instant.

'Little whore,' he rasped and grabbed the hand I had been masturbating with to twist it hard into the small of my back.

I squealed and spread my legs, in utter ecstasy, about to be beaten after hours of sexual torment. Antoine grabbed

112

my other arm and it too was jerked sharply up behind me. I groaned aloud as he held my wrists in one powerful hand, my buttocks tensing in anticipation of the coming pain. My arms hurt as he pushed them further up, then twisted something around them – the belt. Three times he wrapped it round, lashing my arms helplessly behind me. Then he took me by the hair and dragged me stumbling into the bedroom.

'That's what you wanted, wasn't it?' he said, pushing me to the bed. 'Well now you're going to get it.'

I turned bum up, whimpering for mercy even as I presented the target for him.

'You are perverse, to link punishment with love,' he informed me and then began to undress.

I really thought he was going to do it, and stayed there with my bottom raised for whipping while he undressed. Even when he made me suck his cock hard again I was sure it was just a prelude, but when he mounted me I knew that I wasn't going to get any more. I begged for punishment as his cock filled my vagina, but he just called me an English pervert and kept on humping way, using my strapped up arms as a brace on which to pull himself into me. It hurt and had me whimpering with pain and pleasure; but it wasn't a spanking and by the time he came I was calling him a bastard and anything else I could think of. He wouldn't touch my clitty either, but still expected me to come, saying that now that I'd had the punishment I wanted perhaps I could give in to my feelings. In the end the pain was too much and I faked my orgasm as it seemed to be the only thing that would make him come. When he did it was inside me and I was still calling him a dirty bastard as I subsided to the bed with his second orgasm dribbling slowly from my pussy.

Eleven

If my second encounter with Antoine Barras put me in two minds about him, then the same did not work the other way. He had given me a really strong experience, and one that just made me want to come and come even if he hadn't beaten me. In my fantasies he always did, but while we spent the next three nights together I still didn't manage to coax him into it.

He also didn't feel right about bullying and dominating me, although he certainly enjoyed every minute of it. In order to justify his behaviour he liked to believe that he was only doing it because I wanted it. In a broad sense this may have been true, but the details were always his. One thing he was certain about: that I belonged to him. I think the fact that I submitted to his control during sex made him feel he could easily control me in real life – an error which I allowed him to sustain while I went my usual independent way.

He had kept me pretty busy over the weekend, and I saw nothing of Steve and Lydia and very little of Charlotte. He didn't stay with me on the Monday night, and rather than the feelings of loss which I had experienced the previous week I was glad to get some sleep.

The following day was an important one in the wine trade calendar, the start of one of the trade fairs. Knowing that everybody of consequence would be there, I dressed immaculately in a skirt suit of fine pale-grey wool that showed my curls to advantage. My blouse was pure white silk, also my underwear, not because my colleagues were

114

likely to see it, but because it made me feel good. With my glasses on and in neat two-inch heels I looked thoroughly professional and exquisitely pretty.

The hall was crowded, even more so than I had expected. The fair was entirely for private estate wines and almost exclusively European. Having become something of a Burgundy specialist, I made my way to the relevant group of stalls and was soon absorbed in tasting and discussion. Among the first people I saw were Charles and Sophie Carlisle, who were helping promote a group of growers from Epineuil. They had always been friendly to me and I went over at a signal from Sophie. As expected, she handed me a glass of the delicate Rosé d'Epineuil, but then leant forward and whispered to me that she wanted to talk to me in private. I was more than a little surprised, especially as there was a curiously stern edge to her voice. However, I agreed to have a chat when things were less busy and continued with the tasting.

The next stall I visited was exceptionally crowded. They were giving a tasting of cask samples of Grand Cru wines, which not surprisingly attracted plenty of attention. By smiling prettily at the lecherous old Frenchman behind the stall I managed to get a glass of Clos de Bèze. This was simply superb, and I was sipping it happily when without the slightest warning a large hand closed on my bottom.

If I hadn't had a mouthful of wine I would have screamed. As it was I nearly choked before turning to find the fat, beaming face of Percy Ottershaw only inches from my own. Nobody had seen what he had done because of the crowd, and I was still trying to get my breath back and find a suitably crushing riposte when he spoke.

'I hear you've been a naughty girl, Natasha,' he said and then favoured me with an oily grin.

I stopped, my mouth open to frame the first word of the brief speech I was about to give him on his behaviour. He had obviously been talking to John Thurston and knew that I had cheerfully submitted to being sodomised. We were in a dense crowd and several people were already looking at me disapprovingly, so I held my peace, not wishing to risk the line the conversation might take if I gave him a sharp answer. Instead I contented myself with a dirty look and asked what he was tasting in a perfectly civil voice.

'Charmes-Chambertin,' he answered. 'It has plenty of fruit and is certainly a fine wine, yet it lacks something in complexity. I often wonder if the vineyard really deserves its status.'

'Surely your opinion is trivial when weighed against centuries of experience?' I responded, still nettled by having my bottom squeezed.

'Perhaps,' he replied without apparently taking any offence at all. 'Yet you must concede that it is among the poorer Grand Cru. What are you tasting?'

'Clos de Bèze,' I replied. 'It's magnificent.'

'Which rather proves my point,' he answered smugly. 'As it happens, Clos de Bèze is something with which my cellar is rather well stocked. I even have some of the '53 from Lesulot, which I might be persuaded to open in return for an evening of your delectable company. Would Friday suit?'

'No it would not,' I replied and turned pointedly away to ask a question of the producer.

Completely unabashed, he joined in the ensuing conversation and continued to pop up more or less wherever I went as the tasting progressed. I was furious and also intensely embarrassed. My feelings were mainly directed against John Thurston, who had obviously told Percy Ottershaw about seducing me. How much he had told him I could not be sure, but the thought of Ottershaw knowing that I had submitted to buggery and thoroughly enjoyed it was enough to keep my cheeks constantly warm with blushes. The other annoyance was that Ottershaw could have the nerve to think that he could handle me the same way, which he obviously did. John Thurston was a dirty old man, there was no doubt about it. He was big and well muscled though and had certainly been handsome enough in his day. Percy Ottershaw was very different. He was fat for a start. Not plump or cuddly but blatantly fat, with a huge belly, gigantic wobbling buttocks and a puffy face that varied in colour from fresh pink to puce according to how much he had drunk. He was also shorter than me, sixty if he was a day, leery and almost completely bald. The idea that he could think for an instant that I would enjoy sex with him was absolutely outrageous.

Worse still was my certain knowledge that to be given a good firm spanking across his knee would be absolute bliss. I was filled with self-disgust for wanting it, but I couldn't deny my own feelings. As the tasting progressed I kept finding my mind running through the fantasy. Being a dirty old bastard, he would probably make me dress up first, perhaps in tennis kit or as a maid, but in school uniform would be best, complete with big panties in navy blue or white, knee socks and a pleated, tartan skirt. He would probably make me tie my hair in bunches with big green or red ribbons and wear my glasses too. He would probably want to take photographs of me in a variety of rude poses, all of them involving showing my panties. Then it would be over his knee, to be held down and have my bottom fondled with my skirt pulled up so that he could get at my panties. After he had eventually tired of my knickers, they would come down, slowly, so that I could really feel the humiliation of having him strip my bottom. Then he would carry on feeling me, his fat clammy hands pawing my bare bottom. He would pull by bum-cheeks apart and inspect between them. He would put a finger in my vagina. He would rub my clitty to make my pussy juice and swell. He would tickle my anus, maybe even finger my bottom. Then he would spank me, spank me hard on the bare bottom, spank me until I was kicking and howling and blubbering over his lap. When he was done and I was kneeling on the floor with my poor bottom stuck out behind me all hot and red and shamed, I would suck his cock, willingly, eagerly, until he came in my mouth, grunting and sweating as I gulped down his sperm.

'Rather hits the back of one's throat, doesn't it?' a voice spoke close to my ear, startling me out of my fantasy.

It was Percy Ottershaw again, the very man I had been

thinking about, which sent my face scarlet with blushes. I turned away, pretending to admire the colour of the wine I was drinking against the light in a desperate attempt to cover my embarrassment.

For a moment the crowd had cleared and we were alone. He was smiling at me – a dirty, meaningful leer that told me that my worst fears about what he knew were true.

'You really were very naughty,' he said softly. 'Do you know what happens to naughty girls?'

'I ... I have to powder my nose,' I said, hurriedly replacing my glass on the stall and almost spilling it.

A wry chuckle followed my departure, almost as if he had read my mind. I walked briskly in the direction of the loos, almost running in fact, and feeling seriously flustered. He had said it, or as good as said it. The implication of his words was obvious. Certainly I knew what happened to naughty girls – they got spanked.

I was shaking when I reached the lavatory; it took me a good five minutes to calm down. I really hated him and the way he was manipulating me but knew full well that he had no idea of what a powerful effect he was having on me. In fact he wasn't manipulating me; I was manipulating myself, straight into his fat, sweaty arms. His efforts at seduction were no better than they ever had been, even if he did know that I was more pliable than he had previously thought. What had changed was that before he had simply disgusted me. He still did, more so if anything, but it was that very disgust that made the idea of him spanking me so very appealing.

He really wanted me too – using flattery, bribery and perhaps I had even caught a hint of blackmail in his tone. Despite my self-disgust I knew that if he kept the pressure on I would accept an invitation from him, and that once I did that would be that, I'd be lost.

It was as I left the loos that I ran into Sophie Carlisle, who I had entirely forgotten about. She excused herself from the woman she was talking to and steered me gently away by the elbow.

'We really must talk,' she said, her voice gentle but full of authority. 'Come up to the balcony.'

The exhibition was entirely on the lower level of the hall, leaving the balcony to a few reflective drinkers and those who wanted to talk in peace. Sophie Carlisle steered me to an empty section of rail and leant against it, looking down on the throng below.

'This is rather difficult to say,' she began slowly, 'but I really thought I had to tell you.'

'What about?' I asked.

'Well,' she continued, 'it seems that that awful man Thurston has been going about telling people that he slept with you. Nonsense, of course, but I really thought you should know.'

'Thank you,' I answered cautiously.

'It's not that I want to tell you how to conduct yourself or anything,' she continued in a tone that told me that that was exactly what she intended to do, 'but you really must be careful about that sort of thing. It's hard enough being a woman in the trade as it is without giving men like him an opportunity to ruin one's reputation. You were seen leaving the tasting with him the other day, which makes what he says rather difficult to refute.'

'What does he say, exactly?' I asked, equally cross that my suspicions had been confirmed and that she thought she had a right to lecture me on my behaviour.

'It was Charles he spoke to of course,' she went on, 'at the shop the other day. That dreadful man Ottershaw was there too. What he said was ... well, it's really too dreadful; I don't quite know how to put it ...'

I stayed silent, knowing exactly why she was having so much difficulty saying what she wanted to. She was very much of the older generation. In fact she was even a bit reserved by the standards of most people of her age. Sex was hardly something that I could see her discussing easily, and much less the sort of sex in question. Thurston had evidently spilt the beans with a vengeance, telling Percy Ottershaw, Charles Carlisle and perhaps others, not only that he had slept with me as she so quaintly put it, but also that he had buggered me and probably that I had come with his cock up my bottom.

119

'He said he had . . . had the pleasure of your bottom,' she finally managed.

'The dirty bastard!' I retorted, trying to sound as if it was a surprise.

'I know, my dear,' she said, placing a comforting hand on my arm. 'Men really can be quite disgusting and Thurston is among the worst of them. So you see why you must be discreet?'

'Yes, absolutely,' I answered. 'Thank you for letting me know.'

'It's the least I could do,' she assured me.

I excused myself and left, feeling even more flustered than before. For all her slightly patronising – well, matronising really I suppose – attitude, I was grateful to her for confirming what I had suspected. She was not at all surprised that I wanted to be alone, assuming that I was disturbed by the knowledge that John Thurston was spreading rumours about me. Of course the trouble was that it was true.

Being reminded of my session with Thurston really brought it back to me as well: how he had seduced me into accepting his cock, first in my vagina and then up my bottom. For all his despicable behaviour I couldn't deny that it had been good, and I knew that if Ottershaw found me and propositioned me again that I was going to accept. Determined not to subject myself to such utter degradation, I left, but with difficulty and a strong sense of having missed an opportunity.

Feeling somewhat drunk and very muddled, I found a suitable café and ordered coffee and a croissant. It made little difference, and I decided that what I really needed was a long walk and some time to think. I set off in a vaguely north-easterly direction, intending to walk slowly home. Only when I had gone nearly halfway and was in the middle of a park somewhere in Maida Vale did I realise that I wasn't going to make it home without having a pee. Fortunately there was a red brick structure visible at the far side of the park, its discreet location among thick rhododendrons indicating that it was almost certainly a loo.

I was right, although the interior proved considerably less salubrious than it might have been. The cubicles were brick and painted a dull cream that had flaked in places to reveal an even less attractive dark brown beneath. A row of narrow windows illuminated them, the frosted, wire-reinforced glass cracked or even missing in all but one. Reluctant to sit on the seat, I hoisted my skirt up and took my panties off very carefully. Bunching them up in my hand, I held my skirt clear of my pussy and went into a squat over the bowl. It felt pleasantly naughty with my bottom and pussy bare; I held it in for a moment before letting my pee gush into the bowl beneath me. I've always enjoyed the feeling of relief that comes with a good pee and this was no exception. My mouth was a little open and my eyes were shut in pleasure at it splashed into the water beneath me. I even considered playing with myself while I did it and touched my clitty gently, giving an experimental rub.

Only then did I open my eyes and find an eye peering down at me through the cracked window. I jumped, then tugged frantically at my skirt, covering myself only to realise that I had let go of my panties, which where now in the bowl and soaked with water and pee. The eye had disappeared and I yelled a couple of choice insults after it. Fishing my sodden panties out of the bowl with two fingers, I pondered what to do. I was knickerless under a fairly short skirt, but that was all right as long as I didn't bend over too far. More importantly my beautiful white silk panties were soaked and I could hardly walk back home with a pair of dripping knickers dangling from my hand. The way to avoid embarrassment was to wash them quickly in a sink, rinse them as best I could and then put them at the bottom of my bag.

I was pretty cross and slightly scared just in case the peeping Tom turned out to be something worse. Self-confident I may be, but I don't take stupid risks and so set off directly across the open part of the park as I left the loo. To my relief nobody emerged from the bushes behind me and I reached the gate without incident. Only as I crossed the road beyond did I notice an unmistakable figure enter a newsagents some way to my left – Percy Ottershaw.

It could not possibly be a coincidence. There was absolutely no way he would have just happened to be in Maida Vale unless he had followed me from the tasting. And if he had followed me, then it had to have been him who peeped at me peeing. Furious, seething with indignation and burning with humiliation, I ran down the road, determined on a confrontation. Sure enough, it was him in the newsagents, buying a paper and some chocolate. I tapped him firmly on the shoulder and he turned round, his expression a very convincing imitation of surprise.

'Outside, you pervert!' I said in full hearing of the shopkeeper and two other customers.

'What do you mean?' he demanded.

'You know perfectly well what I mean, you dirty old bastard!' I said at the top of my voice. 'How dare you peer in at me in a public loo?'

'I . . . I wasn't, I assure you,' he stammered.

'Then what are you doing here?' I demanded. 'I suppose you just happened to be here did you?'

'Well . . . yes,' he said defensively. 'I live here, just around the corner.'

'So you say!' I stormed.

'No, seriously,' he answered, indicating the shopkeeper, 'ask this gentleman.'

'Mr Ottershaw has been one of my best customers for nearly ten years,' the man replied.

'Well that doesn't mean it wasn't you,' I continued but without any real vigour.

'I assure you, Natasha, that I would not dream of such behaviour,' he replied, now with greater confidence. 'Indeed, I only just returned from the tasting, by taxi. Ask Mr Laymont in the delicatessen if you don't believe me. He saw me get out of the taxi, not five minutes ago.'

'Oh,' I answered, feeling suddenly crestfallen and becoming aware that not just three but eight people were now looking at me as if I was completely crazy.

I rushed out of the shop with the blood coming to my cheeks in a boiling rush. Eight people had just witnessed me make a complete idiot of myself; nine counting Percy Ottershaw, and it was doing it in front of him that was worst of all. If all of them had caught me peeing it couldn't have been more humiliating, and it was with that thought that I hurried home.

When I got there I threw myself down on the bed, absolutely seething with emotion. Ottershaw had managed to get to me at a level I would not have believed possible, and he hadn't even done it intentionally. What he had done was bad enough, telling me I was naughty, with all the implications that not only was I a promiscuous little brat who would benefit from a spanking but also that he would be just the person to do it. What was worse was that without him I wouldn't have been filled with urgent longing and self-disgust. Nor would I have been peeped at in a public loo, with some dirty bastard getting a prime view of my bare pussy gushing pee as I played with my clit. Nor would I have shown myself up in the street.

Reluctantly, but with an inevitable momentum, I pulled up my skirt and put my hand on my bare pussy. I was wet and my clitty was a hard bud between my soft, moist labia. With my eyes closed and my head spinning with shame I began to masturbate over the thought of Percy Ottershaw spanking me.

He should really have done it in the shop for accusing him of being a peeping Tom. The others would have helped, full of righteous indignation that I had insulted him and knowing that a spanking was the best punishment for insolent girls. They would have bent me over the counter and held my legs and arms. My skirt would have been pulled briskly up and they would have exclaimed in disgust at the discovery that I was pantiless beneath it. Ottershaw himself would have beaten me, by hand, making my bum-cheeks bounce and jiggle and revealing flashes of pussy and bumhole to the audience. When he had finished I would have been made to apologise, on my knees with my bum still bare and all red from spanking. Then they would have taken me into the back and used me, making me suck their cocks and lick the women's pussies while they took turns to beat me with a shoe.

I came over that, imagining Percy Ottershaw working my bottom over with a hard shoe while I licked at the pussy of a fat, common-looking woman in pink who had been among the audience. The thought of her plump, hairy lips pushed against my face while I bucked under the slaps and they all laughed at me was in my head as I hit my first peak. Then I imagined them swapping and his cock going into my mouth as she took over the task of punishing me as a second peak tore through me. Then it was the knowledge that someone had watched me pee, not in fantasy but for real, as a third and yet more powerful climax erupted inside me.

Twelve

I awoke to a feeling of acute dissatisfaction, as if I had done something terribly wrong. I had certainly done something embarrassing, and the memory of what I'd said to Percy Ottershaw in the newsagents kept coming back, making me feel nervous and strangely vulnerable. I put on tight jeans, which for some reason usually make me feel stronger but now made no appreciable difference. Writing my column cheered me up a little, especially as I managed to pinch Ottershaw's argument about the Chambertin vineyards and make it sound really clever.

Lunchtime found me toying with some ciabata and ham while I wondered what to do with myself. I felt I should go out and do something, not because I really wanted to or because there was anything to gain, but because it would stop me doing what the darker, dirtier part of my mind was telling me to. The previous day's events had added a new element to my spanking fantasy – one which might be made to involve some interesting experimentation with my own body. The only difficulty was that once I had come I would feel deeply ashamed of myself. Yet unless I made a conscious effort to do something else I knew full well that I was going to end up doing it. The fantasy was wetting myself while undergoing punishment. The more immediate question was: is it possible to have an orgasm while peeing?

It was the fact that I had drunk half a bottle of Chablis and nearly a litre of orange juice that made me decide to give in to my dirty little mind and do it, only at that moment the doorbell rang. My first thought was that it was going to be Antoine, but then I remembered that he had taken a set of keys. Not really wanting company, I went to the balcony and peered carefully down, only to find the globular figure of Percy Ottershaw standing at my front door with a huge bunch of flowers, a bottle and a brown paper bag.

The sight of him put me straight into a panic, and not just because his intentions were obvious. It's bad enough being spoken to by a man like that in public without him coming round with wine and flowers. People might even think I was having an affair with him!

I ran for the intercom, pausing only to hide the copy of my slightly plagiaristic column. A minute later he was bowling into my flat, red faced and puffing from the exertion of climbing the stairs.

'I came round to apologise for yesterday,' he announced, taking an interested glance around and then making for the kitchen. 'I was a little taken aback and I should have been more sympathetic. It must be dreadful to be the victim of a peeping Tom, and I quite understand how you thought it might have been me.'

'Thank you,' I replied uncertainly.

'So I bought you some flowers to cheer you up,' he continued. 'Also that Clos de Bèze I promised and lunch.'

He had certainly brought lunch. I tend to nibble at some good bread accompanied by something tasty and a glass of wine. Percy Ottershaw had no such restraint. He had bought a game pie topped with whortleberries in sweet jelly, oysters, York ham, half a cucumber, bread with olives and sun-dried tomatoes in it, grapes, strawberries, cream and a whole *Amour de Nuits*, which was already trying to escape its wooden box.

'Chablis?' he queried as his eye fell on the vacuum-stoppered bottle I had been drinking with my lunch.

'Yes,' I admitted.

'Ah ha, just the thing,' he said, picking up an oyster. 'May I?'

I nodded, still somewhat taken aback by the swiftness with which he had occupied my flat. He cut the adductor muscle of the oyster with a single practised movement, picked up the Chablis and poured a measure into the shell. His face was set in a look of absolute rapture as he did this, but when the wine was at the brim of the oyster's shell he passed it to me. I accepted it and tipped it down my throat, finding that the wine balanced the flavour of the oyster beautifully.

'Champagne is more traditional,' he remarked as he filled a second oyster for himself. 'Mosel is good too, and most Alsace.'

'Delicious,' I agreed, 'but I've already eaten as it happens.'

'No matter,' he answered, beaming cheerfully as he eyed the food; it would have kept me in lunches for a week.

If he had any dubious intentions he obviously didn't intend to press me, so I relaxed and allowed myself to enjoy first the oysters in Chablis and then the Clos de Bèze '53, a wine for which the superlatives have yet to be invented. Watching Percy Ottershaw eat was a disgusting experience but still held me fascinated, rather like watching one of those snakes that can take in an entire egg. He didn't rush; he managed a lot of conversation in between mouthfuls, but he did eat it all, every single morsel – including the entire cheese. Taste was his major topic of conversation, and he was worth listening to because he had managed to pack more experience into his sixty-odd years than I would be likely to get if I lived to reach a hundred.

'To truly understand sensation,' he was explaining as he took a grape from the bunch, 'one must not be squeamish. Short of the actively poisonous, there is nothing that I will not sample.'

'Come on,' I objected, 'there must be some things.'

'Perhaps a few,' he admitted. 'But you would be surprised at how pleasurable some of the less acceptable sensations are. Drinking a girl's urine, for instance, is a beautiful experience.'

'That's disgusting!' I answered, actually quite shocked and also instantly on edge as his comment brought back the previous day's events.

'Is it?' he answered mildly. 'You young girls claim to be so liberated; it's actually rather droll when put in the perspective of reality. When I think of some of the girls I knew back in the late fifties and early sixties . . .'

He trailed off with a wistful sigh, but his comment had stung and I wasn't going to let it go.

'We are liberated,' I insisted. 'Far more so than back then.'

'Are you?' he answered with a laugh. 'I disagree. It is merely that you think of yourselves as liberated. In fact you are bound by social conventions every bit as rigid as those of earlier days, merely different.'

'That's rubbish!' I protested.

'Is it?' he asked with a lift of his eyebrows. 'You think you do as you please, but you don't. Sexually, for instance. Once girls were obliged by social pressure to create a pretence of being demure and unwilling but that didn't mean they were. Now social pressures oblige you to be sexually aggressive – what we used to call a man-eater. The obligations have changed, but they're still there. What happens to the girl who likes to be taken charge of? But I don't suppose you believe any do?'

'No I . . .' I managed and then stopped.

Of course he had hit the nail on the head and had probably realised that I was like that after talking to John Thurston. That didn't mean I had to admit it to him.

'Let me tell you a story,' he continued, apparently oblivious to the fact that he had managed to unsettle me. 'When I was a young man, still in my teens, I fell in love with a beautiful girl. She was called Elaine and had the most striking red hair that I have seen, before or since. My love was completely hopeless, and I certainly wasn't the only one in love with her either. She was the junior matron at my school you see, and completely untouchable. In practice she was only a couple of years older than me, but she seemed so mature and calm that the idea of approaching her sexually was simply unthinkable. She was demure too, and very proper and reserved, just as the popular image of respectable young women in those days

128

demanded that she should be. She was engaged, but that didn't stop us boys from admiring her. Some of the more romantic ones even gave her flowers and chocolates, which she always accepted with a good grace. Her manner showed that she thought of us merely as children, for all that we were men in the eyes of the law, being eighteen in most cases.

'Being of a more practical disposition than my friends, I realised that there was no chance whatsoever of gaining so much as a peck on the cheek from her. I was besotted though and determined that, if I couldn't have her, at least I could get a good look at her. Not that this was easy; her room was on the top floor and looked out over the playing fields. Logically I knew that every night she undressed and that therefore anyone bold enough to be looking through the window at the right moment would be rewarded.'

'You little pervert!' I interrupted.

'Perhaps,' he replied, 'but there is nothing like the concealment of a woman's body to make men want to see it and at that time I had never seen a naked girl, not even in a picture. Anyway, her bedroom window was out of the question, being set over a fifty-foot drop on to a gravel path. The bathroom was a different matter, because although it had only a tiny gable window – and of frosted glass at that – it looked inwards to the roofs of the school and had one of those spinning ventilators set in the upper pane. Just the thought of what I might see was enough to give me an erection.'

'Didn't you feel ashamed of yourself?' I demanded.

'Certainly I did,' he said, 'but my lust far outweighed any such considerations. My preparations were painstaking to say the least, and not a little risky, with six strokes of the cane the least I could expect if I was caught.'

'The cane?' I broke in as his words intersected my fascination with smacked bottoms.

'Yes, the cane,' he answered. 'In my day masters thought nothing of dishing out six and they used to do it across our naked buttocks as well.'

'Wasn't it exciting at all?' I asked, unable to keep the question in.

'What, being whacked by some grizzled old master?' he retorted. 'Not at all. I dare say it might have been if Elaine had done it, or even Mrs White, the senior matron, but they never did. I suppose some of the fruits – as we used to call gay boys – might have enjoyed it, but not I. I don't suppose they had the cane at your school, not even on the hand?'

'No,' I admitted.

'Pity,' he said, sending a tremor right through·me. 'But I digress. Where was I? Oh yes, preparing my expedition to spy on the beautiful Elaine McKeown. As a prefect I had my own bedsit and so could move around freely at night. The dangerous part was climbing the fire escape to the roof, after which there was little chance of detection. Unfortunately an initial foray only proved that the ventilator provided no more than a frustrating glimpse of her feet and calves. So I waited until one sultry summer's afternoon when everyone else was out on the cricket field watching us play Ilkley Grammar and stole carefully up to the window. Elaine, I knew, was doing the first aid at the match and there was no chance of being disturbed. Working with great care, I dismantled the ventilator, broke off half of one of the blades, rubbed dirt on to the freshly snapped edge and put the whole thing together again. Now I had a clear view into her bathroom and could adjust the broken vane to see either the bath itself or both the loo and wash basin.

'I waited with immense patience for the right night. It had to be both dark and windless to avoid the twin problems of risking being seen against the sky and of the ventilator spinning. Finally the perfect night arrived; I sneaked up to the roof with my heart in my mouth. Of course I had to get the timing right as well, and so I had hung around the medical room with her other admirers until she announced that she was retiring. By the time I got to my station on the roof the bathroom light was on and she had even opened the window a crack because the night was so warm.

'I peeked in and, to my utter delight, found that she was running a bath. She came back in a moment later and

130

began to undress. I watched her strip in fascination. Her uniform was starched white cotton; just watching her take that off had my cock stiff in my trousers. Beneath it she had on all the wonderful, secret underwear that girls used to wear: a suspender girdle, a heavily reinforced bra, big white knickers and stockings. She peeled these off one by one and I was in heaven, especially when she revealed her breasts. By the time she was down to her knickers my cock was in my hand and I was determined to come at the moment she took them down.

'She didn't though, but instead did something that I am never likely to forget. Moving to the loo, she sat down, opened her thighs wide, slid her hand down the front of her knickers and started to urinate through the gusset. I didn't really know about female masturbation, but from the expression on her face and the way her fingers were moving down the front of her knickers I could guess what she was doing. It was when she put her spare hand in between her legs to let her urine trickle over it that my reserve broke completely. I won't pretend that the thought of what a useful piece of information her dirty habit might be didn't cross my mind, but it was mainly a mixture of naive optimism and sheer lust that had me pulling the window up and climbing through.

'She screamed and took her hand out of her knickers, but she couldn't stop the flow of pee. What she did do was try and cover her breasts and in doing so got urine all over them. Feeling bolder than I ever had in my life, I came forward and held my cock out to her. She gave me an absolutely filthy look but took it in her hand and started to masturbate me – as if doing a tedious but necessary job of work. She told me that I was a dirty little boy and that I ought to be beaten but carried on pulling at my prick. Strangely enough she still seemed to have her authority, even though she was masturbating me. It was as if it were one of those things that just needed to be done, like cleaning grazes with iodine or holding our balls and telling us to cough. After a while I took hold of her breasts; she made no objection.

'I came in no time, all over her chest, which she wiped up with tissue just as if she'd been cleaning a cut. Having come I felt a bit awkward and was going to leave, but she had other ideas. She told me to stay and quite calmly took off her pants. She made me lick her, sitting on the toilet with her thighs open. I had the taste of her urine in my mouth while she instructed me on how to do it properly. When she came it was with far more force than my own orgasm. She kissed me afterwards too and told me never to do it again, but I did – three more times before term ended and she passed out of my life. It was that experience which made me realise that, when it comes down to it, women enjoy sex just as much as men, and which also gave me my first taste of a woman's urine. So much for your fifties' women being prim and proper.'

He stopped and took a swallow of his Clos de Bèze. I had been eating grapes in a sort of trance while I listened, simultaneously fascinated and repelled not just by his dirty story but by the fact he was telling it to me. One thought was uppermost in my mind, a question to which I simply had to have the answer.

'Was it really you who watched me yesterday?' I queried. 'Tell the truth, please.'

'No,' he answered bluntly. 'I frankly admit that I would have enjoyed the experience, but a man in my position simply can't go around peering into public lavatories. Besides, since my teenage years I have developed a little more respect for female privacy.'

I didn't answer but popped another grape into my mouth, glad that it hadn't been him.

'Natasha,' he said after a long silence, 'I am not a man to mince my words, and I couldn't help but notice your fascination when I mentioned caning. As a simple proposition, and bearing in mind that we both know that you are no angel, would you let me watch you urinate in return for a caning, if that's your penchant?'

There was a huge lump in my throat that stopped me answering. The thought of him watching me pee and presumably playing with himself while I did it was absolutely gross yet sufficiently in tune with my fantasies to be hard to resist. What was more, he was offering what I needed the most in return, albeit without the thrill of it being done forcibly.

'I also assure you of my absolute discretion,' he continued, sensing my hesitancy.

'Now? Here?' I asked, a question that was as good as saying yes.

He nodded, his round red face shinning with that same look of rapture that he had worn when he had poured the Chablis on to the oyster.

'I ... I'd rather be spanked over your knee,' I managed shakily.

'It will be a pleasure,' he answered with a big beaming smile and that same look of sensual delight.

I got up and walked to the bathroom in a sort of erotic trance. What I was doing was so dirty, so improper that it made the very worst of my behaviour seem mild. He was right about modern taboos though; nowadays it is far less acceptable for a girl to let a dirty old man watch her pee than it is for her to have even the most torrid of lesbian affairs or even group sex. Yet part of the reason I was doing it was to show him that he was wrong, to show him that I, Natasha Linnet, was no puppet of modern social pressures but truly my own woman. Deeper still I wondered if he hadn't carefully devised the entire scenario, including making up the story. If he had then my humiliation would know no bounds if I found out, but the idea was simply too complicated, too devious, to be tenable.

'Floor tiles, how sensible,' he remarked as we entered the bathroom. 'Perhaps you would do it all over the floor?'

The idea sent a shiver the full length of my spine and I nodded, acquiescent to whatever perverse details he wanted to add to his fantasy.

'Naked?' I asked as I turned to him. 'Or through my panties like Elaine?'

'Panties down and squatting with your back to me,' he instructed. 'As if you were doing it in a hedge and were embarrassed because you thought I might try and watch.'

133

I turned my back to him, imagining his eyes feasting on my denim-clad bottom as I prepared to expose myself for him. My fingers were trembling so much that I had trouble undoing the button of my jeans. When it finally popped open I glanced over my shoulder, finding him seated on the edge of the bath with his legs wide apart and his cock and balls protruding obscenely from his fly. He had his balls cupped in one hand and was stroking his cock with his thumb, making no secret of the pleasure he was getting from watching me.

'I like the coy, self-conscious look,' he remarked as I hooked my thumbs into my jeans.

It was genuine. My heart was hammering as I started to pull my trousers and panties down.

'Jeans first, then knickers,' he said, his voice noticeably hoarser than an instant before. 'And stick that fat little bum out for me.'

I adjusted my grip and stuck my bottom out even as his choice of words gave me a new pang of humiliation. My jeans moved slowly down under the pressure of my thumbs, exposing the pink cotton panties I had chosen that morning. They were taut over my bottom, which felt huge as it came on show. I took the jeans down to my ankles, providing him with a thoroughly rude display of my panty-clad bottom. Standing up once more I took a firm hold on my panties and again looked back over my shoulder. His cock was hard, a skinny pink erection that made a truly grotesque contrast with his fat belly. He was pulling at it, his face red and beaded with sweat, his piggy eyes locked on my panty seat.

Again I stuck my bottom out, making it into a plump ball of girl flesh with the panties stretched across the chubby cheeks. He groaned as I started to pull them down and I thought he was coming. I thought he was going to have apoplexy as I exposed my bottom for him – inch by inch with it stuck out far enough to ensure that he got a good view of my pussy and bumhole as I lowered my panties.

As with my jeans, I settled the pink cotton knickers

around my ankles. Still watching him over my shoulder, I sank into a squat, keeping my body forward and my back pulled in to give him a good view between my bum-cheeks. I focused my mind on my bladder, which was full to bursting. It wasn't going to be hard, indeed now that I was in a squatting position it was difficult not to let go. I forced myself to hold it in though, letting the lovely, naughty, humiliated feeling it was giving me build up in my head until I simply couldn't stand it any longer.

Then I let go, gasping as my pee splashed out all over the bathroom floor. It felt so dirty to be doing it on the floor, so rude to be squatting bare bottomed while he jerked frantically at his penis, so wanton to just let my pee gush out as his eyes fixed between my spread bum-cheeks.

He groaned again, and this time he did come, the semen erupting from the tip of his cock to splash on to the floor and mingle with the golden pool of my pee. I knelt down, overcome with pleasure, indifferent to my jeans and panties getting sodden with my own pee. I just had to come, kneeling there in that obscene position while he watched. My fingers were on my clit, rubbing, my pleasure building, my muscles starting to contract –

And I heard the sound of a key turning in the lock of my main door. I panicked, knowing that it had to be one of three people – either of my parents or Antoine. Struggling with my panties and dizzy with my interrupted orgasm I slipped in the pool of pee and fell hard on my side. Somebody called my name and I felt a quite ridiculous flush of relief as I realised that it was neither Dad nor Mum. The relief was short lived. We had left the door open, and as I managed to recover I found myself looking into the astonished face of Antoine.

Percy made an exit of astonishing speed for a man of his age and size. One moment he was sitting on the bath with his cock in his hand, and the next he had risen, barged past Antoine and fled before the rest of us recovered our senses. I heard him clattering down the stairs and even had a moment to worry what my neighbours would think if he hadn't put his cock away in time.

Then Antoine simply went berserk. He stepped forward and grabbed me by the hair. I squealed in protest as he threw me face down into the puddle of my own pee. He was calling me a pervert and a whore as he put a foot on my back. I tried to struggle but only got my face pushed into the floor. As the taste of my own pee filled my mouth I heard a whistle and something hard came down on my bare bum. I yelled, calling him a bastard. He took no notice, once more bringing down what I realised was my big bath-brush across my bum, really hard. It hurt like anything and I yelled out in pain and fury. Again my face was pushed into my puddle, only this time my mouth was wide open. He was calling me a whore, a pervert, a bitch and a slut as he rubbed my face in my piss and thrashed my bottom. I kicked and struggled and beat my fists on the floor but could do nothing against his fury.

He must have given me a hundred hard smacks with the brush. By the end I was blubbering wildly, with tears streaming down my cheeks and deep sobs coming up in my throat. Then it was over and I was lying spent in my own pee, my naked bottom throbbing with pain and my pussy hot and swollen. I lifted my hips and slumped down again; I tried once more, raising my bottom to the bastard who had just thrashed me.

'Fuck me, Antoine!' I pleaded. 'Now, here on the floor.'

'Pervert!' he yelled and hurled the brush into the bath.

The door slammed and he was gone. I was left, beaten and soiled on my bathroom floor, abandoned despite my plea. Feeling completely used I rolled on to my back and slid a hand on to the wet fur of my pussy. I could feel my sore buttocks against the floor, wet with urine as I began to masturbate.

Thirteen

Antoine had made a real mess of my bottom. Both cheeks were purple with bruising and ached like anything. For three days I couldn't sit down on it and spent most of my time lying face down on my bed with my bum bare and well smeared with cold cream. Tight jeans were painful as well and walking was only really comfortable in loose dresses with no panties on underneath. The worst part was teaching my wine class; the chairs at the college are really hard and I had to conduct the entire lesson standing up.

Of course all this served as a reminder of what had been done to me. It was what I had wanted and I spent a lot of time masturbating. This would either be bum-up on the bed so that I could watch myself in the mirror, or kneeling in the bathroom where it had happened. I had some wonderful orgasms and twice wet myself before coming, once when I was already nude and once in my panties, which was the best of all.

He had beaten me considerably more severely than Evan Dunstal, or possibly it was the effect of the bath brush, which was pretty hard. In any case I was still uncomfortable on Saturday but was once more finding that the thrill and immediacy of having been punished faded with the bruises. What I needed was someone who would give me regular discipline and think I hated it, yet not be a complete bastard, like Antoine, when it wasn't time for me to be punished.

I was happy to see the back of Antoine and abandoned his classes without regret. My need for a spanking partner was even stronger though and I was beginning to feel frustrated by the weekend. I knew I could coax Charlotte into spanking me again, but she would be gentle and playful, which would be less than one hundred per cent satisfying. The same was true of Percy, because while I was sure he would make a thorough job of both my beating and my humiliation, he knew I liked it and so would not be perfect. There was one option though, the girl whose nametag I was wearing in my tummy button – Lydia.

My bruises were still prominent on the Saturday, but I hadn't seen Lydia and Steve since the party and so decided to pay a visit anyway and just not get spanked. Given how hard it seemed to be to actually get spanked, I reasoned that avoiding it should be easy. So I made myself up, put on tarty red knickers and bra, a short skirt and my leather jacket and set off for Steve's flat.

He answered the door to me with a big, sloppy grin that let me know exactly what he was thinking. Unfortunately Lydia was with him, slumped on the bed which they had tied me to for my piercing.

'Oh, it's my little slave,' she greeted me. 'We thought you'd run away.'

Her remark brought my mixed feelings for her sharply back. She had tagged my bottom and marked me as hers, which made me want to grovel at her feet but also to take some suitably devilish revenge on her.

'Hi,' was all I said in response, but she was evidently in a wicked mood.

'Let's see your belly button,' she demanded.

I pulled up my jacket, exposing my bare tummy and the piercing.

'You know that means you're mine, don't you?' she asked.

'Yes,' I answered.

'Come and lie on the bed,' she ordered, 'at my feet.'

It was all a bit sudden, but I complied, quite happy to play her games. Climbing on to the bed, I lay sideways and propped my chin in my hands so that I could see the room properly. Lydia had moved her legs to let me on and now put them up on my back in a deliberate gesture of superiority. She had high-heeled boots on, and I could feel the hard outline of one heel through my jacket; it highlighted my feeling of subservience to her.

Having got me where she wanted me she went back to reading her magazine, which was obviously a pose so that when Steve came back in with the coffee he would find me at his girlfriend's feet while she displayed an attitude of easy superiority over me. She had gone into the role really casually, as if absolutely certain that I would do as I was told. Given my behaviour towards them I suppose this was justified, but she didn't really know me, and as I lay there being her footrest I was wondering how she would feel about having her cheeky little bottom smacked in front of her boyfriend. I knew she'd had it done before, although not under what circumstances it had happened. She was tough but small, and I was just considering whether I was in the mood for a fight that I knew would be only half play when Steve came back. He gave a brief, rough laugh at the sight of me lying at his girlfriend's feet – a reaction that gave me a pang of sexual humiliation and put an end to my ideas of turning the tables on Lydia.

'Don't you normally bare their arses?' he said, casually yet hopefully.

'I . . .' I began, but it was too late.

Lydia had reached down and tweaked my skirt up, exposing my panties and undoubtedly a fair area of bruising.

'Hey! You've been whacked!' she exclaimed.

'Let's see,' Steve put in.

I tried to get up, but Steve had put his hand on my back and I couldn't. Amid exclamations of surprise and delight they pulled my pants down and made a thorough inspection of my well-beaten bottom. I lay there shivering with humiliation and pleasure. Their hands were all over me, even pulling my bum-cheeks apart, and I could do nothing about it.

'Who did it?' Steve asked, his tone suggesting that he approved of whoever it was.

139

I know I'm a liar, but I couldn't resist it. The truth was pretty good, but it wasn't the perfect fantasy and I was remembering how Percy Ottershaw had turned me on by telling a dirty story.

'It . . . it was really humiliating,' I began. 'I don't know if I can say . . .'

'Tell us,' Lydia insisted. 'Are you a pervert? Did someone do it to turn you on?'

'No!' I protested.

'I bet it did,' she sneered. 'You little slut!'

'Come on, what happened?' Steve demanded.

'OK,' I agreed reluctantly. 'I'll tell you, but can I pull my panties back up?'

'No,' Lydia laughed. 'Your bum stays bare while you tell us what you did to deserve it being smacked.'

'I didn't deserve it!' I protested. 'Well not so hard anyway.'

'So what happened?' Steve repeated.

'It was this big, fat woman in the laundrette!' I said, having decided on my story. 'She did it because I was making a joke of the size of her clothes.'

Of course I had never been in a laundrette in my life, but it is just the sort of situation that I like, really common and coarse to make my sense of humiliation that much more piquant.

'And?' Lydia demanded.

'Come on, the details,' Steve added.

'All right,' I said resignedly as she began to stroke my bottom. 'I was with my friend Charlotte. We went in to do some washing and there was this huge fat woman already there. Her thighs were so big that there wasn't room to sit down on the seats to either side of her. It just looked so funny; we were a bit pissed anyway, and we couldn't help giggling. She was really common too, all frumpy with her hair up and this huge floral dress like a tent.

'She tried not to pay any attention to us, but I could see she was getting cross and it was just so funny to wind her up. Her clothes were in the dryer, and you could see this huge bra going round and round, big enough to hold a

140

couple of footballs, seriously. I made a joke and she really gave me a glare, but it was just funny, because she couldn't do anything about it – or I thought not anyway.

'When her drier stopped she started taking all the clothes out and piling them in a basket. She put it to the side and started on another lot. While she was putting it in I sneaked round and picked her bra up to show Charlotte how silly it looked. I held it up against my chest and Charlotte started laughing, which made the woman turn around. She saw me and she just went nuts, shouting at me and everything. I just told to her to fuck off and called her a fat cow.

'I walked off, acting really sassy to show off how slim I am. I heard Charlotte call something to me and the next thing I knew the woman had grabbed me. I tried to pull away, but she was really strong, so I slapped her face and called her a fat cow again. She moved back and sat down really hard on the seats, still gripping my wrist. She started to pull me down and I suddenly realised that she was trying to get me across her knee. She was going to spank me!

'As soon as I realised what she was trying to do I really started fighting. I couldn't bear the thought of it. It was just too outrageous. I kicked and screamed and called her names but it didn't do any good, she just pulled me hard across her knee and twisted my arm up behind my back. It hurt and I was almost in tears. Then she started to spank me, really hard, calling me a brat and a little madam while her big hand came up and down on my bottom. It really hurt and there was nothing I could do to stop it. It was really frustrating as well as painful.

'What made it worse was that there were two men in there: one grey-haired old bastard and this really greasy guy with a bald patch. Both of them were laughing at what was happening to me and egging the fat woman on. It was the greasy one who suggested that I ought to have my pants pulled down.

'I didn't think the woman would do it, because she was just punishing me, while the two men were obviously getting turned on by watching. You can imagine how I felt when the spanking stopped and she started to lift my skirt. They all clapped and wolf-whistled at the sight of my knickers and the woman started to spank me again, even harder, while the men made remarks on how wobbly my bottom was and demanded again that my pants be pulled down.

'She did it too, right in front of them. She just took hold of the waistband and ripped them down, then went straight back to spanking me. My bum was bare and I'd never felt so humiliated in my life. They were laughing at me and telling me I was getting what I deserved. The grey-haired man said I'd obviously needed a spanking for a long time, and then the greasy one told me that he could see my pussy!

'I knew it was true, because the woman had me bent right over and my bum was up in the air while my head was down near the floor. I couldn't help kicking my legs about either, because it hurt so much, even though I knew it meant showing them everything, and I mean everything – even down between my bum-cheeks!

'She spanked and spanked and spanked, and when her hand started to hurt she picked up this big wooden scrubbing brush and started to use that. It hurt even more and I burst into tears but she just called me a cry baby and carried on beating me. It went on for ages, and eventually I just didn't care any more. When she finally finished all I could do was lie sobbing over her legs, still with my bum stuck up and those two dirty old bastards feasting their eyes on my pussy and bumhole. I could see in a mirror that it was all red. She made me apologise before she'd let me up, and the last thing she did was pull my panties right off and throw them to the dirty old men.'

I stopped with a groan of pleasure; Lydia had slid her hand between my thighs and cupped my pussy.

'I think you're exaggerating a bit,' she told me as she started to knead me, 'and I also think that, whatever really happened, you enjoyed every second of it.'

'No,' I answered, but not very convincingly because I had really turned myself on, and she was massaging my pussy in a way that kept pressing the palm of her hand on my clitty.

'Let's fuck her,' Steve suggested.

'Yes please,' I purred.

'Oh no, you weren't turned on at all were you?' Lydia said. 'You're a slut, Tasha. What are you?'

'A slut,' I admitted.

She gave me a final rub and pulled her hand away, only to bring it down across my bottom. I squealed and she gave a satisfied chuckle. I think Lydia wanted to spank me, which I would have accepted, bruises or no bruises. Steve had other ideas.

Lydia had rolled round to get at my bottom and it had been Steve who had been holding me down while I talked. Now he took hold of my hips and turned me over, using no real effort at all. Lydia pulled my shoulders and I went with the pressure, turning to lie lengthways on the bed as Steve took hold of my ankles. Her hands stayed at my shoulders, pinning me in place as he held my legs up with one big, strong hand, took hold of my half-lowered panties with the other and peeled them up my legs. They caught on my boots, but he pulled them off one to leave them around an ankle as he opened my legs. I sighed as I was exposed. I was completely open and vulnerable to him, my pussy moist and gaping for his cock.

They stripped me, peeling my skirt and jacket off, then my bra to leave me naked except for my high-heeled ankle boots. Neither of them bothered to undress. It was me who was being fucked, me who was the centre of attention.

'Get it out, Steve; fuck her,' Lydia said, apparently more than happy to have her boyfriend fuck me as long as the session didn't exclude her.

She was kneeling behind me, her arms pinning mine and my head resting in her lap. I could smell the leather of her skirt, her perfume and something else, a hint of hot, turned-on pussy. I watched as Steve unzipped himself and pulled his cock free of his black leather trousers. It was nearly erect, the lovely thick shaft squirming in his hand and the head poking out of the heavy foreskin.

'Show me your balls too,' I begged as he began to ready his cock for me.

'Slut,' Lydia said as Steve pulled his balls free of his fly.

It looked gorgeous. His cock and balls were sticking out, deliciously obscene in a field of black leather. His balls looked big and heavy in their wrinkled pink sack; the shaft reared above them, ready for my vagina. He took hold of my boots again and moved forward, rolling my legs up and stretching my vagina open for him. His cock bumped against me, touching my clitty. I put my hands to my breasts, finding my nipples fully erect, the skin rough and sensitive under my fingers. Steve nudged me with his cock, probing for my vagina, each touch of it sending a delicious thrill right through me. Then it was at the opening to my hole, pushing in, stretching me, filling me. I gave a long moan of pleasure at he slid inside me. Lydia made a low, passionate sound in her throat at the sight of her boyfriend's cock going into me. She leant forward and their mouths met in a kiss as he began to hump himself into me.

Her movement pulled my head forward, in response to which she sat up a little more, letting my head drop back on the bed and giving me a fine view right up her skirt. As usual she had no panties on and her trim little bottom and the furry mound of her pussy were directly over my face and bare. All she had to do was sit back and my face would be smothered in bottom. I could smell her pussy, a rich intensely feminine musk that mingled with her perfume. She was wet and open, her vagina showing as a knot of moist pink flesh, swollen and ready for entry. Unable to resist, I raised my head and kissed her, right over the mouth of her pussy.

'That's right, slut. Lick,' she said. 'No, not there. You can clean my arsehole first, with your tongue.'

The way she said it was so dirty, and I was really trembling as she reached back and pulled her skirt up around her waist. Her bottom was directly over my face, the pert cheeks round and pink with a trace of hair showing between them. Steve had slowed down, allowing me to concentrate on what Lydia was going to make me do. She reached back and looked down over her shoulder with a wicked grin on her face. She was about to make me lick her anus – about the most degrading and subservient act one person can give to another – and she was really enjoying it.

She took a buttock in each hand and pulled them wide. She was really hairy, not just on her pussy but right up between her cheeks. Her anus was a wrinkled pink spot in a nest of hair, the ring slightly distended as she relaxed it for my tongue. I was whimpering softly as she lowered herself slowly on to my face, her buttocks pressing against my cheeks and then my lips touching her anal hair.

'Lick it, you slut,' she ordered.

I obeyed, poking my tongue out to touch her anus. It felt soft and rubbery, the little hole opening under my tongue tip as I heard her sigh of pure ecstasy. I began to lick, tasting her as I lapped at her bottom-hole; Steve once more began to ride me.

'She's doing it,' I heard Lydia sigh. 'She's licking my arsehole out. I really didn't think she would do it. Oh God that's nice. Lick, you filthy little tart. Put your tongue up my arse.'

Her bum pushed harder on to my face and I responded, sticking my tongue deeper up her bottom. It was hard to breath and her scent was thick in my nostrils. She was groaning in ecstasy as my tongue wriggled in her anus. She rubbed her bottom in my face, back and forth over my mouth but never so much that my tongue slipped out of the hole. I lapped, feeling her rubbery little bumhole around my tongue, open over my mouth. I adore a tongue up my own bottom and could appreciate her pleasure, a blend of physical sensation and delight in making me lick her bumhole. Only when I was beginning to wonder if she intended to come with my tongue in her anus did she pull forward, easing her pussy over my mouth.

'Now my cunt,' she said, pressing her pussy hard against my face.

I began to lick, quickly finding her clit. Steve was moving faster and faster inside me, little urgent strokes that had me dizzy with pleasure. My nose was buried in the hair around Lydia's anus and I could just see the soft curve of her buttocks rising above my face. Steve had me lifted on his cock and was holding me by the thighs, leaving my pussy open. Suddenly Lydia moved position, forgetting all about me being her slave and burying her face between my belly and her boyfriend's. Her tongue found my clitty and I had to pull myself up to continue returning the favour. Her sex was spread in front of my face, wet with her juice and my saliva, both vagina and anus looking ripe for entry. I buried my face in her hair, slurping at her vulva with the tip of my nose right against her bumhole. My hands were trapped between her stomach and my breasts, but I pulled one free and pushed fingers into her vagina and anus. Two went into her pussy, which was moist and puffy with excitement. One fitted her bumhole, which was wet with my saliva and tightened on my finger as I probed.

I started to come as her hands curled under my bottom, pulling my cheeks apart. A finger found my anus as Steve's balls began to slap against my bottom. He was coming, right up me, but I didn't care. I felt the sperm squirt out around my vagina and down to where Lydia's finger was working in my bumhole. Then I was coming myself and so was she as my tongue lapped frantically at her clitty. Steve pulled out slowly, allowing Lydia better access. Our bodies locked together, her anus clamping on to my finger as my own started to spasm. I was dizzy, my head spinning from lack of breath yet my mouth still feasting on Lydia's sex.

The orgasm seemed to go on forever, rising and falling and rising to a new peak until I simply could no longer stand it and collapsed back on the bed. She stopped licking, gave my pussy a final kiss and dismounted.

'Thank you,' I breathed and put my arms out to cuddle her as she moved round.

Steve lay down beside me and we stayed like that for a while, with me naked in between them. They had started out using me as if I was a doll, but we finished in each other's arms, content and happy.

Unfortunately the feeling didn't really last. When I

eventually decided that I needed a wash I got up and Lydia and I went to the bathroom together. We giggled and joked and she had a leisurely feel of my tits, admiring their size and firmness. Had we been alone I'm sure everything would have been fine but, as it was, having had the two of us together made Steve just that little bit too cock-sure.

Basically he wanted to treat us equally, both as his girlfriends, and while nothing was said I could tell that Lydia was becoming increasingly jealous. She wanted me to be hers and only available to Steve with her say so. Personally I wasn't fussy and would have happily slept with them. The atmosphere wasn't right though and I eventually left, sexually satisfied but slightly put out.

Fourteen

It would be ridiculous to suggest that my uneven temper over the previous few days had anything to do with my menstrual cycle. After all, what with Antoine, Percy, Steve and Lydia, I had plenty of justification for being a bit emotional. My period did start on the Sunday afternoon though, and by the time it was finished I felt a great deal more balanced and in control.

I had also had a long talk with Charlotte and spent the Monday night cuddled up to her in bed. I told her about Percy Ottershaw and about peeing for him and about Antoine beating me with the bath-brush. When I showed her what was left of my bruising she was horrified and suggested that I should have him charged with assault. The idea had already occurred to me, but to be perfectly honest I simply couldn't be bothered. There was also the thought of Antoine describing the scene he had walked in on in court . . .

Her reaction to Percy was a mixture of giggles and disgust. She admitted that she found the idea of peeing all over the floor really naughty but felt that it was something too rude to ever actually do. The fact that I had been excited by doing it in front of a dirty old man also met with her concern, and she even suggested that I should talk to Evan Dunstal about my perversion. She still hadn't admitted that he liked her to dress up as a man while they had sex, and I felt it was pretty rich to suggest asking advice about my sexuality from a man who clearly had more than enough kinks of his own.

Given her mixed response I refrained from telling her that my spanking fantasy now contained the added detail of wetting myself during punishment, but I did suggest that she might like to cane me later in the week. This suggestion was greeted with giggles and blushes and we agreed to do it really formally early on the Friday evening, when I would report to one of the college's gyms to which she had the key.

My other thoughts were of Percy Ottershaw. The idea of contact with someone so gross still disgusted me, but I couldn't deny that it was also a turn on. More importantly, perhaps, he had offered a simple deal: my kink for his with no emotional attachment or implication that he had any rights over me whatsoever. He had skill too, of a sort, and technically he still owed me a spanking which he might well come round to claim if I didn't come and ask for it.

Never having previously been told I was going to have something sexually painful happen to me several days before the event, I had never really appreciated the part anticipation can play in spanking games. Waiting for Friday was agony and ecstasy. I knew I was going to have my bare bottom caned and the knowledge had me in a permanent tizzy all week. I must have masturbated over it a dozen times at least, and it hadn't actually happened!

It was going to though. Every time Charlotte saw me she would give me a smile and a remark about my coming discipline. We had agreed the ritual in detail, a complex, subtle piece of fantasy play. Despite it not having the shock value of a genuine beating, I knew that the experience would be both painful and humiliating. By Friday afternoon I was biting my lip with apprehension.

Following Percy's story, Charlotte and I had agreed that although neither of us had actually experienced it, the natural place for a girl to be caned was at school. This was the basis for our scenario and I had spent the morning at the shop with the franchise to supply uniforms to my old school. To my delight the woman behind the counter not only accepted me as an eighteen-year-old schoolgirl but was actually quite bossy to me while she helped me choose my uniform. I have always been proud of my complexion and do look young, especially with my glasses on. Nevertheless it was still flattering to be accepted as eighteen without the least hesitation. If anything, she seemed to think I might in fact be younger and be trying to pretend that I was eighteen!

I got the full works, exactly as my real uniform had been when I was at school, even down to the underwear. Confident in my size, I made the purchases and went home, eager to get dressed up. Putting on big knickers and a sensible bra, both in plain white cotton, rolled away the years as if they had never passed. White knee socks, a neat white blouse, the original black ribbon tie, a pleated skirt in the regulation Royal Stuart tartan and sensible shoes added the final touches. A comparison of me standing in the mirror and my leaving photo showed that there really was very little difference. Putting my hair in bunches with big red ribbons completed the effect. I'd never actually worn my hair like that, but it did look cute. In fact, I looked far more girlish than I really had when I was a sixth former; but it felt right and so I stuck to it. Feeling very daring indeed, I decided to walk up to the gym in my uniform. This added a delicious frisson to the whole thing, and I could always pretend to be going to a fancy dress party if any of my other neighbours saw me.

What I hadn't counted on was Percy Ottershaw, who was bowling down the street as I came out of my front door. I was caught dead, standing there in full school uniform in front of the one man who was really not going to believe any stories about fancy dress parties.

'Up to mischief, Natasha?' he asked, his fat red face split by a knowing grin.

'I . . . er . . .' I managed, not really sure what to say at all. 'What are you doing here?'

'I came to see you,' he said. 'Partially to make sure that you were all right after that thoroughly unpleasant fellow burst in the other day and partially in the hope that you might still wish to indulge your half of our deal.'

'I'm not sure,' I answered hesitantly. 'Look, let's walk.'

I wasn't sure what I wanted to do, and I find it's always best not to make hasty decisions when that happens. Telling myself that I could easily get rid of Percy if I wanted to, I set off in the direction of the gym with him puffing along beside me. While I was getting myself up as a schoolgirl I had thought that it might add a nice touch to being punished by him; it had always seemed somehow appropriate. Now I had the opportunity, but I wasn't sure what Charlotte would think.

As we walked over the bridge into Chalk Farm, I decided that it didn't really matter what Charlotte thought. She had always preferred to follow my lead, and just because I was the one who was going to get whacked didn't mean that I wasn't calling the shots. During this process, I had been assuring Percy that I had no intention of bringing charges against Antoine Barras, which he accepted with considerable relief.

'If you come with me now you can cane me,' I offered, putting a big smile on his podgy face and an expression of incredulous outrage on that of a passing woman.

I giggled, wondering if she thought he was my father and that I was a genuine schoolgirl agreeing to a disciplinary caning.

'Excellent,' he answered. 'I shall enjoy that immensely. May I suggest turning right then?'

'It's the other way,' I pointed out. 'We go up Haverstock Hill.'

'A small detour may prove rewarding,' he chuckled and steered me to the right with a proprietorial pat on my bottom.

Nobody took any notice of us as we walked in the general direction of Kentish Town. I suppose we really did look like father and daughter, or possibly an uncle treating his niece to a day out. London is like that though. I sometimes think I could walk naked down Bond Street and that everyone would politely ignore me.

I had no idea where he was going and was surprised when he went into an antique shop in a back street off the Kentish Town Road. Whatever he wanted wasn't there and I followed him out and to another shop with a distinct feeling of puzzlement. It was just about to close when we got there, but the proprietor seemed to like the idea of having me in the shop; he locked the door behind us and said we could browse.

Percy thanked him and started to poke around, while I was getting a little concerned about getting to Charlotte in time. Then he gave a quiet exclamation of satisfaction and I turned from the old fireplace I had been admiring to see him drawing a long deep-brown cane from a stand of walking sticks.

'I thought we might be lucky,' he said happily and flourished the cane in the air.

It was an evil-looking thing, long and thin with knobbles and a crook handle at the end. I remembered pictures of similar ones from my father's collection of old Giles cartoons and had always giggled over the idea of someone getting a whacking. Never had I imagined that the recipient might be me!

'This should do,' Percy was saying. 'Pull your skirt up, my dear, and stick your bottom out.'

The way he said it was wonderful, so casual, so matter of fact, as if it were perfectly reasonable to test a cane across the seat of a young girl's panties in a public place. I pouted my lower lip out in a little moue of resentment and then reached back to lift my skirt. The shopkeeper's eyes were bulging out of his head as I stuck my bottom out and presented Percy with the taut white cotton seat of my panties, absolutely bursting with what appeared to be teenage bottom. The shopkeeper so obviously wasn't going to stop us that I couldn't resist taking the fun one step further.

'Do I have to take my pants down, Dad?' I asked shyly.

'No I . . .' Percy began and then changed his mind. 'Yes, I think it's best that you do.'

I slipped the back of my panties down, making a big show of reluctance and leaving them so that my bare bum was just peeping out between skirt and panties. Percy swung the cane, landing it across my bottom with a meaty smack. It wasn't very hard, but it stung enough to make me jump and drop my skirt. He left me rubbing my bottom and looking sorry for myself while he paid the shopkeeper without so much as a flicker to suggest that what he had done wasn't completely normal. The shopkeeper dropped the money because he was trying to watch me struggle my panties up under my skirt. When we got outside I was laughing so hard I could barely stand up.

Charlotte was expecting me in less than ten minutes, but we were lucky enough to get a cab and were dropped off outside the gym with a minute to spare. She was surprised to see Percy and perhaps a little put out, but our good humour was so infectious that she soon cheered up, especially when we told her about the shop. There was also something deliciously conspiratorial about meeting together for a punishment session.

Charlotte was in her gym outfit and looked gorgeous and wonderfully stern. Tight shorts worn over a body really showed off her elegant curves and I could see her nipples through the material. I don't imagine she had been wearing the shorts to teach aerobics, which is what she had been doing earlier. For a start they were so tight that I could make out the lips of her pussy; they also left a good slice of creamy white bum-cheek spilling out on either side behind her. I was dying to be beaten by her and she was certainly having a strong effect on Percy as well – though I imagine rather a different one.

'Charlotte was going to cane me over the vaulting horse,' I explained to Percy. 'After giving me a good telling off.'

'That sounds an excellent idea,' he answered. 'I'll just watch at first, if I may?'

'Sure,' I assured him. 'Come on then, Charlotte. Let's go.'

They really put me through my paces. Charlotte did the actual work while Percy gave advice. He had no shortage of it either, and it helped build a rapport between the two of them, a rapport built of their mutual pleasure in my exposure and discipline.

First I was put over Charlotte's knee and given a firm

spanking to warm me up. This was a classic in its way, and perhaps how I might really have been treated had I attended school fifty of more years before I did. She pulled a chair into the middle of the floor and sat down. I was then told to go across her knee, which I did, with my bottom to Percy. My imagination really began to run as she lectured me, and then, in a horribly matter-of-fact manner, lifted my school skirt and took down my pants. It was done swiftly, methodically, with a delicious disregard for my dignity. It was as if by being naughty I had forfeited my right to modesty. I was going to be spanked, and when a girl was spanked her pants came down – and that was that. I was imagining myself not just over the games mistress's lap with an older, male master watching, but also with a dozen or so tittering classmates, all of whom felt that watching me get a bare-bottomed spanking was the height of entertainment.

So there I was, with my bum all bare and everyone watching me – admiring the plump swell of my teenage buttocks, feasting their eyes on the pouted rear view of my vaginal lips, considering my puckered, pinkish-brown anus and enjoying the knowledge that I knew it was showing. Then my spanking began, her hand coming down across my poor, defenceless bottom with firm, disciplinary smacks, each of which made my cheeks wobble and drew a squeak from me. My bottom quickly began to warm and my excitement rose with the pain. I could feel my panties stretched between my thighs and knew that they offered no concealment. Indeed, they only enhanced the view of pussy as it began to swell and juice in an involuntary and deeply shameful response to my spanking.

I lost control of myself pretty quickly, bucking and wriggling over her lap as she spanked and spanked and spanked. The way she did it gave me no chance to compose myself; smack followed on smack with an insistent, merciless rhythm that left me sobbing with frustration as well as pain. My bottom was really hot, and I could hear Percy, or rather Mr Ottershaw, chuckling over the sight.

Just when I thought I was going to commit the final

154

indignity and put my hand back to play with myself while she punished me, it stopped. One moment I was lost in a dizzy haze of pain and humiliation, my hot bum the sole focus of my body, then the stinging slaps stopped, and I was lying over her knee, limp and breathing hard. There was also the sure knowledge that I was in for more, which filled me with both dread and delight. It was at that point that I remembered the detail of peeing myself. It would have been wonderful to have peed my panties while being spanked across the gym mistress' lap; but there would be plenty of time later as well.

Their next entertainment was to put me over the vaulting horse. This piece of equipment provides endless possibilities for punishing girls, as I quickly discovered. Having found out how much a gentle cane stroke stung, I was shivering in anticipation of what an old fashioned six of the best was going to be like. They had guessed this and seemed determined to torment me until the actual punishment came as a merciful release.

I was made to pose on the horse, each position more revealing than the last. Charlotte, now Miss Petersham, had told me to pull my knickers back up, but they didn't stay that way for long. First I had to bend over the end with my legs together – a pose that left my bottom the highest part of my body. My skirt was tucked up into its waistband and my panties pulled down. They admired my bottom from various angles, commenting on the pros and cons of beating me in the position. Finally it was decided that it gave me too much opportunity to kick my legs and I was told to pull up my pants and stand to attention.

Next it was kneeling on the top with my face down and my knees together. Once more they pulled my pants down and again commented on how I looked. My bottom was stuck right up and my cheeks were open wide, providing them with the rudest possible view of my pussy and anus. I felt utterly humiliated and very vulnerable, and had they beaten me that way I would have had to stay still for fear of falling off. As it was they decided that my bum was too high up to be accessed properly, presumably in case fat old

Mr Ottershaw wanted to fuck me afterwards. So I was told to get down, cover my bottom and once more stand to attention with my knickers on show.

Miss Petersham then suggested bending me over the long side and having me open my legs to stand on two weights. I got into the position and she pulled down my pants again, but with my legs apart they wouldn't come down far enough to ensure that my pussy showed properly and that my upper thighs were completely unprotected. Several times they moved the weights and adjusted my panties, but they were never satisfied; the position left me too much modesty and they were determined that I should be allowed none whatsoever.

I had braced myself for punishment each time, only to be let down. The mental effect of this was so strong that as I adopted yet another position – rolled up on my back along the top of the horse – I could smell the scent of my own pussy. They decided that this position was too awkward and risked caning my vaginal lips, which they felt too harsh. Once more I was told to get down.

They had seen every detail of my body. They had made me pose in rude positions. They had discussed the exposure of my pussy, bum-cheeks and anus. They had spanked me. I was wet with sweat and hoarse with excitement and apprehension, keen to be thrashed and yet dreading the pain and exposure. I was also wondering what they would think if, in the heat of punishment, I lost control completely and wet myself.

Their final choice of position was superb, leaving me helpless, exposed, vulnerable and thoroughly rude. They adjusted the legs of the horse, raising it to its maximum height. I was then told to get over it and found that I could only touch the ground with my feet or my hands, but not both. Miss Petersham then produced skipping ropes and tied my wrists to my ankles. With the ropes looped off around the legs of the horse I was left spread-eagled over it, completely unable to move and with my bum stuck up and spread wide.

Then they took my big white pants down for the final

156

time, stretching them tight between my thighs so that the cotton was pulling into the soft flesh of my thighs. It was all showing: pussy, bumhole, the lot, every rude detail of my sex. I could see back between my legs as well, to where Miss Petersham was flexing her cane thoughtfully and eyeing my naughty bottom.

'I trust you appreciate the shame of your position, Linnet?' she asked.

'Yes, miss,' I answered.

'I trust that you realise that your privates are showing?'

'Yes, miss.'

'And do you appreciate that being in this position of vulgar exposure is entirely your own fault?'

'Yes, miss.'

'And are you sorry?'

'Yes, miss.'

'I doubt it, but I am also sure that you will be after I have decorated your bottom with six red lines.'

She lifted the cane, knowing full well I was watching. I was shivering with anticipation, so hard that I was sure my bottom would be wobbling like a little round jelly. She was still, holding the cane high over the target. There was a lump in my throat and I was whimpering as I watched the dreadful cane that was about to be used on my naked bottom.

Then it happened. She brought the cane down in whistling arc that ended on my bare skin. It was agony, a sharp sting followed by a burning sensation that made me cry out and left me whimpering and sobbing. It wasn't just the pain either, but my helplessness. They were beating me and there was nothing I could do about it. I couldn't even do more than wriggle my bottom, which did nothing to dispel the pain but just amused my tormentors. Then the second stroke came down, before I had really got over the first. I squeaked, only to receive the third immediately and then the fourth.

I completely lost control. Each stinging stroke followed the last, burning into my bottom in a way that allowed me no time at all to arrange my thoughts or brace myself.

They just came down, one after another as I struggled and yelled and thrashed against my bonds. She didn't stop at the agreed six either, but just kept on, beating and beating me into a state of dizzy ecstasy and pain. Nothing mattered but my poor, punished bottom, the ropes on my wrists and ankles, and the ready, open feeling of my vagina.

When she finally stopped, my whole bottom was burning. My eyes were hazy with tears but I could see her standing there, cool and poised with the cane in one hand. The contrast between her, dressed and calm, and me, bare bottomed and well thrashed, was extraordinary and gave me a desperate need to grovel at her feet. I wanted to kiss her shoes, put my lips to the taut white material where her shorts covered her pussy; I wanted to kiss her high, firm buttocks and then for her to take her shorts down and allow me the privilege of licking her anus.

But I was helpless and it didn't matter what I wanted.

'Mr Ottershaw, you seem to have become somewhat excited,' she said from behind me. 'Perhaps I could offer you some relief?'

They did it. While I hung upside down with my school uniform disarranged and my severely punished bottom on show, she went down on her knees and sucked his cock while he stroked her hair and admired the view. It was supremely frustrating, to be used as the wank object of a dirty old man while I could do nothing whatsoever to pleasure myself. Only when I was sure he would come in her mouth did she suddenly stop. I was untied and led over to him. She pushed me to the floor and grabbed my hair, then pushed my face on to his erection. My bum was left bare as I sucked; his eyes were locked on it as he came in my mouth. I was told to swallow and did it. Then with my red bottom stuck up high and my mouth full of the taste of penis and sperm, I masturbated, quite shameless in front of them. The orgasm was exquisite, the peak of sexual torment that had lasted well over an hour, yet even as I concentrated on the image of myself as a schoolgirl and what they had made me do, there was something missing.

It was ecstasy, but it was a fantasy. For all the care and

158

preparation, for all Charlotte's beauty and Percy's skill, for all the very real pain and shame of the punishment, it was, in the end, fantasy.

Not that that meant I wasn't up for another session at another time, but despite everything the experience lacked that vital ingredient – reality.

Fifteen

I slept with Charlotte that night. We hadn't specifically intended to, but after she had spent a while rubbing cream into my bottom it was inevitable that we would get carried away.

She had enjoyed caning me. So much so in fact that she had been sufficiently turned on to want to suck Percy Ottershaw's cock. As with me, having sexual contact with such an obvious dirty old man produced in her a mixture of self-disgust and delight. Discussing our feelings, we decided that a lot of the pleasure came from taboo breaking. It's nice to do something that is generally disapproved of. It feels naughty, and both of us had been brought up to make a strong connection between 'naughty' and 'sexy'. It is expected that old men will lust after pretty young girls, and it is also expected that the girls will turn them down. When a woman accepts such sex, particularly if she actually starts a relationship, society excuses the action at least partially by saying that she is doing it for money. In our case there was no such excuse. We had done it for the sheer, rude, naughty delight of doing it.

Even though he was not with us, it was Percy who gave impetus to our sex that night. As she creamed my bottom we discussed the fantasy and how it had felt to be in our roles. We then began to speculate on how things might have changed.

Our first thought was of how it would have felt to be dealt with side my side, cuddling each other while we were first spanked and then caned. Afterwards he might have made us get down on our knees and give his cock a long, indulgent lick before he came over our faces and made us lick each other clean of sperm. It made a lovely picture: the schoolgirl and the gym mistress, side by side in uniform and gym kit, sucking on some fat, dirty-minded old bastard's penis and then licking his come from each other's pretty faces.

From there we went on to how he could have cheerfully fucked us both. If he had asked we would both have done it, but for both of us an important element of accepting sex from him was that we should feel somewhat coerced. True, Charlotte had volunteered to suck his cock, but it had already been out of his trousers and it had been pretty obvious that he wanted some attention given to it. On the other hand, had he but asked she would happily have peeled down her tight shorts and let him give her rear entry over the gym bench. I could then have crawled up beside her and he could have taken turns with us, enjoying two trim young bottoms, one of which had been thoroughly whacked in advance.

We were lying side by side, both masturbating as I described how it would have felt to kneel for him. He would have rested his heavy belly on my sore bottom, poked for my entrance with his cock, found it, filled me, ripped my school blouse apart and begun to hump me while he groped my breasts. Charlotte gave a contented moan at what I was saying and increased the speed with which her finger was working on her clit. I leant across and took her hand off her pussy, replacing it with my own and starting to knead as she turned her attention to her breasts. Her eyes were closed and her mouth a little open, a picture of female ecstasy. I rolled to the side, putting my thigh on her legs so that I could rub my pussy while I masturbated her.

'Think how it would feel,' I continued. 'He would have pulled my blouse open and got my tits out. My nipples would be stiff under his fingers. He would be grunting and groaning like the fat pig he is, fucking me and feeling my boobs. All the time you'd be watching and knowing that you were next. Your shorts would be down and your bum all bare and ready, with only the thin strip of your leotard to protect your pussy. You'd be wet too, really wet with a big damp patch showing over your hole.'

'Describe him mounting me,' she breathed as she pushed her leg out to increase the pressure against my pussy.

'He'd pull out of me,' I said, 'leaving me to play with myself, my little school skirt still up and my panties around my thighs. You'd be watching as he shuffled over to you, all red-faced and fat and sweaty, with his little cock sticking up under his belly. You'd feel really disgusted with yourself as he took hold of the rear of your leotard and pulled it aside so that he could see your wet pussy. He'd be able to see your bumhole too, and he'd touch it to let you know it was showing. It would be wet with your sweat and his finger would go in a little way, up your anus, down between your pretty little bottom cheeks.

'Then he'd come closer and you'd feel his cock pressing into you, the balls against your clitty, the base of the shaft hard between your lips and up between your bum-cheeks, touching your vagina and anus. He'd lean forward, his fat belly squashing out on your bum. His hands would grip your leotard and pull it down over your boobs. He'd start to feel them, touching your nipples to make them even harder than they already were. He'd start to probe with his cock while he fondled your boobs, butting it against your clitty and your bumhole in his eagerness to get it up you. Then it would go in and you'd really be filled with self-disgust as he began to fuck you in the doggy position – a fat, blubbery pig of a man mounted on you, his soft, clammy hands feeling your tits, his cock filling your sweet pussy.'

She groaned and turned her head to me, opening her eyes in a mute appeal for more. I started to frig her faster, moving my finger on her clitty in small, fast circles.

'Then,' I said, 'just when you thought the experience couldn't get any dirtier, he would pull out. You'd wonder what was happening and think he was going to finish off in me, only to feel his prick touch your bumhole and realise

162

that he was going to bugger you. Yes, Charlotte, bugger you; put his cock up your sweaty little bumhole. You'd try and squirm out from under him, but his weight would be on you and you'd be helpless. You'd try and close your anus but it would be moist with sweat and his cock would be slick with your pussy juice. You'd call him a filthy bastard as the tip of his cock forced your ring open, but he'd ignore you. You'd feel the head of his cock pop into your anus. His shaft would slide in, inch by inch up your rectum while you cursed and swore at him. All you'd do was turn him on more; when it was all in and his balls were up against your empty pussy, he'd start to sodomise you, humping your anus, grunting and panting and sweating while he buggered you. His balls would be slapping on your pussy and his fat belly would be smacking on your bottom as if you were being spanked. You'd hate yourself, but you'd be coming, cursing him even as your orgasm hit you, squealing in revulsion and ecstasy as he came up your bottom. That's right, darling, he'd have spunked up your bottom, right up your dirty little bumhole. Then he'd pull out and you'd feel your anus close slowly, pulsing, oozing sperm from a dirty, fat old man's cock. You'd love it though and he would know it. The sperm would be dribbling down your pussy. You'd put a hand back and start frigging in it, squelching it around your clitty, masturbating in front of him like a dirty little slut, making yourself come again and again . . .'

And she had, screaming out loud as her orgasm tore through her. I wasn't far away either, and locked my thighs around her leg as she came. I could feel her body tensing in her ecstasy and was coming myself even as her spasms began to subside. The fantasy was burning in my mind, the beautiful, elegant Charlotte on her knees with Percy Ottershaw's cock stuffed firmly up her bottom. My pussy was hot and open against her thigh, my clitty like a bead of fire on her skin, my bottom tingling from my beating. I said her name and called her a filthy bitch as I came, clamping my legs on to her as her arms came around me.

Then we were cuddling, lying soft and yielding in each

other's arms, our mouths meeting and opening to kiss, long and passionately until we were completely drained. We stayed like that for ages, just lying on her bed in each other's arms, neither moving nor speaking. Eventually I drifted off to sleep, only to wake at some later time to find her hand stroking my right breast in slow, somehow timid movements. I responded and we made love again, only more gently and without anything but each other to inspire us.

I awoke when Charlotte moved her shoulder from under my head and let me down with a bump.

'What's the matter?' I asked blearily as I opened my eyes to find her already halfway to the door.

'I'm supposed to be in church!' she answered as she ran for the shower.

'Never mind that,' I called after her. 'Come back and give me a cuddle.'

The hiss of water cut off her reply and I lay back, my senses slowing clearing to leave a sense of annoyance. Surely she could have foregone church after sleeping with me, especially when our lovemaking had been so intense.

Evidently the church was still too important, because while she apologised and kissed me nicely, she refused to give in and resisted my efforts to drag her back into bed. I was left face down among tangled sheets, stark naked and seriously frustrated. It wasn't even Sunday, but she had abandoned me for Evan Dunstal and his bloody crack-pot religion without hesitation. I had expected the morning to be a long, soft period of sex and cuddles, perhaps with breakfast thrown in somewhere along the line. Instead I had been left alone.

I suppose my behaviour for the rest of the day could be described as sulking, although I felt I had every right to be cross. My bottom was in a fine state, purple and red with bruising and too sore to sit on comfortably. I needed sympathy and cold cream followed by a willing tongue. Instead I had to content myself with my vibrator; for once it was unsatisfactory.

* * *

My thoughts for Charlotte were less than charitable and included a long introduction of her pristine bottom to the cane that Percy had so thoughtfully left at my flat. Once I had given her twelve strokes, for each of which she would have to thank me, I might then allow her to apologise. She would have to go down on her knees, of course, and I'd probably make her kiss my bumhole, but after that I'd be prepared to forgive her and go back to bed for the rest of the weekend.

Knowing the times she usually spent at the services, I could guess that she would either come back at around one or indulge herself with Evan and perhaps not get back at all until the next day. Had she not returned I would have been really cross and so was relieved and pleased when my bell went shortly after one.

I had put on black silk underwear and calf-length leather boots for her and was carrying the cane in my hand as I went to the door. After pressing the intercom and leaving the door open an inch I returned to my living room and sat down with my legs crossed and the cane in my lap, looking stern and sexy at the same time and leaving no doubt as to what I intended. As I heard the door click I raised my chin, projecting both hurt and authority to what I was sure would be a contrite Charlotte. Instead it was Evan Dunstal.

The scene held for perhaps a second, both of us staring at the other in disbelief. He was the last person I had expected, and not someone I was very pleased with.

'What the hell do you think you're doing?' I demanded, managing to recover my wits first. 'This is my flat, and private, so get out!'

'We need a serious talk, Natasha,' he replied firmly, apparently unfazed by my fury.

'What about?' I asked, somewhat taken aback by his statement.

'Your tendency to perversion,' he continued, his voice full of self-righteousness and smug, holier-than-thou tones.

'My tendency to perversion?' I retorted, stung not just by what he had said but also by the hypocrisy of it.

'I fear from what Charlotte tells me,' he carried on just as pompously, 'that you have allowed yourself to be seduced by abnormal lusts ...'

'Abnormal lusts?' I interrupted.

'Sexual sensation seeking is a regrettable trend in modern society ...' he went on.

It was too much. I had been saving up my knowledge of his own kink for the right moment, and now was that moment.

'I may enjoy a smacked bottom,' I declared loudly, 'but at least I don't go around dressing girls up as boys and buggering them!'

He stopped, his face the most beautiful shade of scarlet imaginable.

'But ... but Charlotte promised ...' he began, stammering his words out.

'No, Charlotte didn't tell me,' I said with immense satisfaction. 'I saw you, through the skylight, that first day I visited you. So don't talk to me about perversion!'

He stood there, red in the face and unable to decide what to say. I felt really pleased with myself. He had come to give me a lecture, to put the dirty-minded little sinner in her place and instead he had been left feeling confused and dirty himself. One thing I was sure of: while he might be just as bad as me, he couldn't handle his own sexuality. I could.

I was about to deliver the *coup de grâce* in the form of a few well-chosen words that would have shown him up both as a pervert and a hypocrite when I realised that I was handling things the wrong way. On my present course all I would do was anger and humiliate him and he would be able to paint me as a bitch to Charlotte. Far better was to seduce him and then say that he had come on to me, balancing my story just right so that she would be disgusted by him without actually running to the police. Of course to do it I needed some specialist, and intimate, knowledge.

'Look, we don't need to argue, do we, Evan?' I said softly in place of the frosty retort I had been planning.

166

He said nothing.

'You see,' I continued, turning to show him the elegant curve of my back, the fullness of my breasts and the soft swell of my bottom, 'there's really nothing wrong with liking kinky sex. It doesn't do any harm, does it?'

He opened his mouth, but all that came out was a sort of cough.

'I wouldn't mind dressing up for you,' I purred. 'What do you like best? A smart suit? An army uniform? I'd look cute as a corporal, don't you think? How about leathers? I've got leathers; I'd make a good gay man in my leathers, especially from the back . . .'

He made another sound in his throat, which I think was supposed to be a denial, but it was no use. I had him. No man, but no man, resists me if I really want them. I'm just too cute. Even if he did have strange half-homosexual fantasies, the sight of me in black lacy underwear and boots was far more than he could resist. I could see him trying though, and wondering if I was teasing him, so I swung round on my chair and stuck my bottom out towards him.

'You can put it up my bottom,' I offered sweetly, 'and I'll dress anyway you like. I love the idea of having sex like a boy, with your lovely big cock up my bottom.'

He swallowed and took a step forward, completely lost. I suppose that if Charlotte had told him even half of what we had been up to he would have been pretty excited, but now he was desperate. I wiggled my bottom as he came forward. He was moving as if in a trance, his eyes fixed on the taut black silk that covered my cheeks.

'Don't you want me to dress up?' I asked, feeling that if he was going to bugger me then we might as well get the most out of his fantasy.

'Yes please,' he gagged, his former stern, self-satisfied manner now vanished beneath his lust.

I giggled and dismounted the chair, wiggling my hips deliberately as I walked towards the bedroom. He followed like a puppy-dog eager for a treat. Having got him that far, it was easy, my only problem being that my wardrobe was pretty thin on anything even vaguely resembling male attire. I'm naturally feminine and have always gone for lace and silk and clothes that make the best of my curves. I also have a great deal more chest than Charlotte, and while she had made a very pretty boy in a suit, I was never going to look like anything except a girl in boy's clothes.

Not that I allowed this minor detail to daunt me. Being clever and inventive I simply suggested that I dress up in his suit. His response was eager to say the least and I realised that I had really hit the nail on the head. We stripped together, and I must admit that he had a fine body, muscular and smooth. I had seen his cock before, but now it was mine, and that made a lot of difference, especially as I had offered him access to my bottom-hole.

Once I was dressed and had rolled the trousers legs and sleeves of his suit up to make it fit me at least roughly, I took a look in the mirror. To say that I looked masculine would be an overstatement, but there was a definite male element about me. Only the delicacy of my face and my full brown curls really gave the lie to it, though, as the suit was big enough to hide the line of my chest and hips.

I gave him a twirl and then asked if he would like to be sucked. Of course he said yes and sat himself down on the edge of my bed so that I would have to kneel between his knees. Down I went, and was soon sucking cock as eagerly as any gay man ever did. It felt strange pretending to be a boy while I sucked on a man's penis – a purely mental thrill but quite a nice one. I suppose at the end of the day a lot of the pleasure of cock sucking is in the mind. After all, your average heterosexual man would be horrified if it was suggested that he might like a blow-job from another man, yet it wouldn't feel any different from having a girl do it. Of course there's an element of power and control in having someone give you oral sex, especially if you don't return the favour.

He was soon hard in my mouth and the experience of sucking him had begun to make my pussy juice. It was my bottom that was due to be filled though, and as I knelt up on the bed I was conscious of a strong pang of the same sort of deliciously subservient feeling I had had when John Thurston buggered me.

'You're only the second man to do this,' I told him as he put his hand to my trouser buttons. 'So be gentle and use lots of lubricant.'

'I will,' he grunted, his fingers fumbling my fly open.

I've always found the feeling of exposing myself for sex really exquisite, and now was no exception. He pulled my trousers down and settled them around my knees, then put his hand on my pants and slid them slowly down off my bum. They were big Y-fronts, which created an unfamiliar feeling as he adjusted them to cover my pussy but leave himself access to my anus. It was his disinclination to expose my sex that started my feelings of humiliation. After all, I'm a girl and a very attractive one, so it's not surprising that being treated as a boy is humiliating.

He left me like that, kneeling with my bare bum in the air, while he went to fetch some lubricant. I had to tell him where to look, making for added indignity as I was actively having to help him to bugger me. He came back with my big tub of cold cream and got behind me. I could see our images in the mirror, me kneeling and actually looking boyish except for my head and the undeniably girly curve of my bottom. Other than that I looked like a curate with my trousers and pants down while I was prepared for buggery. He was behind me, nude, with his finger in the cream tub, a wonderfully obscene image, especially with the colourful marks showing that I had been given physical discipline across my nates.

I watched him pull the finger out and then felt the cool, slimy cream down between my bum-cheeks as he applied it. It went right on my bottom-hole, and then up it as he slid a finger in to grease me inside. I squeaked slightly as my anus was penetrated, but was quickly moaning as the big finger worked in and out of my bottom. He put the cream down and scooped some more out, using it to smear his still fully erect cock.

His erection was sticking up from a thick nest of pubic hair, the greasy tip almost touching my lowered pants.

Despite the feeling of a finger going in and out of my anus, my eyes were wide open and glued to the fat penis that was about to replace it. Having a cock up the bum is a pretty daunting prospect for a girl, and I had only done it once before; I was more than a little nervous as he knelt up to penetrate me.

His finger came out of my anus with a sticky pop and I watched him in the mirror as he raised himself and put his penis in its place. Remembering John Thurston's advice, I relaxed my anus just as the firm, rubbery knob pushed into me. I must have been very well lubricated, because a good three inches of his erection slid straight up my bum on the first push. I gasped as my anus stretched, then began to pant as my rectum filled with cock, inch my inch as he forced himself slowly up my behind. When he was in, his belly was pushed against my buttocks and his pubic hair was rubbing in my crease.

My bottom felt tender, and not just in the hole that was stretched around a thick cock shaft. My cheeks also smarted. As he began to bugger me I was given a sharp reminder of what it means to have been caned. He had made no comment whatsoever on the state of my bum, but as he rode me he began to stroke the bruised parts that were visible to him. I could imagine him fantasising not just that I was a junior priest who had submitted to anal sex, but that he had beaten me first, presumably as discipline for some sort of religious infraction.

As with John Thurston, it felt lovely to have a cock up my bottom at first, a wonderful breathless feeling that is less physically pleasurable but mentally dirtier than being fucked properly. He took his time, buggering me for a bit, then pulling it out and putting it in again, apparently fascinated by the sight of his cock going into my bumhole. I was thoroughly enjoying the experience and had reached back to play with myself, intending to come while he was in me.

The painful parts of buggery come at first entry and when the man is approaching climax and really begins to push. Evan was no different and really started to ram it

170

home when he was nearing orgasm. I squeaked in protest but he just seemed to enjoy my reaction. It was also impossible to frig with him using me so roughly; all I could do was gasp and squeal until he suddenly gave a jerk and came deep up my bottom.

I finished myself off with his sperm dribbling down over my pussy, just as I had imagined it while fantasising with Charlotte. It was a great orgasm, centred on the disgusting and wonderful feeling of having sperm running from my anus as the ring pulses and contracts after a nice big cock has been up it.

As I suspected, he was full of guilt and uncertainty after coming. I helped him wash and gave his clothes back, sending him home satisfied but guilty while I was satisfied and thoroughly pleased with myself. If I now decided that Charlotte should no longer associate with him, I had all the knowledge of his anatomy and behaviour needed for a convincing description of his clumsy attempt to force me to go to bed with him.

Sixteen

I played it beautifully. When Charlotte returned at close to midnight she asked what Evan had said to me. She wasn't at all happy with him anyway as, while she had wanted to talk to him about her sexuality, she hadn't expected him to immediately come and remonstrate with me. He had insisted on going alone and it had taken her the rest of the day to pluck up the courage to face me. I really gave it the works. First I forgave her for talking about private things to someone else. Next I asked if she didn't think that his insisting on coming to me alone was a bit suspicious. Then, pausing dramatically and biting my lip, I told her that he had come round, got his cock out and told me that if I didn't suck it then my sexual preferences were going to become common knowledge. Refusing to bow to his blackmail, I had thrown him out.

I didn't even need to go into the more complicated details of my story. Charlotte was furious with him and grovellingly apologetic to me. She easily accepted my argument that it was best not to go to the police and we spent the night together. On the Sunday morning she didn't go to church, and we spent a lazy day in bed with her playing maid for me.

By the Monday morning we were more than simply sex partners. Nothing had been said, but from the worshipful way she treated me she was clearly infatuated and it was a feeling I was happy to return. I had been expecting Evan Dunstal to come round at some point on the Sunday, or at least ring, and had been ready for either eventuality. As

172

it was, he didn't, and I was feeling that I had sorted things out nicely to my advantage.

For the rest of the week I was in a pretty perky mood. Charlotte and I were now sleeping together full time, although we were being careful not to let our other neighbours find out. The bruises on my bottom kept me on a pleasant sexual plateau, while on the Tuesday night I put six red stripes across Charlotte's pert rear. The only thing she didn't particularly like were peeing games, but on the Thursday afternoon I was made an offer that promised something special in that direction.

This was from Charles Carlisle, the last of the trio of my colleagues that included John Thurston and Percy Ottershaw, and was not entirely unexpected. I already knew that John Thurston had told him about buggering me and suspected that Percy might have told him rather more.

I had always known he fancied me – they all did – but he had never done anything about it. Despite being much the same age as his two friends, he lacked much of the dirty old man quality. Instead he was small, dapper and polite, but with a slightly firm edge to his character which made him appeal to me as a possible spanker. Of all my older wine colleagues, he was the only one I might ever have actually considered having an affair with.

Men being married is not something that normally bothers me if they make a pass. After all, a married man can hardly expect me to be faithful, although I've know ones who did – briefly. Charles wasn't just married, though: he was married to Sophie Carlisle, and not only was she influential among the wine press, but I was actually slightly scared of her.

I frequently use his shop to buy samples for my wine class and was doing so that afternoon. He was always generous and had opened a fine old Beaune Grèves, something for which I have always had a particular taste. Taking a deep sniff at his glass, he had pronounced that it had *'sente du merde'*, literally the smell of dung. Beaune doesn't actually smell like shit, but can have a rich, intensely earthy scent that I suppose is not dissimilar. I was a little surprised to hear Charles use the expression; it is a little rude and he was normally polite to the point of obsession.

When I agreed with him there was a quality to his answering smile that reminded me firmly that he certainly knew that I enjoyed being buggered and possibly knew that I enjoyed both spanking and peeing games. With him there was none of the reluctance and self-disgust that I had felt with both John Thurston and Percy Ottershaw, and as I raised my glass to my lips I was wondering if in Charles I had not met the man to keep my bottom regularly warm. There was, of course, still Sophie, but if he was going to want to spank me then it was a risk I was prepared to take. Not that I could tell him. My experience with Percy Ottershaw had taught me that while arranged spankings are nice, they lack the erotic power of being genuinely punished.

While all this was going through my head he had been sipping his wine, very casually, apparently lost in contemplation of its nuances.

'So few people of your age really appreciate old Burgundy, Natasha,' he remarked. 'You really should come to dinner sometime.'

'I'd be delighted,' I replied. 'You and Sophie live somewhere out near Henley, don't you?'

'I was thinking more of a restaurant,' he answered. 'Just the two of us and perhaps a decent bottle afterwards.'

'I'd love to. Next week perhaps,' I assured him, mindful of the cane bruises on my bottom.

'Friday, then,' he said with satisfaction.

I took another sip of wine, my mind already full of the delightful possibilities for naughty behaviour that the coming date provided. He shifted his glass to his left hand and back, then leant forward to glance into the shop.

'I, er . . . I suppose you know that I am a close friend of John Thurston?' he asked.

It was a very polite way of saying that he knew I liked anal sex, but that was what it was. I nodded in response and his next comment was even better.

'Given that I think we understand each other,' he began diffidently, 'would you perhaps enjoy a brief *entré*, as it were?'

It took me an instant to realise that he was offering sex in the shop and another to decide that I liked the idea. It was naughty, wonderfully naughty in fact to think of us indulging ourselves in the back office while he kept half an eye on the shop.

'If you like,' I answered coyly. 'What did you have in mind?'

'Possibly you would . . .?' he said, indicating his fly.

I smiled and began to sink to my knees, sure that it wasn't just my hand he wanted me to make use of. His chair was invisible from the shop, but all he had to do was lean forward to see it. This meant that he would be able to watch for customers while I sucked his cock, which seemed a deliciously rude thing to do.

'I was thinking, perhaps, in the toilet?' he said as my fingers reached his fly.

'I wanted to do it here,' I protested.

'I, er . . .' he objected as his zip slid down under the gentle pressure of my fingers.

'Come on,' I urged. 'I want to suck you while you talk to a customer. It would really turn me on.'

'You are a very naughty girl, Natasha,' he said as I burrowed my hand into his fly. 'But seriously, here we can be seen from the window of the café next door.'

He was right. I already had my hand on his cock, which felt nicely firm. The window was certainly a risk, but no one was there so I pulled his cock out and gave it a quick kiss before standing up.

'OK,' I agreed. 'I'll do it in the loo, but shouldn't you lock the door in that case?'

'I'll hear the bell,' he replied with an urgency mirrored in the rapid stiffening of the penis in my hand.

I led him to the loo by his cock, tugging at it so that by the time he was seated and I was kneeling between his knees it was fully erect. There's something extremely dirty about kneeling on a lavatory floor with a man's cock in your mouth; I greatly enjoyed giving him his blow-job.

He had a nice cock, not all that long, but thick and fleshy so that it made a really good mouthful. He stroked my hair while I sucked him, very gently so that I felt I was being soothed to encourage me to accept having a cock in my mouth. After a while he opened his trousers properly and took his balls out so that I could stroke them and jerk at the base of his cock while I sucked.

With me masturbating him into my mouth it isn't surprising that he didn't take long, and just as he was about to come he told me I was naughty again and said I needed to be punished. Then my mouth was full of sperm and I was swallowing frantically to stop it going all over my clothes.

When we had tidied up he gave me my wine samples free, which was in a way payment for the blow-job and made me feel even naughtier. I was in need of my own orgasm, and I suppose could have sat on the shop loo and masturbated myself to my heart's content. I was in the mood for something messy though, and instead I left the shop with the intention of going home, wetting my panties in the shower, sitting down in my own pool of pee and coming off like that.

As it was, I was halfway across Fitzroy Square when I saw Lydia coming the other way. I hesitated, wondering if I should greet her while I was conventionally dressed and then realising that it was too late as she gave me a wave.

'Been to an interview or something?' she asked as we came together, her tone suggesting that any such behaviour was scarcely acceptable in her eyes.

'Visiting a friend,' I said. 'He's a bit old fashioned.'

She nodded, either accepting my explanation or disinterested in the whole subject.

'What are you doing?' I asked.

'Nothing special,' she answered, although when I had first seen her she had been walking pretty purposefully in the direction I was coming from. 'In fact I think I might take you back to my flat and make you lick my bum again.'

The comment was designed to humiliate me and allow her to assert her power, which it did, but I still couldn't suppress a giggle.

176

'You're a dirty little whore, Tasha. What are you?' she demanded.

'A dirty little whore,' I replied meekly.

'You think it's just a game, don't you?' she continued with surprising vehemence. 'You don't really realise that I have a natural dominance over you, do you?'

Well, it was a game, to me; and for all that I'd enjoyed every humiliation she had put me through, that was all it was, a game.

'I like being your slave,' I ventured, keen to play with her and not wanting the argument she seemed to be angling for.

'You just don't see it, do you?' she answered. 'So it looks like I'm going to have to teach you a lesson in front of everybody.'

I had no idea why she was so impassioned, but in my current mood being taught a lesson in front of Steve, Sally and the others really appealed to me.

'If you say I need it,' I answered, bowing my head to her.

She told me to follow her, and as we walked it became clear why she was so antagonistic towards me. Steve, apparently, had been trying to pursued her that a *ménage à trois* was a good idea, with me as equal partner. It was typically arrogant of him that he hadn't even considered asking my opinion, and he had really managed to wind Lydia up. She wanted me as her slave and hers alone. It amused her to let men fuck me, including Steve, but at the end of the day she wanted control. Darren, ostensibly my partner among them, didn't even get a mention.

Her complicated emotional problems were none of my business. As long as she continued to provide me with such exciting sexual experiences, I really didn't care who was with who. She did, and had got it into her head that I needed this 'lesson' to really be shown my place. Personally, I think she was just finding an excuse to bully me sexually, but I was happy to play along.

She certainly felt strongly about it in any case, because our chance meeting put whatever she had been doing before completely out of her head. She hustled me back to the flat and sat me down, then started to make some phone calls. Steve turned up while she was doing this and was surprised to see me, especially so conventionally dressed. It was a hot day and I had chosen a skirt of plain grey silk and a white blouse, not exactly formal, but very different from what he was used to seeing me in.

Lydia told Steve to put the bed in the middle of the room and continued trying to get hold of people. I had no idea what she intended, but knew that it was certainly going to involve me being punished in some way and would undoubtedly be sexually humiliating. She seemed pretty cross, and I was conscious of a measure of apprehension despite my confidence in enjoying whatever she had in mind.

Only when Sally turned up with her tattooing equipment did I realise that what Lydia intended wasn't actually acceptable. The idea was to give me a good spanking, then tie me to the bed, shave my pubic hair and tattoo 'Property of Lydia' on my pussy mound.

The idea was exquisitely humiliating, but out of the question. Tattoos last, and I wasn't spending the rest of my life with one stating that I belonged to another woman, no matter how exciting the prospect and despite the fact that it would normally be covered by my pubic hair. I explained this to them, and while Sally and Steve agreed with me, Lydia was less than happy about it. Of course the worse thing was that Steve took my side, and so she was faced with the prospect of having to back down and really loosing face.

'You can spank me,' I offered, trying to defuse the situation. 'Even though my bum's a bit bruised from a caning I got last week.'

'Oh yeah? Let's see?' Steve asked.

It really was not a tactful thing to say.

'You want to see, do you?' Lydia demanded, turning on him with fire in her eyes. 'Well I'll bloody show you, then!'

She leapt at me, taking me completely by surprise and pushing me down on the bed. I giggled and gave way, expecting to be rolled over and soundly spanked. Instead

178

she pulled my glasses off, which was a big mistake. A girl had done it to me once at school, and I had had a thing about it ever since. Because I had been allowing her to control me sexually, Lydia thought of me as someone she could push around. She didn't really know me at all, and as my temper flared I decided that the time had come to show her another side of my personality.

She was on top of me and had grabbed my hair. She really expected me to submit and had raised a leg so that my body would turn beneath her as she pulled me over by the hair. Instead I twisted, caught her off balance and quickly mounted her. She still had my hair and pulled hard, forcing me to the side. It hurt and I really got in a temper. For all her tough behaviour and hard image, at the end of the day she was a shrimp, not just a lot shorter than me but lighter too and not as fit. For a while we were struggling on the bed, neither really getting the better of it. Steve thought it was hilarious to have two girls fighting over him and Sally also seemed to think it was pretty funny. I was vaguely aware that Chloë and Teo had joined them, but I was too interested in getting on top of Lydia.

Finally I did it, my weight and strength telling against her sheer viciousness. I had several scratches, but I was mounted on her with her arms pinned down.

When I fight, I don't try and hurt – I try and humiliate. Pulled hair and scratches quickly fade, but the memory of having your knickers pulled down or your tits popped out of your bra really lingers. I had managed to get Lydia's skirt up, and as the little tart had no knickers on as usual, her bare pussy was on show to everyone.

She was exhausted, flushed and hot and, I was sure, turned on by being forced to submit and by having her pussy put on show. I knew I would have been and I was still pretty furious. I decided that the moment had come for my long-awaited revenge.

I freed my arms by pinning hers under my knees. She made no attempt to struggle but turned her head to the side as I pulled up her top. Her little tits came on view, heaving slightly from her exertion. Her nipples were erect and the piercing rings were wet with sweat, confirming my suspicions of her arousal.

'Make her lick your arse!' Steve suggested helpfully.

Lydia shivered, a sure sign that she was accepting her defeat. I thought of how her tongue would feel on my anus and decided to have it, but not yet, not until I had utterly humiliated her. She lay trembling beneath me, her eyes fixed on mine as I pulled my skirt up to my waist. Then, as I pulled my panties aside to show her the pussy she was going to have to lick, she changed the angle of her gaze to my sex and opened her mouth ever so slightly.

She looked up at me, defeated, pleading for me to claim my prize and have her lick me to orgasm, perhaps after tasting my anus. I pulled my panties further aside and spread the lips of my pussy, presenting her with my open vulva, just inches from her face. She opened her mouth and stuck her tongue out in a beautiful gesture of acceptance and then I began to pee, straight into her open mouth.

There was a general gasp of shock as my jet erupted in her face, then her mouth was full and it was bubbling out of the sides as she tried to close it. I was laughing as I sat up further, directing the jet of urine into her face. She was spluttering and struggling, trying to unseat me as I casually pissed on her. Once I had soaked her face and hair, I moved down, splashing it on her breasts and wetting her top. Then I sat back, with my pussy right on hers and let myself go. She gave a moan of mixed disgust and ecstasy as my hot pee ran down over her sex.

She was soaked. It was in her hair, her mouth, all over her breasts and pussy. Her top and skirt were sodden, while the bed beneath her was a soggy swamp of piss. Sitting proudly astride her, I peeled off my top and bra and threw them aside, then turned and, still on top of her, took of my skirt and panties. She had given in and made no resistance as I turned and poised my bare bottom over her face. I was in ecstasy as I lowered myself on to her, making sure my bumhole was directly over her mouth. She had made me lick her bottom and now she was going to find out how it felt to have to tongue another woman's anus.

The only difference was that when I had done it she hadn't pissed all over me first.

When her tongue touched my bumhole it gave me a magnificent feeling of superiority. I had beaten her and now she was licking my bottom in front of her friends, lapping at the little hole as I perched, victorious, on her face. For all my excitement I managed to restrain myself from making her transfer her attentions to my clitty until she had had a really good lick of my bottom. It was bliss having her tongue in my bottom-hole, but it wasn't going to bring me off and so after a bit I moved a little and she began to lick my sex.

The sensation was lovely, too lovely in fact to worry about maintaining my pose of forcing it on her. With a shrug to the audience I leant down and buried my face in her pussy, finding her clitty as her thighs went up and around my head. The others were silent as Lydia and I licked at each other on her pee-sodden bed; not even Steve found anything to say.

It didn't take long to come, and when we did it was together – a perfectly matched orgasm that had us holding tight to each other and both licking frantically as we climaxed.

The following week saw some of the best sex of my entire life. Every night I slept with Charlotte, accepting her gentle caresses and the occasional playful punishment to spice things up. I even let Percy Ottershaw spank me in a hotel toilet after a tasting and then treated his cock to a leisurely suck.

When I wasn't with Charlotte I was quite often with Lydia and Steve, having now reached an agreement on who was what to whom. After my fight with Lydia and the subsequent messy sex we had had a long talk, the upshot of which was that I managed to convince them that I was no threat to their relationship but simply a fun playmate. Steve was more than eager to accept this, and Lydia, while perhaps somewhat chagrined by the way I had treated her, seemed happy enough.

Three times during the week we had sex together. Each time I faithfully played my part as Lydia's slave, but there was no more nonsense about me doing anything other than what I wanted. After all, she knew what might happen if she didn't behave.

Best of all, the coming Friday was my date with Charles Carlisle and what promised to be a chance to have my bottom smacked as a proper erotic punishment.

Seventeen

In my limited experience of oral sex in toilets, it generally comes after dinner dates and not before. Twice in my life I had sat on restaurant toilet seats with my panties off and my knees up while some obliging boyfriend licked me to ecstasy. With Charles it was the other way around, in both senses; but having sucked his cock in the shop toilet removed a lot of the awkwardness that often comes at the start of a date with a new man. He wanted it again when I arrived at his shop, but I told him to be patient and wait – the first step in my carefully laid plan to get spanked before the evening was out.

Of course we had a lot in common as well, both being in the wine trade and, in particular, specialists in Burgundy. This also meant that I could place myself in his hands when it came to choosing a restaurant, which is a rare luxury for me. There are only a handful of restaurants in London with worthwhile wine lists, and the majority of young men need to be carefully steered in the right direction. With Charles there was no such difficulty. As soon as we had left his shop he took me gently by the arm, a courteous but masterful gesture that I would have resented from a lot of men. A short cab ride found us at *Au Bouef Farci* in Westbourne Grove, a restaurant that I had given an especially flattering write-up only the week before.

In the circumstances it was hard to act the brat, especially as I needed to be cheeky without actually spoiling the evening. I was sure he wanted to spank me though. He had been on the point of orgasm in my mouth when he had said I needed to be punished, and that is not a time when somebody lies. I knew that he had spoken to John Thurston as well, and possibly Percy Ottershaw.

I was determined to do my best, though, and made a point of doing slightly embarrassing things, things which I hoped he might use as an excuse to put me across his knee at the end of the evening. For a start I was in a little black velvet dress with just a tiny pair of white silk panties underneath. This left a lot of cleavage showing and hinted at my nipples, a display that a lot of men would have thought was overdoing it. Charles complimented me on my appearance but showed none of the strict disapproval I had hoped for.

Flirting with the waiters was my first bit of cheek, an action always guaranteed to irritate dates. They were all smart young Frenchmen with polished manners and big egos, so it wasn't difficult, but Charles took it in his stride, giving nothing more than a paternal chuckle at my girlish spirit.

The meal was excellent and by the time we were sipping our '72 Armagnac I was feeling thoroughly mellow and ready to be bedded, spanking or no spanking. I was still determined to get it if I could, though, and tried my next tactic on the ride to his flat. This involved being amorous in front of the cab driver, which is usually guaranteed to embarrass all but the most thick-skinned of dates. I kissed Charles and he responded briefly, but when I became more passionate and tried to get his cock out he simply took me by the wrists and held my arms firmly behind my back. He was surprisingly strong, presumably from lifting cases all day, and I found myself helpless. Eventually I had to promise to stop teasing before he would let go, but as soon as he demanded it of me I knew I had won. His tone was unmistakable. He wasn't exactly cross with me, but he had picked up on the game I was playing.

'You're very bad sometimes, Natasha,' he said gently as the cab drove away.

That was all, but it was enough. I knew we were going to bed together as we walked up to his flat, a split-level

affair that he used during the week. He had taken my arm
again and there was never a question of whether or not I
was coming in. Charles turned his key in the lock and then,
putting his hand gently but firmly on my bottom, steered
me through the door.

'I hear that you enjoy it wet,' he said, really more a
statement than a question.

It was pretty blatant, especially for him, but there was
no point in pretending to be outraged. In fact, to have
asked for wet sex and then pretended that Percy Ottershaw
had not told him about me would have been an insult to
my intelligence. I was blushing and feeling more than a
little ashamed of myself at the realisation that he, and
presumably several other men, knew what I had done for
Ottershaw. On the other hand, Percy had promised
discretion, so I couldn't be sure.

I giggled and smiled down at Charles, feeling naughty
and not a little drunk. The application of his hand to my
bottom had been firm, almost a smack, as if to chivvy me
along – a bad, drunken girl who needed to be guided by
having her bottom patted. I had been bad, he'd said so,
and it seemed more than likely that he'd want to punish
me with the spanking I so desperately wanted. Maybe he
would even make me pee in front of him and then spank
me as well, which would be lovely. In any case I was lost,
willing to do just about anything for the chance of getting
my bottom smacked. There was something cool and
dominant about Charles too, for all his small size, and I
could feel myself responding to his desire to control me.
Maybe he sensed some of this, because his grip on my bum
became tighter, more possessive.

'Run along upstairs, then, and get dressed in what's on
the bed,' he said.

It was an order, although pitched with just a touch of
humour to allow him to back out if I protested. I didn't,
but the implication of his remark came home to me even
as I scampered up the wrought-iron spiral staircase that led
to the upper level of the flat. The bastard had had it all
planned out. If he had laid out whatever costume he wanted

me in, then he had clearly been confident in his ability, not only to seduce me, but also to make me play his dirty little games.

So I wasn't the only one who had been planning the encounter in advance, and the smoothness with which the evening had gone was as much the result of his will as mine. Normally, this would have been the point where I exerted myself to take control of the situation, making the man do as I wanted. Now what I wanted was my spanking; so I needed to let him take control.

When I saw what was laid out on his bed my heart went straight to my mouth. It was a traffic warden's uniform, neatly pressed and laid out, accompanied by sensible heels, stockings, a suspender belt, bra and panties, all the underwear in ridiculously frilly pink nylon. I hate nylon and never wear it, but now the itch to put it on was overwhelming. It was girly, and tarty, and tacky, just the image to bring out my feelings of erotic humiliation. The uniform was better still, giving a distinctly lower-middle-class image. It was also an image of which every motorist in London must have bitter memories. There's only one reason a man who regularly parks his Jaguar in central London wants a girl to dress up as a traffic warden: to punish her. I could just see Charles wanting to take a pretty traffic warden across his knee in the middle of St James's or Regent's Street. Her neat little uniform skirt would come up as she thrashed and struggled, threatening him with her authority. Then her fury would double as she found that her panties were coming down, only to turn to pleas and sobs as she was given a well-deserved spanking on her bare, wiggling, fat, lower-middle-class bottom. Only it wouldn't be her; it would be me.

I was trembling as I dressed, fumbling the clothes on in my eagerness. I was nervous too. A spanking may be a turn-on, but it hurts just the same and it was possible that he would want to use a cane or something. I could hear Charles doing things below me, presumably getting something ready for me. Finally I was ready and checked my appearance in the mirror before going down to him.

Everything from the little hat to my sensible walking shoes was perfect. I really looked the part: a pretty, haughty, thoroughly annoying little busy-bodying brat – perfect spanking material. Unable to resist a peep at what Charles would see, I turned my back to the mirror and pulled up my skirt, revealing my stocking tops and the absurd frilly pink panties nicely filled with my chubby bottom. I couldn't believe any man, especially Charles, could see such a sight without wanting to smack my cheeks.

I went down the stairs, finding Charles in the kitchen area. His eyes lit up at the sight of me and I smiled back. He had pulled a stool out from the table, a round-topped one of polished oak. It was ideal for bending over, and my trembling became more pronounced.

'Stand up straight,' he said, now a definite order.

I obeyed, coming smartly to attention as if I was about to be ticked off by a superior. I felt more than a little ridiculous and also deeply humiliated. I have to admit it was exciting though, not especially because I get anything out of being dressed as a traffic warden, but it was so nice to be really used without the slightest thought for my preferences or dignity.

'You're going to be punished,' he said firmly. 'Bent over and punished.'

I could have come on the spot. He was going to punish me too; and given the stool and the position he wanted me in there was only one thing that could mean – a good, hard spanking on my naughty little bottom.

'Bend down over this,' he said in a voice thick with lust.

He turned the stool over so that the legs stuck up, making what was effectively a cage for my middle. I went down, resting my tummy on the cross pieces of the stool's legs.

'Put your hands behind your back,' he continued.

I obeyed as he came to kneel beside me. He was smiling like a happy schoolboy as he unwound the rope. I waited passively as he tied one end to a leg of the stool and began to lash me into place. He did it with his normal obsessive neatness, creating a spider's web of rope that bound my waist firmly to the stool.

Once I was firmly strapped into position he moved behind me and took hold of the hem of my skirt. I looked back, shaking violently as he pulled it up, exposing my nylon frillies. Then they came down, eased slowly off my nates and settled around my thighs to leave my rear view on display without the slightest reserve. I knew my pussy would be showing, swollen and wet, also my anus, brownish pink and wrinkled. My position was so utterly humiliating, and he was going to punish me like that: beat me and then fuck me. I sighed out loud, unable to restrain myself. He gave a little chuckle and turned his attention to my chest. I was purring as he pulled my jacket open, undid the buttons of my blouse and flopped my breasts out of the pink nylon cups of my bra to swing loose and bare beneath me. For a moment he toyed with my nipples, then he stood up.

'You look beautiful,' he breathed. 'The uniform suits you, and so do those tarty pants and bra. I'd love to do this to a real traffic warden, but you make a great fantasy. Anyway, I'm going to punish you now.'

This was it, the moment he announced that he was going to beat me, something that I would receive as if it was a horrid shock rather than my deepest desire. Then he would thrash me across my nude bottom until I was howling and my breasts were swinging back and forth as my body bounced in reaction. Next he would mount me and fuck me with his thighs slapping against my red-hot buttocks as I blubbered and snivelled over my beating. Finally he would come in my vagina and finished me off with his fingers while he gave my bottom a few more slaps.

He left the kitchen area. I knew he would be fetching the punishment implement, perhaps an English school cane, a leather whip or a big wooden brush – anyway, something that would really hurt. Instead he came back with a bottle of Pommard, a half-pint glass and an enormous syringe.

'What are you going to do?' I asked, feeling slightly worried despite my excitement.

Charles merely grinned and began to pour the Pommard slowly into the half-pint glass, stopping only when it reached the brim.

'Seriously, what are you doing?' I asked as he put the nozzle of the syringe into the Pommard and began to suck it up.

'Nothing painful,' he replied cheerfully, 'but something I've always wanted to do. I'm going to give you a wine enema.'

'An enema?' I echoed, my bottom-hole suddenly feeling very prominent and very unprotected.

'Yes, with Romier-Congé's *Pommard les Epinots* 1989, as it's you,' he continued, holding up the full syringe and expelling the air from the top exactly like a doctor preparing to give an injection.

'Isn't that a bit good to waste?' I replied, trying to sound jolly despite my violent trembling at what was about to be done to me.

'Oh, we're not going to waste it,' he answered, applying butter to the nozzle. 'You're going to taste it – after it has been up your pretty bottom.'

I could have protested. In fact I could have stood up; though I was tied to the stool, it wasn't fixed to anything else. I almost did, but I couldn't resist and just hung my head and shut my eyes, feeling utterly ashamed of myself as I prepared to accept a degradation worse even than what I'd done for Percy Ottershaw. Charles laughed, as if he had never doubted my reaction.

A moment later I felt the cold, metal nozzle of the syringe touch my anus. It was slimy with butter and went in easily, popping my little hole open as I relaxed to accommodate it. For one instant I wanted to back out; then it was too late. The wine was flowing into my rectum, creating a strange, cold sensation around my anus. I gasped as the cavity started to fill, a weird pressure not unlike having a cock up my bottom but without the stretched anal ring. It began to hurt, just a little, and my breath was coming faster as the pressure in my rectum built up. I could hear my moans and pants as the combination of ecstasy and humiliation threatened to overwhelm me, then the full half-pint was in place up my bottom and he was withdrawing the syringe. My belly felt swollen and heavy, like a round ball dangling beneath me, an exquisitely dirty sensation. I clenched my anus to stop the wine coming straight back out, holding it up myself in a desperate effort to keep it in and prevent myself from committing the final indignity and spurting it out all over the floor.

I managed to hold it but found I had to wiggle my toes and kick my legs to do it – a reaction that drew a sadistic chuckle from Charles. Their was a picture in my mind of myself bent over and tied up in my uniform. I would look at once absurd and obscene, with my bottom bare and my cheeks well spread, my anus greasy with butter and damp with wine, clenched tight to stop me from soiling myself. Then I'd give in and the wine would spurt from my anus and dribble down into my ridiculous panties, a sight too obscene to contemplate; only I couldn't help it.

I knew that the alcohol would go straight through the lining of my rectum, but was still taken aback by the sheer speed with which I started to become dizzy. The pleasure of having the enema in me also built with my drunkenness, and I knew I was going to have to do it. I resisted though, wriggling frantically and clenching my buttocks tight. I hadn't peed when I'd changed either, because I'd thought Charles might want to watch. The pressure in my bladder was making it worse, adding to my breathlessness and pain. Within minutes I was gasping and moaning, barely able to keep my anus tight but no more able to endure the humiliation of letting go.

Then it just happened. I screamed as my anus gave in and the enema erupted from my bottom. I felt it spurt out and heard it splash behind me. A great pulse of emotion hit me, the blend of physical relief at emptying my rectum and the overwhelming mental shame of coming close to the pleasure of orgasm.

It splashed against the door of the units behind me, a stream of dirty wine gushing from my bottom with extraordinary force. For a long moment it continued, then my scream was dying to a long sigh of utter bliss as the rush died to a trickle that ran down the insides of my thighs and into my panties. I could feel my anus pulsing and dribbling behind me and was thinking of what a state I must have looked to Charles. I was tied and helpless. My boobs, bum and pussy were all bare; what clothing I did have on served not to cover anything at all but only to make me all the more humiliated. Worst of all my bumhole would be a moist pink flower, open in the centre, while the evidence of what had been done to me was behind me and in my panties.

Even though Charles had done it to me, I felt deeply embarrassed for making a mess of his kitchen floor, which may have been ridiculous but added to my thrill. He swallowed loudly enough for me to hear and I wondered if he was going to forget about the next step in my degradation and simply bugger me on the spot. I wouldn't have blamed him at all and looked round to see if he had his cock out for me.

He did, a thick, stubby erection with a lot of flesh on the shaft. It was sticking out of his trousers with his balls protruding beneath it. He was stroking it with his left hand while in his right he held a large, clear-glass water jug. This had a good measure of rather cloudy red wine in it; I realised that I was going to be spared nothing.

I was breathing really heavily as he shuffled round to my front, and I knew that it wouldn't have taken much to bring me to orgasm. Unfortunately my hands were tight up in the small of my back, and I could only pray that he would have the decency to bring me off when he had taken his pleasure with me.

He moved so that his cock was in front of my face, pointed directly at my mouth. I opened wide obligingly and he slid it inside, moaning as I sucked eagerly on his shaft. I was in the mood for a good, long suck, but for him it was just an interlude, perhaps done merely so that he could say he'd had his erection in my mouth. I suppose that perhaps I wanted to suck for a long time in order to postpone the inevitable, because I knew full well that my resistance was broken and that I'd do as I was told and enjoy it, no matter how disgusting it became.

He pulled out quickly, leaving me with my tongue sticking out, lapping hopefully at thin air. I looked up as he raised himself a little, then swallowed as he took a wine glass from the table. My eyes followed it down, hypnotised as he slowly and deliberately poured a half-measure of Pommard. He began to play with his cock again, directly in front of my face as he lifted the glass.

'Taste,' he ordered thickly as he put the glass to my lips.

I felt the cool, hard glass touch my lips, a sensation I had experienced untold times before but never in such circumstances. The scent was rich in my nose and I let out a little, involuntary whimper as he tilted the glass and the wine moistened my lips. Almost before I knew what I was doing I had parted my lips and was drinking, tasting myself mixed with the wine. I swallowed a little, an act so dirty, so rude, that the tears started in my eyes even as my desperation for an orgasm rose to an unbearable level.

'Make me come!' I begged, pulling back momentarily.

He didn't disappoint, putting a knuckle to my clit and rubbing at me while his other hand went on to my bottom. I was moaning out my thanks through my filthy mouthful as a finger penetrated my anus, then started to come as he masturbated me with exquisite expertise. I screamed as I reached orgasm, my anus clamping tight on his intruding finger and my mouthful bursting from my lips as I hit an incredible peak. My head was swimming and my whole body seemed to be on fire, a plateau of ecstasy which I rode while he continued to rub at me and fingered my bottom-hole. Only one thing remained to complete my soiling; wetting myself. I felt so wonderfully dirty and the pressure in my bladder was too much anyway. I began to pee, moaning as it gushed out over his hand and began to fill my lowered panties. The weight of pee bagged them out, making the slippery nylon pull against my thighs. Charles kept rubbing, and I hit another peak as my pee died to a trickle. Every muscle in my body seemed to contract at the same time, then again. I looked back between my legs to see a wide golden pool spreading out rapidly between my knees, hit a final peak and then I slumped in my bonds, exhausted, sore, filthy and so, so happy.

Unlike many men, Charles was really good to me afterwards. When I had come down from my orgasm I was guilty and ashamed and a little tearful, but instead of telling me not to be a baby, he gave me a cuddle and helped me to the bathroom to wash. He wouldn't hear of me helping him clear up either, but sat me down in a bathrobe with a glass of Pommard, unadulterated this time.

The taste of the Pommard that had been up my bottom hadn't actually been too bad, just a bit earthier than usual, and I admitted this to him. He jokingly suggested putting a bottle into the next blind tasting we attended, which made us both laugh.

I stayed the night, having sex twice more before we went to sleep, both times in rather more conventional fashion. The first time was just a little kinky, with me kneeling in the traffic warden's outfit with the skirt up and my white silk panties pulled to the side. The second was actually quite loving, with Charles between my legs and my arms wrapped around him. It was nearly dawn by the time we got to sleep and my last thought before drifting into a satisfied stupor was that this one was definitely worth a replay.

Eighteen

Not surprisingly I awoke with mixed feelings. I'd been really dirty, filthy in fact. Not just allowing a man to give me an enema but actually tasting some of it. It had been ecstasy though, and the memory of the sheer pleasure, both physical and mental, was so strong that I knew it wouldn't be the last time I allowed someone to poke a nozzle up my bottom. The sensation of fluid filling my rectum and the odd, heavy feeling in my tummy had been best; or maybe the point when I just hadn't been able to hold it any more and it had squirted out all over the kitchen floor; perhaps even when I'd been forced to taste it, for sheer mind-blowing intensity.

In any case I felt I needed to share the experience and so told Lydia, who seemed to be the most dirty minded of my female friends. She was amused, turned on and a little shocked, which I found pleasing. I had to embroider the story a little but ended up telling her about Charles, sucking his cock in the shop toilet and the traffic warden's uniform – everything, in fact – all of which she listened to with increasing amazement. I countered her question as to whether I felt used by pointing out that I had accepted another date on the coming Friday and was thoroughly looking forward to it.

We might have ended up in a clinch then, and it would probably have been a messy one, but Steve returned to the flat at that point to suggest playing some game on motorbikes. This sounded boring to me until I got the details. Essentially the girls would be let loose on a piece of wasteland and the boys would chase us. If they caught us they could fuck us; it promised to be quite an experience.

Lydia was keen too and eager to show off Steve's new motorbike. This was a huge, powerful thing, and obviously brand new. How Steve had got hold of it I didn't like to think, given that I had never seen him do a minute's work in the time I'd known him. It was nothing to do with me though, even if he'd stolen it, and the sight of it added to the exciting idea of being chased. Teo also had a bike, while the idea was for the rest of us to travel up in Sally's clapped-out Metro. Given that this meant six of us in a small car I abandoned my last pretence of being poor and admitted that I had a car. They had always thought I was a rich girl after a bit of rough anyway, but they were still suitably impressed when I returned with the TVR. Lucy even insisted on riding with me, much to Phil's annoyance.

The wasteland turned out to be the site of an old factory somewhere on the outskirts of Romford. It was just the sort of place I would have been terrified to go alone, full of quiet corners among piles of rubble and dim buildings smelling of damp. This made it the perfect place for our game, with a built-in atmosphere, so to speak. Just seeing Steve and Teo sitting astride their bikes with the others standing behind looking tough scared me – with that delicious thrill of being really frightened but knowing that you are in fact perfectly safe, rather like watching a horror film.

They gave us five minutes and we ran into the wasteland. The place was huge, and it would have been easy to find some secluded nook and just hide. That wasn't the idea though; we wanted to be caught. But that didn't mean we had to make it easy. The largest of the intact buildings was a big warehouse with doors tall enough for full-size lorries. We entered this so that the boys couldn't see us and had a quick discussion, agreeing to split up to make it last longer. We scattered, most of the girls heading for the areas of sunlit rubble outside while Sally went for the maze of old offices at one end of the warehouse and I climbed on to the roof.

This allowed me to see what was going on, while, by keeping low, there was little chance of being spotted until I needed to be. I had decided that I wanted to watch at least one of the other girls getting caught and fucked before enjoying the same treatment. That way I would be really turned on to the idea and wet enough to be entered easily if they got a bit carried away.

Being men, they appointed a leader, Steve, and set out a strategy. This involved Steve and Teo riding noisily to either side of the warehouse while the others advanced quietly in the middle. The idea was obviously for the bikes to scare the girls into the centre, where they could be caught and held down until the other boys arrived. As I was on the roof it made no difference to me, and I was sure Sally and Lydia were far too cool-headed to be trapped so easily. Lucy had run for the far end, making herself vulnerable only if another girl wasn't caught first, and so it was Chloë that their initial run put up.

It was better than any film, perhaps even like it must have been to attend the Colosseum in ancient Rome. Hearing Steve approaching, she ran for the cover of the warehouse, exactly as they intended. Phil, Darren and Paul were already inside. As I heard Chloë's laughing scream I risked climbing down at the end so that I could watch from the offices. Sally was already there, watching her little sister with an excited grin. Chloë was in the middle of the warehouse, standing still as Steve and Teo circled her on the bikes. Each time she tried to dodge away they would move, blocking her path. They were just tormenting her as she had no chance of escape and it was putting her in a fine panic. The boys closed in, the three on foot coming closer then suddenly darting in and catching her by the arms.

She was laughing, squealing and struggling as they dragged her down on to the concrete floor. Paul took her arms and Phil and Steve a leg each, spread-eagling her on the ground. Darren tugged her top up, exposing her big bra-less breasts, while Teo pushed her skirt up. I put my arm round Sally, both of us watching delightedly as Chloë's legs were held up and her knickers pulled off. We had agreed that it would only be the actual boyfriends who fucked the girls; Teo had already pulled his cock out and was stroking it, preparing his erection while the others held her down. His cock was long and thick, the shaft a glossy dark brown and the head red-brown, just the sort of big, black cock so many white girls like to fantasise over.

'Make her suck it, Teo,' Sally whispered hopefully.

It was not Teo, but Steve who pulled his cock out and offered it to Chloë's mouth. She began to suck him as Teo mounted her. I felt a hard lump rise in my throat as I watched. Chloë, sweet, curvaceous, mischievous Chloë, was being held down by three men while a fourth made her suck his cock and a fifth fucked her. Her lovely breasts were bare and her panties had been pulled off. She had a good nine inches of black cock inside her pussy and a nice, thick white one in her mouth. Rough hands were feeling her tits and her face was set in an expression of utter bliss while she was being so thoroughly used.

My own pussy was beginning to feel more than a little wet. Sally's arm was tight around my waist, as mine was around hers. She smiled at me and I transferred my hand to her bottom, treating myself to a leisurely feel while we watched her little sister get fucked. Sally had jeans on and her bum felt really nice in the taut denim with it stuck out to allow me to explore. After a while they turned Chloë over and made her do it on all fours with her puppy-fat bottom stuck up in the air and her tits dangling in the boys' hands. Steve kept it in her mouth and she sucked eagerly, bobbing her head up and down on his prick as her body shivered with Teo's pushes. Steve seemed to tense and then withdrew, leaving a trail of white semen joining his cock to Chloë's lips for an instant before it broke and was left hanging from her chin. She opened her mouth and I could see the come in it, white and dribbling from the edges as Teo's strokes became harder. She squealed really loudly and then he pulled out, grabbing his erection to jerk it frantically over her bottom. He came, spurt after spurt of white semen erupting on to her plump, naked bottom, spattering her full buttocks and soiling her turned-up skirt.

My hand was between Sally's thighs, feeling the swollen lips of her pussy though her jeans from the rear. I wanted to have her, but the boys were already tidying up and discussing their next move. I could see that they were seriously turned on and felt the thrill of knowing that if was caught I was going to get just the same treatment as Chloë. I didn't want to be the next, though, and reluctantly abandoned Sally's bottom to retreat silently from the danger area.

Sally came with me, climbing on to the roof with an athletic ease that I supposed came from stripping. The roof was covered in a tarry substance, black and hot in the burning sun. A low parapet gave us shelter and we ducked down behind this, both full of nervous anticipation as our arms once more came around each other. We heard the motorbikes start up and ducked, giggling, beneath the parapet as the boys emerged from the warehouse Somebody came out of the office doors directly beneath us and as he spoke I realised it was Paul.

'When I get Sally I'm going to fuck her up the arse,' he announced with relish, drawing a grunt of appreciation from his companion.

Sally's arm tightened on my waist on hearing this and we ducked further down, exchanging looks of mock terror For a while all we could hear was the roar of the motorbikes and then there was an excited scream and the sounds of pursuit became louder and more urgent. We couldn't resist looking and raised our head to see that the boys had reached the end of the compound and had flushed Lucy out into the open.

They had her in a clearing among piles of shattered brick and the end wall. A rusting car stood in this space, its broad bonnet offering a wide surface across which they had thrown her. Paul and Darren were holding her arms while Phil was behind her, his arms around her hips to get at the button of her jeans.

As with Chloë, it was really exciting to watch Lucy getting fucked. She made a big fuss about it, kicking and squealing, pretending to be unwilling, which I freely

198

confess was an extra turn-on. The boys held her easily though, Steve and Teo just watching while Paul and Darren gripped her arms. Phil dragged down her trousers and panties, exposing her lovely bottom, all pink and bare in the hot sun. She looked back over her shoulder as he got his cock out, watching as he stroked his cock to erection for her. Then he took her by the hips and put it in; her expression changed to ecstasy as he started to fuck her.

He was humping her from the rear in a way that made her bottom bounce and wobble delightfully, which I found especially appealing. After a while Paul let go of her wrist and pulled her tits out, feeling them while Teo took over the job of holding her down. Sally and I were feeling each other's bums as we watched, getting more and more turned on by the sight of our friend being used over the bonnet of the old car.

When Phil pulled out and came into Lucy's lowered panties it was just too much for me. I folded Sally in my arms and kissed her, thinking of how Lucy was going to have to go home with her knickers full of come as Sally responded. We sank down together on to the hot roof, our hands groping for each other, finding breasts and bottoms to stroke and explore.

As I lay back, her hand went between my legs, easing them apart to move up my skirt and find the front of my panties. She began to play with me as we kissed, rubbing my clitty through the silk, her finger in between my pussy lips. More of her weight came on to me and her breasts pressed against mine as my arms went around her back.

'I'm going to lick you out, Tasha,' she whispered hotly. 'Open your legs nice and wide.'

As my thighs came apart fully she mounted me, coming down between my legs like a man would. Her hands were on my breasts, her mouth on my neck. I pulled my top up and scooped my boobs out, eager for her kisses. She took a breast in each hand and squeezed gently, making me purr with pleasure.

A noise caught my attention, the clang of a boot on metal. Alarmed, I looked up to see Steve's grinning face emerge over the parapet. Sally was up like a hare and had bolted before I could really react. Then Steve's hand closed on my ankle and he was pulling himself over.

'Got one!' he called triumphantly. 'Tasha!'

I struggled but he held me easily, and as Phil joined him I knew I was going to get it. The others followed, eager hands spreading me out on the hot roof. They pulled my bra up and pulled down my panties, leaving me exposed and vulnerable to entry. Looking back I could see Sally. She was standing on the far parapet, keen to watch them do me but able to run should any move her way.

'Strip her!' Sally called sadistically.

They responded immediately. I felt every instant of being stripped: my top being wrenched off, my bra being ripped away, my panties being slipped off my ankles, my skirt being pulled free . . .

When I was stark naked they spread me out again. Ted and Paul had my legs, Phil and Steve my arms, while Darren stood over me, grinning as his hand went to his fly. It came out, the cock that was about to be put in my vagina while I was held by four men. I was going to be fucked in front of them, and probably made to suck too – perhaps even be sodomised.

'Put it in her mouth, Darren,' Steve suggested.

Darren's grin grew wider as he flopped his cock and balls on to my mouth.

'Suck my balls,' he ordered.

I opened my mouth, taking his testicles in. He groaned as I sucked on his scrotum, then put his hand to his cock and began to slap the half-erect shaft against my cheek. It grew quickly, rearing up over my face.

'Give me a lipstick ring,' he demanded, pulling his ball free.

I moved to allow him to put his cock in my mouth, taking in all I could and then closing my lips on the base of his shaft. He pulled back, flourishing his cock, the ring of glossy red lipstick clear proof that his prick had been in my mouth.

'Now I'm going to fuck your posh twat,' he announced, rising to hold his cock out over my face.

I could do nothing, only relish the sensation as Teo and Paul brought my legs up to present their friend with my open pussy. It was a really exposed position, and I knew it showed my bumhole too.

'Nice cunt, Tasha,' Paul remarked, then looked over to where his girlfriend was watching. 'Hey, Sally, when we get you it's going up your arse!'

Sally just laughed. Darren knelt down, holding his cock. I relaxed, intent on the full appreciation of the moment. The four of them had good grips on my limbs, a cock was about to be put in me and there was absolutely nothing I could do. Darren moved forward and slapped his erection on my pussy. It touched my clitty and I moaned aloud.

'Come on, Tasha, at least struggle a bit,' Steve said.

I responded, thrashing my hips just in time to prevent Darren's cock from slipping inside me. He protested and the others took firmer grips on me. I tried to struggle, putting all my strength into it so that they had to use both arms to hold me and keep me spread for Darren. Steve was right, it was much better with them holding me really hard and the feeling of being forced was really strong as Darren finally got his cock to my vagina. I continued to struggle as his erection filled me, then began to swear and spit at him as he mounted properly and began to fuck me.

He hesitated, only to be told not to be a prat by Steve. I kept up the game, but the pleasure of his cock inside me was rising and I was about to give in when he came, right up me. I groaned in resignation, lying back as he pulled out and mumbled an apology.

'I want a bit of that,' Steve said. 'Take her arm, Darren. Really struggle hard, Tasha.'

'I'm exhausted!' I protested.

'Come on,' he insisted. 'I'll make Lydia lick you when we get her.'

'I'll try,' I promised. 'Come on, then.'

Steve and Darren swapped places. After a fair bit of sucking I managed to get Steve's cock hard and he entered me while I put up as much resistance as what remained of my energy would allow. He seemed to enjoy it, because like

Darren he came inside me and once more I was left with a pussy full of come.

As soon as Steve had finished they abandoned me and tried to rush Sally. She jumped down from the parapet, laughing, and disappeared. They followed, climbing down from the roof to leave me soiled and exhausted on the hot surface.

What I needed more than anything was a drink. Fortunately I had a bottle of mineral water in the car and some much-needed tissues. Chloë saw me as I was climbing down, and together we walked to the car, giggling over the game and wondering what had become of Lydia.

After finding Lucy and sharing the water we made our way back on to the wasteland, where the boys were chasing Sally. She was giving them a good run and despite their motorbikes she was still managing to elude capture when the three of us had climbed back on to the warehouse roof. We could see her, crouched behind a slab of concrete, not ten yards from where a puzzled Phil was looking around him. She saw us and made a sign with her fingers, indicating the stupidity of men in general and the boys in particular. The temptation to give her away was too much, and, after all, she had stood there laughing while I had been stripped and fucked.

'Behind the slab, Phil!' I called, pointing to Sally's hiding place.

He glanced around, unsure where I meant. Sally panicked, dashing from her hiding place only to run full-tilt into Darren as he came around the corner of what had once been some sort of hut. He grabbed her and managed to hold on with his arms around her waist, despite her furious struggles.

We watched her mock rape in delight, although from the way she fought it might almost have been real. Paul, Steve and Teo came quickly to the sounds of Sally struggling with Phil and Darren. For an instant Sally stopped fighting and I saw her point to Steve's bike. Phil nodded and then grabbed her by the neck. Kicking and struggling, she was dragged to the motorbike and thrown down over the seat with her bottom stuck up over the tail bar. Steve fixed his chain around her waist and the body of the bike, securing her in place. They put her hands behind her back and tied them in place with some old flex, then undid her jeans and pulled them off, taking her knickers and boots with them.

I put my hand down the front of my panties, unable to resist playing with myself. Lucy giggled and smiled at me, while Chloë was too intent on watching her sister being raped to notice me. I began to masturbate as they spread Sally's thighs across the rear of the bike, displaying her vagina and anus for their use. They tied her legs in place, leaving her utterly helpless, nude from the waist down, her bottom raised and open and her beautiful long legs strapped to the sides of the motorbike.

Steve and Teo held the bike; Sally was gaping for Teo's thick black cock as he got it out and put it to her mouth. Phil was already behind her, his erection in his hand.

'Up her bum! You said you would!' I called out, keen to watch Sally sodomised over the bike and to come over the sight.

'Cunt first!' Phil called back. 'She likes it slimy.'

Teo's prick was beginning to stiffen in Sally's mouth as Phil mounted her firm little bottom. It was a slightly awkward position, but it looked great as he began to hump her and I was having to control my urge to come. He fucked her slowly, taking his time in her vagina and then pulling out. His cock was glistening with her juices – a rigid pole of hard penis that I would just love to have sucked clean. Then he put it between her bum cheeks and greased her anus with her own juice. I began to masturbate faster, watching Sally tense as Phil's knob touched her bumhole. For an instant her eyes shut in pain and I knew it had gone in. Then her expression was once more blissful as she sucked on Teo's now hard cock and accepted Phil's length slowly into her back passage.

I watched him bugger her, masturbating myself as his cock moved in her bumhole, imagining how she felt, strapped over the bike and sodomised in front of us. My head was spinning, my legs weak as my eyes locked on her pretty bottom and the obscene way his penis protruded from between her cheeks. It was quite clearly in her anus, pumping away, filling her, stretching her. Suddenly I was coming, my muscles tensing as the orgasm welled up in me. Even as I climaxed Phil pulled back, his cock squirting sperm as he did so. For one exquisite moment I saw Sally's bumhole as an open black hole as a jet of sperm erupted right into it. Then it closed and the come oozed out, dribbling down her pussy as I rode my climax on and on.

As Phil stood back Chloë started to clap and cheer, breaking the trance. Teo was still in Sally's mouth and she was bucking her hips, cleverly rubbing her pussy against the bar at the rear of the bike. I could see every detail between her legs as she rubbed herself, her open pussy wet with juice, her anus pulsing and oozing sperm. Teo was masturbating into her mouth while beside me both Lucy and Chloë were following my example and masturbating shamelessly over the sight.

Lucy had her trousers down and I gave her bottom an encouraging squeeze, then pulled her panties up tight into her crease, spilling her buttocks out on either side. She groaned and I began to smack her bottom, still holding her panties up. Below us, sperm squirted from Sally's mouth around Teo's cock, then she was coming herself. She wouldn't let Teo go, but sucked hard, draining his sperm as she went through a long climax. Chloë came next, with a little whimper, perhaps of shame, as she climaxed over the sight of her sister in ecstasy. Lucy started to squeal and I gave her a harder smack as she went into orgasm, tensing her buttocks and bowing her legs in abandoned pleasure.

That was that, except for one thing. Nobody had seen Lydia since the beginning of the game. After a few minutes' recovery we all joined in the search, girls as well as boys. Finally we found her, hidden in a half-collapsed lavatory among the old offices. She had watched Sally being fucked from the window and was desperately turned on and keen to be given similar treatment. The rest of us watched from the doorway as Steve and Phil tied her down over the lavatory, then, on some sadistic impulse, changed her position so that her head was actually down the bowl.

They pulled her skirt up and she began to moan and lift her bottom, desperate for entry. Steve got his cock out and began to pull at it as he admired his girlfriend's degraded position. He'd come twice and not many men can manage three times in an hour or so. The view was good though, and he eventually managed an erection by pawing Lydia's buttocks while Chloë obligingly went down on her knees and sucked him.

With his cock finally hard he got down behind Lydia and entered her, making her sigh. Her arms were tied around the lavatory bowl so that she couldn't frig, so I motioned to Chloë to help. She moved around, sliding one hand between Steve's legs to feel his balls and the other under Lydia's belly to masturbate her.

She must have been incredibly turned on, because she started to come almost as soon as Chloë's finger found her clitty. As she went into orgasm a really mischievous urge came over me. I pushed through the door, reached out and pulled the chain. I hadn't really expected it to work, but it did, starting with a rusty creak and then a low rumble. Filthy brown water spurted out around Lydia's head as she came, soaking her hair and filling her mouth. She lifted her head, spluttering and gasping, still in orgasm despite what I'd done to her. The look she gave me was wonderful and promised a long and humiliating punishment at some later time.

Unfortunately Steve couldn't come and eventually had to abandon the task of fucking Lydia. Even then she wouldn't have minded too much, having come herself, but the idiot Darren had to spoil everything. As tactless as ever, while Lydia was being untied, he made a joking remark about Steve coming with both Chloë and me. She was furious, and nothing we could say would cheer her up. I seemed to be the one she was most annoyed with, although as I had been held down when Steve fucked me I didn't see that it was in any way my fault. I said this, which only made her go into a sulk, refusing to speak to anybody except Sally.

Inevitably the bad feeling brought the day's fun to an end and I drove back with Chloë, feeling upset when I should have been really happy.

Nineteen

On my return to the flat my annoyance was quickly pushed to the back of my mind. Charlotte was waiting for me and was in a worried and uncertain mood. As it was Saturday she would normally have been at the church had it not been for my successful disposal of the unctuous Evan Dunstal. Unfortunately he had not given up so easily and had called when she didn't turn up. She had pointed out frostily that she was not inclined to see men who attempted to force sex on to her friends. Dunstal had denied doing anything of the sort and had argued that I was not to be trusted. The words he had actually used, apparently, were 'scheming, manipulative little bitch'. Charlotte had stuck up for me and eventually put the phone down on him, but he had managed to sow the seeds of doubt.

I had to rally my thoughts really quickly, but with my knowledge of Evan Dunstal's intimate anatomy and personal habits I eventually managed to convince her that I had been telling the truth. She threw her arms around me and burst into tears, which really did make me feel like a scheming, manipulative little bitch. I didn't let it worry me for long though, because she was sobbing in my arms, warm, soft and intensely female. I kissed her and she responded, a gentle loving kiss that went straight to my head and also to my pussy.

An hour later we were lying together in my bed, naked and snuggled together in the warm afterglow of really good sex. We had taken turns to lick each other, slowly and sensuously, working over each other's bodies in detail before the final flurry of urgent flicks to our clits. Twice more that night we had sex, and this time, when the morning came, she stayed with me, curled up like an obedient little puppy.

I had been sipping the coffee she had made for me and we hadn't spoken for perhaps ten minutes when she lifted her head.

'I'm sorry I doubted you,' she said softly. 'Do you think I ought to be punished?'

'Yes,' I replied without hesitation, 'and you can start by kissing my pussy while I decide what to do with you.'

She burrowed obediently down the bed and between my thighs. As her mouth found my labia I began to invent a suitable punishment. As she licked, my fantasy became juicier and juicier, until, as I started to come, I couldn't resist speaking.

'I'm going to have you buggered,' I moaned. 'Buggered by a big, fat pig, really hard, right up your tight little bumhole . . .'

I lost my words as I started to come and just moaned out my ecstasy as she lapped at my clitty. Only when she had finished and her head re-emerged from beneath the bedclothes did she reply.

'You're joking, aren't you?' she asked in a sweet, worried little voice.

'I meant Percy Ottershaw,' I replied, 'not a real pig.'

'I suppose I should thank you,' she answered.

'You will by the end,' I assured her.

Percy was delighted by the prospect of helping to punish Charlotte; what sixty-year-old dirty old man would not be by the offer of unrestricted access to a beautiful young woman? It put Charlotte in that delicious mood of uncertainty and erotic humiliation that I knew so well, and she was already trembling by the time we arrived at his flat.

This wasn't just at the prospect of being sexually punished either; it was partly at the way she was dressed. I had wanted to humiliate her, but because it was Sunday it hadn't been practical to go out and buy a Brownie uniform, incontinence pants or any of the other things that had come to my wicked and inventive mind. Instead I had taken a really big white beach towel, and, with the aid of large safety pins, put her in a pretty convincing nappy. Her blushes and giggles while I was doing this told me that I was on the right track, and by the time I was finished she looked very sweet indeed, and very unsure of herself. I let her put on a loose summer frock and sandals, but nothing more, and marched her off to Maida Vale.

Percy was in a thoroughly cheerful mood and quite happy to let me organise things. I started by making Charlotte take off her dress and show him her nappy – first standing with her hands on her head so that he had an unobstructed view of her neat little breasts, then crawling on all fours and finally standing with her hands on her knees and her bottom stuck out. I had brought my camera along and photographed all three positions, a practice I intended to continue for the whole of her punishment session. She was becoming increasingly excited, but I was determined not to rush and told her to do exactly as she was told while I finished the film.

I took photos of her sucking his cock, with him sitting fully clothed in an armchair while she knelt, nappy-clad bum stuck out, little boobs dangling and his erection in her mouth. Close-ups followed, so that every detail of her face was captured as she sucked on his skinny, pink shaft. I added ones of her masturbating him while she sucked his balls and some of her simply sitting on his lap in her nappy with his cock in her hand.

The contrast between them was truly wonderful: Percy fat and red-faced with his skinny cock sticking out under his fat stomach; Charlotte slim and young and beautiful. Even the nappy didn't look out of place, and anyone who saw the photos would just think that she had been made to wear it by the dirty old pervert whose cock she was handling. The scene really fuelled my dirty old man fantasies and was certainly turning her on too, as I could see when she happily went back to sucking his cock when I had taken my pictures of her handling it.

I had her spanked next, over his knee with her nappy rolled down to expose her bum. The first couple of shots showed her having the nappy taken down, then about to be punished with her pussy peeping out from between her thighs at the rear. As he began to slap her buttocks I took the whole sequence, with her bum getting redder and redder and her pose becoming more and more undignified. By the end her whole bottom was a lovely glowing red and her thighs were splayed apart as far as the nappy would permit, giving me a fine view of her tight brown bumhole and her now obviously moist pussy.

She was ready to have her bottom entered, but I had other ideas. I made her bend over the sofa and gave her six with a bamboo from one of Percy's pot plants. She yelped at every stroke, and by the time I had finished her bum was decorated with six sets of lines. Percy and I then inspected her bottom, admiring the way each stroke had produced two thin red lines in parallel on the already flushed skin. Caning her was immensely satisfying, fun as well as sexy. There is something deeply amusing about seeing a girl with her bum bare getting a good whacking. Having experienced it myself, I can really feel her humiliation at the exposure of her bum for punishment and also her pain as it's delivered. It looks so beautiful too, and it was more than I could resist not to give Charlotte another six.

This left her in a sweaty, trembling, slightly tearful state, immensely turned on and fully obedient to me. Rather than get up and cover herself, she stayed over the sofa with her naked bottom thrust out in the hope of attention from my fingers or Percy's cock. Instead of granting her wish I said that she looked an absolute disgrace and told her to pull her nappy up. She gave me a lovely shamefaced look and did as she was told.

Giving the camera to Percy, I marched her into the bathroom and told her to wet her nappy. She blushed deeply, but hung her head and folded her hands across her stomach. For a moment nothing happened, and then I heard the gush of pee and saw the wet stain begin to spread at the front. I was laughing as the camera clicked and the pee began to run down her thighs. Soon she was standing in a pool of it, which spread out gradually on the bathroom floor while she blushed and snivelled over what I had made her do.

I was beginning to get to the point of wanting to come myself, and, while I was quite happy to make Charlotte wait for her orgasm for hours if it amused me, I wanted mine to order. It was also time for Percy to fuck her, and I wanted her to watch as her trim, pretty body was mounted by an obese old man. I had her remove the nappy first and wring it out over her own head. The expression on her face as the pee trickled down over her was wonderful; I was laughing so much I could barely stand. Making her clean her mess up with her dress was also satisfying, and of course we photographed her doing it. Then it was into the bath for a rinse and out of it for a brisk rub with a towel, the whole process watched by Percy's beady little eyes.

His flat was a bit short on mirrors, but I managed to move one on his dressing table so that Charlotte could kneel on the bed and watch herself being mounted from behind. She was nude now, while neither Percy nor I had taken off so much as a stitch. I had told her that she could back out at any time she liked, but she was completely happy and evidently in the same sort of sexual trance that I get into during a long punishment session. She crawled naked on to his bed and parted her thighs so that she could see not only her red bum but also her pussy in the mirror. Her eyes were wide and her mouth slightly parted, a very different image from the demure fitness instructor I had first met.

Keen to give Charlotte the full impact of being fucked by a dirty old man, I told Percy to strip. He began without hesitation, Charlotte watching him undress while I admired his room. It had the perfect image. All the furniture was antique and well used, creating an old-fashioned atmosphere that was added to by the smell. This was entirely masculine, yet also spoke of age and respectability. Possibly it was the camphor, which I remembered from my grandfather's house, or his talc, which was in a silver shaker that appeared to date from at least the last century.

Percy was now naked. His body was fat and pink and pig-like, hardly the image of masculine good looks, but ideal for when I was going to watch him mount Charlotte. She had watched him undress with a sort of fascinated dread, but now had her face pushed into the pillows. Her bottom was raised and she was clearly ready for entry, her pussy moist and swollen and her buttocks red from her spanking and the cane. Percy was nursing his cock back to erection and admiring Charlotte's bum, waiting for my command to enter her.

'Watch,' I ordered her. 'Look in the mirror. Concentrate on the view. Feel the humiliation as he mounts you and puts his cock in you.'

She moaned and turned her face to me with a look of pure need.

'A little less eagerness, slut,' I told her. 'Go on, Percy, fuck her. In her pussy first, but don't come.'

I photographed it all. First Charlotte naked on the bed with her red bum stuck in the air. Then Percy climbing up behind her, his little erection poking out from under his belly and his face red with lust. Then him settling his stomach on her bottom as he probed for her vagina. Finally him inside her from underneath, his cock in her pussy and his balls dangling down towards the lens. Her face was a picture as he humped her. Her eyes were fixed on the mirror, watching the reflection of herself kneeling, naked and beautiful, while a fat old man used her from the rear.

As I watched I slid a hand down the front of my jeans and began to massage my pussy mound through my knickers. Seeing what I was doing, Charlotte stuck her tongue out in a clear invitation to join in. It was more than I could resist, and a moment later I was struggling to get my jeans off. Percy turned to watch me strip, slowing his pace inside her and grinning as I peeled my clothes off. I had a need to retain control, and so I stripped only to my

T-shirt but took my bra off underneath. This worked. Despite having a bare bum and pussy and my nipples being clearly visible under my top, I still felt that it was me who was in charge. They, after all, were both stark naked.

I slipped into position in front of Charlotte and spread my thighs to offer my open pussy to her lips. Her tongue darted out to dab on my labia, bringing me a lovely tingling sensation. I lay back, resting against the headboard of Percy's bed and watching him fuck her while she licked me. He was enjoying himself hugely, bouncing away on her bottom and taking in the view of her giving me oral sex.

I let it go on for a long time, my pleasure slowly building towards orgasm. Percy showed no signs of coming too soon and spoiling the fun, which is one advantage of older men. He was getting tired though, but I wanted Charlotte to think she had got away without the supreme indignity of being buggered by him. When she put her hand back to play with herself I slapped her cheek gently and told her to stop being dirty. She gave a little whimper and started to lick more firmly at my pussy, almost making me loose control.

'No,' I ordered. 'Not yet you don't. Percy, put it in her bumhole.'

Charlotte whimpered again but continued licking. I pulled away, forcing myself not to just relax and let it all happen. He had pulled out and his cock was resting between her bum-cheeks, just the tip showing under his belly, purple and glistening with her juice.

'Open me first please,' Charlotte said quietly; from where she had once more pressed her face into the pillows.

'Naturally, darling,' I answered. 'Do you really think I'd let him bugger you without greasing your dirty little hole first?'

She nodded; and I gave her a slap on what I could see of her bottom.

'What can I use, Percy?' I asked.

'Try lard,' he suggested hoarsely as he continued to move his cock between her bum-cheeks in little jerks.

The idea was perfect, painless for the sensitive areas of skin yet somehow exquisitely humiliating. I ran to the kitchen and found some in the fridge, a big half-pound bar of it, barely used. Back in the bedroom I passed it to Charlotte.

'Grease your bottom,' I ordered, picking up the camera.

I only had four pictures left, but made the most of them. The first was of Percy holding Charlotte's bum-cheeks apart while she rubbed a blob of lard on to her anus with the packet balanced on her bottom. The second showed her with her finger well up her bumhole and the lard smeared liberally around it. The third showed the head of his cock poking at her anus, the greasy hole just beginning to stretch to accommodate it. The last was taken from underneath and showed his cock in her bumhole, her anal ring stretched taut around his intruding shaft and the lard squishing out around it. I was giggling again as I described the picture I had taken to Charlotte, who gave me a look of utter chagrin despite already being open-mouthed and breathless from having Percy's cock up her bottom.

'You can play with yourself now,' I told her, 'but don't come until he's done it up your bottom.'

Now was the time for me to come as well. I got back into position on the bed and pulled Charlotte's head against my pussy. She gave a contented squeak and began to lick. I was immediately in heaven and could feel my orgasm approaching as her tongue began to lap at my clitty. Percy's cock was well in her bottom and I could feel each push coming through her as she was sodomised. He was grunting and his belly was making dirty little slapping noises against her bum. I could smell the scent of sex and sweat as I pulled my top up to get at my boobs and began to caress a nipple.

Percy came first, right up Charlotte's bottom, groaning loudly as his sperm flooded into her.

'Stay in her,' I said as she immediately began to rub more urgently at her clitty and increased the pressure of her tongue on mine.

I fixed my eyes on the sight of Charlotte's neat little

buttocks sticking out from underneath Percy's fat, hairy belly as I started to come. That was the true piquancy of it for me; the delight of watching a beautiful young girl spanked, fucked and finally buggered by a grossly overweight, red-faced old man, a dirty-minded old bastard, a lecherous old sod who liked nothing better than to wedge his cock up a pretty girl's back passage. I screamed as I came, my pussy burning under Charlotte's tongue and my nipple hard between my fingers. Every muscle in me tensed and for a moment my vision went red. Everything was swimming around me and I was vaguely aware that she was coming too, and still licking me. The thought of her anus tightening around his prick came into my head and I was coming again, wishing it was me with a cock up my bottom and sperm in my bowels.

Later it was me, bent over his sofa in the nude while Charlotte took her revenge and put me through a humiliating ordeal not dissimilar to her own. This was after a leisurely meal made by Percy and a couple of bottles of fine Meursault to wash it down. He dressed while we stayed nude. It felt completely natural to be wandering around his flat without a stitch on, even with the knowledge that his eyes were feasting on our naked bodies, particularly our bums and tits.

Once we had all relaxed a bit Percy suggested that it was only fair for me to at least take a spanking. I crawled over his knee without hesitation and again tried to wet myself while I was being punished. It didn't work though, because I simply couldn't concentrate on peeing while enduring the pain of having my buttocks slapped. When Percy had finished with me Charlotte took over, bending me over her knee and smacking and teasing until I was thoroughly chastened and ready to be used by Percy.

Just as I had done to her, she let him fuck me before it went up my bottom. I wasn't allowed to come though, but was made to lick her bottom-hole while I masturbated. I was completely open in front of him, pussy spread wide as I frigged and licked at her anus, then coming with my tongue well up her bottom and a finger in my own.

The effort of buggering two girls in a day had exhausted Percy, and despite our best efforts to tease him back to erection we had to call it a day. We even put on a show for him, with the two of us stark naked on the living room floor, licking and pawing at each other's bodies. It was no good and, with the promise that we would be back next time either she or I needed to be punished, we left.

We walked back hand in hand, kissing occasionally and indifferent to the jealous or shocked stares of passers-by. Charlotte was nude under her dress and I lifted the back of it to flash her legs and bottom at a particularly disapproving woman. She was perhaps fifty and looked very prim and formal, but when she saw not just a bare bottom under a dress but one that had so obviously been recently whacked, her expression turned to something more often seen on a goldfish.

Back at the flat we got into the bath together and had a nice long play, now completely at ease with each other and quite definitely lovers. As we snuggled down together for the night I felt happy, sexually satisfied and, above all, immensely pleased with myself.

Twenty

I stayed thoroughly pleased with myself for the entire
week. True, my original plan for finding a partner who
would keep my bottom warm and genuinely believe he was
punishing me hadn't come to much, but my efforts had
certainly created some interesting offshoots. Best of all I
had a really devoted, worshipful girlfriend who was not
only gorgeous but would do exactly as I told her. Lydia, I
was sure, would come out of her sulk soon enough,
perhaps if I gave Steve a little less attention. Percy
Ottershaw would do what I wanted when I wanted, and if
that involved beating and humiliating me, then he was just
the man for the job. Finally there was Charles Carlisle,
who seemed to have a knack of taking my dirtiest fantasies
and bringing them to new heights of perfection.

The spanking fantasy had become too complicated
anyway. For perfection I now needed to be dragged across
someone's knee for genuine punishment, put through the
skirt-lifting and panty-lowering ritual and spanked until I
was in tears. It also required an audience and that I lose
control of my bladder and wet myself during the
punishment. The person who did it had to be just right too,
older than me, naturally strict and someone who considered
smacking a girl's bare bottom to be a perfectly reasonable,
even necessary, thing to do. I was asking too much of life
and would have to stick to pretty girls and older men, who
at least could provide more playful discipline.

Charles failed to meet the criteria for a perfect spanker,
but he was the one I was thinking of on the Friday. He had

rung to give me two instructions; to dress perfectly and to drink at least two pints of water before I came out. I had giggled at the second order, knowing full well that it meant some nice dirty, wet sex later in the evening. He refused to explain, but hinted that he was going to make me wet myself, hence the smart dress. Possibly he would even make me do it in public, the idea of which had me trembling with excitement. As long as he chose somewhere I wasn't actually going to be recognised I was game, in fact more than game.

I drank not two, but three pints of water before I left, and when I set off for his town flat I was already beginning to get the naughty, mildly uncomfortable feeling of a full bladder. As I walked I imagined the scene that might be coming. I was in a scarlet knee-length dress of Chinese silk with gold and emerald embroidery. It was very tight and clung to my figure in a way that accentuated my curves and would make it blatantly obvious what I had done when I wet myself. Beneath it I had stockings, suspenders, panties and bra, all in fine ivory silk, with high-heeled court shoes completing the ensemble. I looked smart, beautiful, rich and perhaps a little haughty, all of which was guaranteed to make people envious. I had no glasses on either and had done my make-up to accentuate my 'superior-to-you' look.

The whole look was deliberately as brattish as possible for a very good reason. If someone, say a cabbie or a secretary coming home from work, sees a sweet, pretty girl wet herself in the street, he or she is likely to feel sorry for her. On the other hand, if they see it happen to a stuck-up rich girl in a dress worth their month's salary, their attitude is more likely to be amusement than sympathy. If Charles was going to make me humiliate myself in public I wanted to do it properly, because at the end of the day that was what was going to give me the best orgasm.

I was almost skipping as I climbed the outside steps and rang his intercom. The door buzzed and I pushed it open, then ran up the stairs to his flat. The door was ajar, just a crack, making me wonder if he hadn't prepared something special for me inside.

'Hi, Charles,' I called as I went in, closing the door behind me and turning to bounce into the main room.

I stopped dead. Seated on the sofa were two people, and neither of them was Charles Carlisle.

'Good evening, Tasha, you little whore,' Lydia said, venom dripping from every word.

'There's no need for that, Lydia.' Sophie Carlisle spoke calmly yet with a firmness that had my lower lip trembling.

Now that they were sitting together the resemblance was obvious. Take away the outrageous hair, the piercings and add about twenty-five years and Lydia *was* Sophie Carlisle. I suddenly felt stupid for not realising that they were mother and daughter when all the signs had been there to read, but it was too late now; I had really put my foot in it.

I couldn't think of anything to say, but just stood there looking at my feet and numbly envisioning professional disgrace.

'Come here,' Sophie Carlisle ordered.

I stepped forward, feeling far too uncertain of myself to do anything other than obey. There was a set, determined look on her face, not so much anger as cold intent. She reached out as I approached and took me by the wrist. I realised what she was doing an instant too late as she pulled hard and caught me off balance. I came down across her lap with a yelp of indignation. It was happening – she was going to spank me!

'No! You can't! You can't!' I squealed as Lydia caught me by the hair and pushed my face down into her lap.

I kicked out as my arm was twisted expertly into the small of my back. Sophie Carlisle cocked a leg up, forcing my bottom high.

'No, not this, not a spanking!' I begged as my body was adjusted into the right position for a beating.

'Hold her while I get her ready,' Sophie said, still very calm.

I was feeling anything but calm as Lydia's hand twisted hard in my hair. She took the arm her mother had put up behind my back and pulled it harder; it hurt and meant that all I could do to save myself from the coming punishment was to smack my free hand against Sophie Carlisle's legs.

'Stop that, you little brat,' she ordered. 'You've had this coming for a long time, so at least try and take it like a grown woman.'

I stopped, but more because of Lydia tightening her grip in my hair than because of what her mother had said. I didn't want to be brave about what was happening to me; I wanted it to stop; yet I also wanted to give in to it, completely.

Not that I had any say in the matter. They had me helpless and all I could do was whimper pathetically as Sophie Carlisle began the agonisingly humiliating process of baring my bottom. She was very matter-of-fact about it, clearly regarding a bare bum as a necessary prerequisite for a girl to be spanked. My dress was tight and could only be tugged up with some difficulty. This meant that my thighs were exposed inch by inch, my shame increasing as more and more flesh came on show.

I could feel it all coming on view; first my stocking-tops, then the area of chubby white flesh between stocking-tops and bum, then the base of my panties and the tuck of my buttocks, then the crest of my bottom and the full expanse of my panty seat, then the waistband of my panties, the two little dimples at the base of my spin and finally my suspender belt. She tucked the dress under my arm where her daughter had it twisted behind my back, ensuring that it wouldn't fall back during my punishment.

As I lay there with my knickers on show I could hear the sound of my own breathing, deep and regular with a slight catch that came from my shame and anticipation of the pain of my coming beating. Lydia had my face pushed hard into her lap and I could smell the leather of her skirt, her expensive perfume and a faint whiff of pussy. I was trembling and whimpering faintly, keeping still only because they had me in a painfully awkward position.

Then Mrs Carlisle took my panties down. It's easy to say that, but quite another thing to be held down over a woman's lap and have your last scrap of protective modesty peeled down slowly over your bottom to leave it bare and vulnerable to a coming spanking. It produces a quite extraordinary feeling of helplessness and inferiority, both emotions that are normally quite alien to me. They weren't now. I felt utterly in thrall to her. She had me over her knee and was taking down my panties so that I could be spanked properly – spanked on my bare bottom, spanked as a punishment, spanked because I deserved it.

A great bubble of shame was swelling in my head as my bottom was exposed. I felt it every inch of the way as the silk glided down over my bum-cheeks, baring me, humbling me. Bit by bit they came down, revealing my big pink bottom, the full cheeks ready for slapping. She opened my panties when they were about halfway down and Lydia laughed as she got a view right down the back of them. Then my bottom was completely bare and I was sobbing out my emotions into Lydia's lap with the air cool on my unprotected rear, the bubble still growing as my panties were inverted around my thighs. Then Mrs Carlisle cocked her leg up further; my thighs and bum-cheeks opened; my pussy and anus came on show and the bubble burst.

'Baby!' Lydia said vindictively as my tears started.

I made no effort to reply, but could only wait for the actual spanking to start. Sophie Carlisle hadn't finished preparing me though, and had a final degrading touch to add to my exposure and helplessness. Taking my panties down to my knees, she lifted her leg and put it between my thighs. As she curled her legs around mine to clamp me firmly in place, I found my bare pussy spread over her legs with my clitty in direct contact with the nylon of her stockings. I could feel my panties too, stretched taut between my knees and held in by her leg.

'I'll take her arm now, thank you, Lydia,' Sophie Carlisle said and once more took a firm hold of my wrist. 'Right, you dirty little tart, this is for trying to seduce my husband.'

And she started to spank me. Her hand came down hard across my bare bottom, drawing a yelp from me and making my cheeks bounce. Lydia laughed, a delighted chuckle directed at the state I was in and what was happening to me. The second smack fell and Sophie began to beat a rhythm on my bottom: hard, regular blows that stung and made me yelp and buck. Lydia was laughing at me, gleeful as her mother turned my bottom a rosy pink, keeping her hand twisted firmly in my hair and my face pushed into her lap.

It stung crazily, and Mrs Carlisle never paused long enough to let me get control. Soon I was crying freely, and I knew that my frantic bucks and wiggles were making a fine show of my pussy and bumhole. I had to thrash about though; the pain was too much for me to worry about my modesty. Her smacks were also making my pussy rub on her legs, the touch of nylon on my clitty bringing me on heat whether I wanted it or not. Soon I was begging her to stop, pleading and apologising in between sobs and yelps.

'Miserable, snivelling brat!' was all I got for my efforts. 'When I've finished with you, you really will be sorry!'

She went on: slap after slap on my poor nude bum. She ignored my pleas and my yells, spanking and spanking until I was dizzy with pain and the heat in my crotch. Soon I was blubbering and kicking my legs in a manner that must have looked utterly pathetic from the way it made Lydia laugh. Suddenly she stopped, just when I had been about to lose my last vestige of control and start rubbing myself on her leg.

'I hope you feel suitably chastened,' Sophie said, resting her hand on the crest of my throbbing bottom.

I did feel chastened. I felt like the snotty little brat I am at heart, spanked and humiliated; snivelling as much because I knew I deserved the beating as from the actual pain and sense of disgrace. I could feel myself coming on heat too. From the waist downwards I was showing everything: my round, red bum, my open pussy and my wrinkled brown bumhole. It was all open, every little detail of my sex, exposed not because anyone wanted to see it but because to have it all bare humiliated me and made my beating more effective. In contrast they were fully clothed, not a stitch out of place, while I wasn't even allowed the decency of keeping my anus hidden. If they just wanted to ensure my bottom was unprotected they could have simply pulled my panties tight up between my bum-cheeks. No, they had had to come down, purely so that I had to suffer the knowledge that my swollen pussy and the puckered brown ring of my bumhole both got an airing while I was beaten.

It was all so unbearably shameful, and there was also the pain in my bladder – a dull ache that reminded me just how dirty my intentions had been that evening. Peeing myself in public didn't seem so sexy now that my panties were down and the wife of the man who had been going to do it to me had reddened my buttocks as a punishment. It still seemed rude, but something for a girl to be punished for rather than enjoy.

'Yes, I'm sorry,' I snivelled. 'Please, Mrs Carlisle; please stop. I won't do it again. I promise. Haven't I been spanked enough?'

'No,' she declared firmly. 'Lydia, pass me the hairbrush; I want to make sure that she remembers this for a long time.'

'No!' I squealed, remembering just how much more a hairbrush hurts than a hand does.

She took no notice, and the instant she began to smack my bum with the hairbrush I knew it was going to happen. The pain was far worse than her hand had been. It was both heavy and stinging and applied at a relentless speed that immediately had me blubbering and yelling again. Each smack pushed my crotch against her leg. With my pussy spread on to her thigh the whole of my vulva was in contact with the textured nylon of her stockings. My clitty was being rubbed and there was nothing I could do to stop my pleasure rising along with my pain.

I began to go dizzy as my orgasm approached. My whole world was centred on the sensations of my body, principally my blazing bottom.

'No,' I whimpered as it started, 'Sophie, no, I'm ... I'll ... oh God!'

I gave up, unable to hold back. The sound of the hairbrush on my bum, the pain as each smack fell, Lydia's cruel laughter, the hands twisting my wrist and hair, all of it blurred into one as my climax hit me. I screamed, a very different note to my tormented yells. I clamped my teeth on the leather of Lydia's skirt, tasting the bitter flavour and pushed my bottom up, now desperate for more, harder smacks.

'She's having an orgasm! The dirty little slut!' Mrs Carlisle exclaimed in amazement.

'Yes I am,' I called. 'Yes I am. Beat me. Come on, beat me; punish me! Hurt me, Sophie; I'm coming!'

'You filthy, filthy, filthy!' she screeched, pounding away at my bottom with the hairbrush in a vain attempt to make my pain drown out my pleasure.

It didn't work. I was coming on her leg and nothing could stop me. I screamed as I climaxed and the muscles of my pussy contracted fiercely in uncontrollable spasms. I screamed again as she brought the brush down on my bottom with every ounce of her strength. Then I lost control of my bladder. I was in the middle of orgasm, rubbing myself frantically on Sophie's stocking, squealing and wriggling in an ecstasy I had never known before. Then the pee was gushing from my pussy, spraying out behind me, splashing on her legs and trickling down mine to the floor. I heard Sophie Carlisle's exclamation of utter disgust and with that a new climax hit me, even stronger than the first, making my body spasm, bringing the blood to my head. I screamed again, the world turned red and I was fainting from sheer pleasure. As if in the distance I heard Sophie give a gasp of indignant fury and then it was just too much – everything went black, and even as it happened I realised that I was fainting.

Epilogue

I lay on the bed, my red, smarting bottom uppermost and visible in my mirror. Four times I had come since returning home, and my vagina and anus were as sore as the rest of my rear from my frantic stroking and probing. I had been spanked, spanked for real, just as I had wanted since the fantasy first came to me. Mrs Carlisle had beaten me like the snivelling, pathetic little brat I am. I'd come on her lap, to her disgust and her daughter's delight. I'd wet myself too, all over her lap. Then I'd fainted, overcome by the sheer power of the experience.

They had taken my pants and sent me home. I'd walked back snivelling and rubbing my bottom through my dress. My make-up had been smeared from my crying and my stockings were wet with my pee. People had seen, a lot of people, but I hadn't cared. In fact I'd wanted them to know I'd been spanked. When I'd finally reached the flat I'd locked my door and stripped naked. I had fallen to my face on the bed, humped my red bottom up and put my hand to my pussy. I was still in tears as I masturbated, and after a while I sneaked a hand back to the fullness of my bottom and poked a finger into my anus.

I shivered at the memory, and the memory of the next orgasm and the next. I'd felt I needed to pee again after that and had simply done it on the bed, taking my fourth orgasm in a pool of my own urine. Now it felt warm and wet against my belly, as much a reminder of the state I was in as my throbbing bottom.

Wiping a stray tear from my cheek I pulled my legs up,

focused on the reflection of my poor, punished bottom, put my hand on to my pussy and started to do it again.

NEW BOOKS

Coming up from Nexus, Sapphire and Black Lace

Nexus

Taking Pains to Please by Arabella Knight
June 1999   Price £5.99   ISBN: 0 352 33369 3
It can be a punishing experience for willing young women striving to please and obey exacting employers. On the job, they quickly come to learn that giving complete satisfaction demands their strict dedication and devotion to duty. Maid, nanny or nurse – each must submit to the discipline of the daily grind. In their capable hands, the urgent needs and dark desires of their paymasters are always fulfilled: for these working girls find pleasure in taking pains to please.

The Submission Gallery by Lindsay Gordon
June 1999   Price £5.99   ISBN: 0 352 33370 7
For her art, Poppy the sculptress seeks out and recreates the heights of submission and domination. Each sculpture she creates is taken from life – a life of total sensual freedom where she meets a strange cast of brutal lovers. From strangers in restaurants to tattooists, from a baroness to a uniformed society of fetishists, Poppy experiences rigorous obedience and tastes power for the first time. The result is her Submission Gallery.

The Handmaidens by Aran Ashe
June 1999   Price £5.99   ISBN: 0 352 33282 4
Tormunil can be an exceedingly harsh place for pretty young serving girls. Destined for a life of sexual slavery at the hands of merciless overlords, the chosen ones are taken to the Abbey – a place where strength is learned through obedience to those who follow the path of the Twisted Cross. Taken into this strange world, the young and beautiful Sianon and Iroise are allowed few privileges. Tormented to the peaks of pleasure, but punished if they seek release, their only hope of escape lies with the handsome young traveller who has fallen for their charms. This is the fifth in a series of Nexus Classics.

NEXUS NEW BOOKS

To be published in March

DIRTY LAUNDRY
Penny Birch
£6.99

Natasha Linnet is back, and with her pet dirty old man in France, she is feeling deprived of kinky sex. Unfortunately, Gabrielle Salinger, the therapist from hell, has found out about Natasha's sex life. Not wanting to end up as a case study in perversion, Natasha tries to keep her nose clean, and walks straight into the flabby embrace of the awful Monty Hartle, whose main joy in life is the humiliation of women. Before long, Natasha finds that she really can't handle the filthy Monty, and that what Gabrielle *really* wants is not work-related at all! That leaves only one way out, and Natasha exploits it to the full.

ISBN 0 352 33680 3

TEASING CHARLOTTE
Yvonne Marshall
£6.99

Young debutantes Imogen and Charlotte are about to come out for the London season. The girls, however, feel little need for the company of the stuffy and reliable bankers and diplomats to whom they're introduced. They're fascinated, instead, by the legend surrounding the mysterious Kayla, a society beauty infamously caught on camera doing a very special favour for an unidentifiable but clearly very important man. But when they get close to the heart of the mystery, the truth proves more bizarre than gossip ever could – in ways that even Imogen and Charlotte's fertile imaginations can scarcely have perpared them for.

ISBN 0 352 33681 1

DISPLAYS OF INNOCENTS
Lucy Golden
£6.99

The twelve stories in this collection reveal the experiences of whose who dare to step outside the familiar bounds of everyday life. Irene is called for an interview, but has never before been examined as thoroughly as this; Gemma cannot believe the lewd demands made by her new clients, a respectable middle-aged couple; and Helen learns that the boss's wife has a wetly intimate way of demonstrating her authority. For some, it widens their horizons, for others, it is an agony never to be repeated. For all twelve, it is a tale of intense erotic power.

ISBN 0 352 33679 X

To be published in April

WHIP HAND
G. C. Scott

Richard and his German girlfriend Helena continue to live out their private fantasies of submission and domination, with all the elaborate touches that their England rural idyll can afford. Even Helena's imperious aunt Margaret no longer wants to spoil the party – or does she? As Richard's tame dominatrix she seems to want nothing more than to join in their fantasies. But can Richard be sure that she doesn't want to keep him all to herself? The latest in G. C. Scott's powerful series of novels about the reality of male submission.

ISBN 0 352 33694 3

SLAVE-MINES OF TORMUNIL
Aran Ashe

Leah, the pretty young slave from the Citadel, has been claimed as body-slave by Josef, the handsome outlander who must now assume the responsibility of training her in the Tormunite ways of lust. Together they embark upon a quest for the lovely milk-slave Sianon, reportedly abducted by soldiers as a vessel for their pleasure and cruelty. Josef's worst fears are confirmed when he discovers that Sianon is being held in the notorious fleshpots of the mines of Menirg. The third novel in Aran Ashe's classic *Chronicles of Tormunil*, some of the finest erotic fantasy fiction ever produced.

ISBN 0 352 33695 1

THE INDIGNITIES OF ISABELLE
Penny Birch writing as Cruella

Nineteen-year old Isabelle is a refined young woman of cultish tastes and a deep sexual yearning which she's yet to reveal. The pleasures of domination and the female form are obvious to her, but now, in her first year at university, she's set to discover that there are many more excitements of the flesh. As she traverses the pathways of willing sexual degradation, Isabelle's sensual education is about to begin. A Nexus Classic.

ISBN 0 352 33696 X

If you would like more information about Nexus titles, please visit our website at www.nexus-books.co.uk, or send a stamped addressed envelope to:

Nexus, Thames Wharf Studios,
Rainville Road, London W6 9HA

NEXUS BACKLIST

This information is correct at time of printing. For up-to-date information, please visit our website at www.nexus-books.co.uk

All books are priced at £5.99 unless another price is given.

Nexus books with a contemporary setting

TIE AND TEASE	Penny Birch	☐
	ISBN 0 352 33591 2	
TIGHT WHITE COTTON	Penny Birch	☐
	ISBN 0 352 33537 8	
THE TORTURE CHAMBER	Lisette Ashton	☐
	ISBN 0 352 33530 0	
THE TRAINING OF FALLEN ANGELS	Kendal Grahame	☐
	ISBN 0 352 33224 7	
THE YOUNG WIFE	Stephanie Calvin	☐
	ISBN 0 352 33502 5	
WHIPPING BOY	G. C. Scott	☐
	ISBN 0 352 33595 5	

Nexus books with Ancient and Fantasy settings

CAPTIVE	Aishling Morgan	☐
	ISBN 0 352 33585 8	
THE CASTLE OF MALDONA	Yolanda Celbridge	☐
	ISBN 0 352 33149 6	
DEEP BLUE	Aishling Morgan	☐
	ISBN 0 352 33600 5	
THE FOREST OF BONDAGE	Aran Ashe	☐
	ISBN 0 352 32803 7	
MAIDEN	Aishling Morgan	☐
	ISBN 0 352 33466 5	
NYMPHS OF DIONYSUS £4.99	Susan Tinoff	☐
	ISBN 0 352 33150 X	
PLEASURE TOY	Aishling Morgan	☐
	ISBN 0 352 33634 X	
THE SLAVE OF LIDIR	Aran Ashe	☐
	ISBN 0 352 33504 1	
TIGER, TIGER	Aishling Morgan	☐
	ISBN 0 352 33455 X	
THE WARRIOR QUEEN	Kendal Grahame	☐
	ISBN 0 352 33294 8	

Period

BEATRICE	Anonymous	☐
	ISBN 0 352 31326 9	
CONFESSION OF AN ENGLISH SLAVE	Yolanda Celbridge	☐
	ISBN 0 352 33433 9	

------------ ✂ --------------------------------------

Please send me the books I have ticked above.

Name   ....:...

Address   ....

            ....

            ....

            .... Post code ....

Send to: Cash Sales, Nexus Books, Thames Wharf Studios, Rainville Road, London W6 9HA

US customers: for prices and details of how to order books for delivery by mail, call 1-800-805-1083.

Please enclose a cheque or postal order, made payable to **Nexus Books Ltd**, to the value of the books you have ordered plus postage and packing costs as follows:

UK and BFPO – £1.00 for the first book, 50p for each subsequent book.

Overseas (including Republic of Ireland) – £2.00 for the first book, £1.00 for each subsequent book.

If you would prefer to pay by VISA, ACCESS/MASTER-CARD, AMEX, DINERS CLUB or SWITCH, please write your card number and expiry date here:

....

Please allow up to 28 days for delivery.

Signature ....

------------ ✂ --------------------------------------